# In HEELS, *She* GOES

## A Cheney Manning Novel

by

## Donna Kelly

ISBN: 9798840465578

# CONTENTS

# SNOWFALL

*February 2nd*

A snowfall at midnight holds the truth. There is a purity in it, a simplicity of silent language: a lonely rushing of thousands of scattered messengers, spiraling downward, searching for a place to land. And, as she lies in her bed, watching the flakes tumble and skate along the wind, illuminated by the outdoor-security lights, she wonders if this loneliness will last forever.

Almost as if her smartphone knows that each snowflake carries with it the mark of despair, there is a ping of an incoming text message. She doesn't customarily sleep with the phone next to her head, so it's across the room on top of her antique-writing desk beneath the window along the west wall. She continues lying there for a moment, staring up at the ceiling. She really doesn't want to get out of bed. It's cold, and even though she can't sleep, she's snuggled in for the night. Who would be texting her at this hour anyway?

The only one who usually texts her this late is Manuel's little sister, Carmen, if she is scared and can't sleep or if she misses her brother and wants to talk about him. Sometimes Carmen says she hears gunfire or hostile voices coming from the streets outside of her mom's house, so she calls Cheney "just to talk." Other times, Carmen reaches out to Cheney to share stories about Manuel. But it shouldn't be Carmen texting, because Cheney just talked to her last night, and Carmen said she was going to spend the weekend over at her cousin's house in Indiana.

1

She has visited with Carmen virtually at nine o'clock sharp each Thursday evening of every week since December for their two-person book club meeting: officially named the Spinach Omelet Book Nerds. Those discussions are usually confined to the topic of their reading progress and analyses of chapter assignments for their mutually-selected book of the month. Carmen usually doesn't talk about Manuel during their official meetings. Rather, it's the occasional post-midnight calls or texts in which Carmen shares stories and expresses grief about her brother. It's been more than two months since Manuel was stabbed and killed in the Cook County Jail, but his death still seems fresh to Cheney. She understands why the child seemingly has such difficulty grasping that her brother is dead. After all, she too, struggles with accepting the notion that he's not coming back.

Cheney first met Carmen at Thanksgiving at Manuel's mother's house, with Cheney's shoulder still in a sling from having taken a bullet. Carmen was smaller than Cheney had pictured her to be. For some reason, Cheney had mistakenly thought that she would appear more like Manuel: strong, tough, defiant, all bravado and swagger. But she was just a tiny, introspective girl, with a round face peering out from behind oversized black-rimmed glasses.

When Cheney had introduced herself and said that she was a friend of Manuel's, the child had squinted at her and said, "Manny told me all about you. You were more than just a friend. He said you were his girlfriend."

Cheney had been a bit taken aback, and had not known how to immediately respond to that; so, at first, she had just nodded, silently. She was not used to talking to kids, really wasn't around them much, and had never really mastered how to communicate with them. She had never wanted to have children, and part of the reason for that was that she preferred intellectual conversation with adults to small talk with children. Rearing a child just simply did not interest her, and she was

2

convinced that taking care of a child was not how she wished to occupy any part of her adulthood.

So, she wasn't quite sure how to take the bluntness of the nine-year-old sister of Manuel Rodriguez. After an awkward momentary silence, Cheney had changed the subject, a typical lawyer tactic, and had said, "Manuel told me that you like to read and that you like horses. What are you reading now?"

"*The Lion, the Witch and the Wardrobe*," the child had answered.

"Oh, that's a good one," Cheney had said. "C.S. Lewis."

"Have you read it?"

"A long time ago," Cheney had said.

"Will you talk to me about it?" Carmen had asked.

Cheney had been surprised by the child's question, and had asked, "What do you mean?"

"When I'm finished reading it, can you talk to me about it? Momma doesn't know how to read, and Miguel and Elias never have time for me," Carmen had said.

Cheney had just met Manuel's mother, Lupe, that same day. Cheney's Thanksgiving visit had been arranged a few days after Cheney had been released from the hospital, when she had received a call on Dan's old cellphone. At first, she had been puzzled, because she had not recognized the number with the Chicago area code, but when she had answered, and heard a voice asking for her in Spanish, she knew imme-diately it was Manuel's mother.

During the call, Lupe Rodriguez had entreated upon Cheney to come to the house in Humboldt Park for Thanksgiving. At first, Cheney had hesitated; but then, she had quickly capitulated, because she had felt compelled to go. After all, Manuel had done so much for her. Actually, he had given his life for her. She had to go. There was no way she could say 'No'.

So, she drove to the west side of Chicago on Thanksgiving and met Manuel's family in a crowded bungalow, full of cousins and other relatives. She had also met two of Manuel's younger brothers on that day, neither of whom he had ever mentioned. Manuel had only talked to her about his mother, his older brother who had been murdered, Freddie, and his little sister, Carmen.

She had been surprised when Lupe had introduced her to her other sons, Miguel and Elias. At first, Cheney wondered why Manuel had never mentioned either of them. Carmen, however, with the naïve innocence of a child, had filled in the blanks when she had whispered to Cheney a blunt and telling explanation as to why her brothers were too busy to discuss *The Lion, the Witch and the Wardrobe* with her. "They're both always too busy slinging dope. Momma doesn't know that about them though, so don't tell her."

Cheney had felt such empathy for the child then, that she had agreed to discuss the book with the child. "Of course, of course, as long as you check with your mother, and she says it's okay with her, you can call me and I'll talk about the book with you."

The child had immediately sprinted over to her mother, rattled off something in Spanish of which Cheney only caught bits and pieces, and then had joyfully returned to Cheney exclaiming, "It's okay with my mom!" And, so had begun an unlikely friendship between Cheney Manning and Manuel Rodriguez's kid sister and the formation of their virtual book club that convened each Thursday evening.

4

The phone messaging pings again. Carmen wouldn't be texting her from her cousin's house, but maybe she'll just wait until tomorrow to check to find out who it is. It just seems like a lot of effort to get up from beneath the warmth of the comforter just to see who is texting her.

Although she had turned the heat up to a decent temperature earlier in the evening, it's still chilly in her bedroom, for the wind outside is fast-moving and relentless: Its icy palms slap against the frigid glass of the two double-paned windows above Patton's couch. Even the massive Rottweiler, with his fur coat, looks a bit uncomfortable with the cold, howling wind. He lifts his head up and stares at her, as if he is contemplating whether the bed would be warmer than the old couch on which he usually sleeps. Even though it is dark, she can see the shape of his massive head, and the glint of his eyes, and she knows he is thinking about abandoning his customary spot and jumping into the bed.

Her curiosity gets the best of her, and she begrudgingly stands up to get the phone. When she does so, Patton leaps off the couch and onto the foot of the king-sized sleigh bed, as if this is his opportunity to claim as much space as possible.

She looks at the face of the phone before she gets back under the covers. It's a message from Brian Patterson, the police officer who was with her husband on the night he was murdered. Though it has been three months since Dan was killed, the grief is still with her, and it really hasn't subsided much, if at all.

The text doesn't say a lot, just: "Hi. Checking to see how you're doing. Figured you'd be awake."

And she is. She had received a couple of post-midnight texts from Patterson around this hour, back in January or late December, but she hasn't heard from him since then. She had conveyed to him that it was

5

okay to text her at this late hour, because she is usually wide awake anyway. The last she had heard, Patterson was still on midnight-shift probation, which meant that he had a field training officer alongside him in the squad. The only time Patterson texts her is when he is on duty. She figures that his doing so is a way for him to avoid a direct one-on-one conversation with her, while still trying to appear as if he has some level of genuine concern for her. It's an obligatory text. That's all. Psych 101.

She snuggles back down into the bed beside the warmth of the mammoth Rottweiler, and sends a lazy thumbs-up emoji back to Patterson, with a half-hearted, "Thnx for checking. All is well."

His next text reads: "Do you need someone to shovel you out tomorrow? The snow is coming down pretty good here. It may be up to ten inches near you."

"No, thnx," she texts back. "Someone is coming here to plow my driveway tomorrow."

He replies with a thumbs-up, but what he sends next surprises her, though only mildly so. It's actually her reaction to his text that surprises her more, for she feels a stir of what might be the faintest tinge of interest. His text reads: "Would you like to meet for lunch sometime?"

She doesn't hesitate in responding. "Sure."

What she's not really certain of is whether he is asking her on a date, or if this is just a well-being check to make sure she's not in the throes of depression. She rules out the former. It must the latter. She's never had the feeling that Patterson is romantically interested in her, and in fact, he always seems like he finds her a bit annoying. Besides, he certainly wouldn't be putting the moves on her only three months after Dan was killed.

Still, it would be nice to get out of the house and talk to someone. She has barely left the premises since she finished with her physical therapy sessions three weeks ago. She went with her parents to see Kate's performance in *Steel Magnolias* at Northern Illinois University in DeKalb two Saturdays ago, but, other than that trip, and excursions to the grocery store, she's been pretty much homebound.

His reply text reads: "How is Monday at noon? Downtown Meskwaki?"

He must have something to tell her. Why else would he all of a sudden be pushing for a lunch meeting? This has to be about something more than just checking to make sure she's doing okay. But what could it be? Dan's murder case has been resolved for months. Solomon Wilson was released, and the case against him was dismissed: that happened way back when Cheney was still in the hospital in November, recovering from her gunshot wound.

Even though she's puzzled why Patterson wants to meet with her, she sends a thumbs-up and asks, "Where?"

He specifies a restaurant along the Fox River, and she writes back: "See you there at noon."

She's not surprised he chose Meskwaki to meet. She had heard from one of the Loomisville police officers that Patterson had moved there in December, even though he had not mentioned it to her in any of his texts. But then again, why would he? She really knows nothing of his private life. She only met him after Dan was murdered, and she has had fairly limited contact with him since she has been released from the hospital: a handful of text messages and one awkward phone conversation.

The sound of the gathering wind is so strong it is almost frightening, as if it is going to bring the house down; it whistles like a sinister firecracker. Patton raises his head briefly, stares out the windows and then puts his head between his outstretched paws and sighs, as though he shares her concern about the prospect of being swept away in the snowstorm. These winter nights in the farmhouse make her feel even more isolated than ever, and she is grateful that she at least has her faithful dog to lay beside her, a reminder that she is not really all alone in this world.

The snowflakes look they are being punished by the wind, flailing, drowning, spinning out of control, insubstantial pieces of crystalized water, but beautiful in a stark and strangely comforting way. This sad parade of six-armed symmetrical ice queens almost prods her into getting out of bed, retrieving her journal from the desk, and writing a poem. But she really needs to sleep. She has a video conference early in the morning with the director and a couple of board members of a non-profit organization in Chicago that assists the families of fallen police officers. The organization paid for Dan's funeral expenses back in November, but now they want to pay off the mortgage on the farm too.

Cheney is torn over this. She doesn't want to refuse to accept help, and she is grateful for it; but, on the other hand, Dan and she didn't have children, and she has the ability to earn a great deal of income in her career. It seems wrong somehow to accept charitable assistance when she has decades of earning capacity ahead of her and no dependents. Besides, with the line-of-duty death benefits and Dan's life insurance policy proceeds, she can live comfortably for a couple of years without working if she wants to take a break.

Right now, she has no desire to go back into the office at all, perhaps ever again. She hasn't been to work since Dan was killed three months ago, but she is still – technically - employed as an assistant public defender in Stickney County. Derek Strozak shot her in the shoulder in

November, and she's been on FMLA leave ever since. Maria Calderon, her supervisor, called her a few weeks ago to check to see how she was doing, but Cheney could tell she was really trying to figure out if and when Cheney was returning to the office. Cheney was ambivalent.

She's running out of time though, now, and she'll either need to return to work soon, or be let go. She's been thinking about it a lot lately, and the notion of taking a year or so break from the practice of law sounds inviting. She could really use a reprieve from the demands of clients, taxing trial preparation, unreasonable prosecutors and ill-tempered judges. She really needs to let Maria know that she's not coming back, so that they can find her replacement. It's not fair to the rest of the attorneys in the office that she's been out for so long and that she is waffling on whether to return at all. She'll call Maria in the morning and let her know her decision.

Even with that box checked, she still can't sleep. She closes her eyes, but her mind is still processing information on overdrive, like most nights. She replays the events of November. It all seems so bizarre and surreal. The murder of her husband is difficult to accept and there are moments when she thinks he is going to walk through the front door as though nothing has happened. The fact that her former client, Solomon Wilson, was indicted for Dan's murder still shocks her a bit, like it did on the night the police came to give her the news about Dan. It's hard to believe it really happened. But it did. Dan is dead and Solomon Wilson was the one whom the police arrested for the murder.

Cheney never believed it. Solomon didn't have it in him to kill anyone. Yes, he was a troubled kid, with a significant juvenile history, but he wasn't a killer. He was a petty drug dealer, that's all. But the police wouldn't believe her. Jeff Cantoni, Dan's best friend, the lead detective on the case, had scoffed at her when she had tried to convince him that Solomon was innocent.

Ultimately though, she had proved Jeff Cantoni had been wrong. It wasn't Solomon who was the killer. Instead, it was her ex-boyfriend, Derek Strozak. How she arrived at that conclusion is the part that seems like something out of a dream, as though it happened to someone else, not her. Her confrontation of Strozak replays in her mind, and culminates with the stinging bullet that struck her in the shoulder. She remembers lying on the floor, thinking she was going to die. The days in between Strozak's murder of her husband and Strozak's subsequent attempt to murder her are fuzzy, at best, and she struggles to get a sense of whether certain things actually happened or whether they are fantasy. Sometimes she lies in bed wondering whether Manuel Rodriguez was a real person, or whether he was just part of some dangerous and passionate dream.

She rolls over and starts to fade into sleep, and it is not long until she is entranced with a memory of a man kissing her, his lips warm, but fierce. It is not Dan's face in the dream, nor, thankfully, Derek Strozak's. Instead, it's the coal-colored brooding eyes of Manuel Rodriguez that she soaks in with her somnolent breaths.

And she is so enraptured by him, by his touch, that she continues sleeping even when she hears a doorbell ringing. The noise is harsh, an intrusion into her private moment with Manuel, and she ignores it, right ear on the pillow, sound asleep. Even when it continues, and there is intermittent frantic knocking, she works it into the romance, so that she and Manuel continue touching each other, laughing at whoever is trying to get them to come to the door. It is only when she hears Patton charging down the stairs, barking furiously, that she wakes up and realizes that this is not a dream.

There is a blizzard. It is nearly one in the morning. She is alone with the closest neighbor nearly a half of a mile away. And, there is someone at her door.

# CONCEALER

Only bad news comes at this hour. The last time she had opened the door so early in the morning was when two police officers from Loomisville had showed up three months ago to tell her that Dan had been killed in the line of duty. Back then, when she had heard the doorbell ring so late at night, her sixth sense had told her that it was probably the police coming to the house to tell her that Dan had been killed. She had been right. But now, she has absolutely no idea who would be at her door at this hour, particularly in the middle of a blizzard. Her heart literally feels like it is going to break loose from the walls of her chest, and she looks out the window to scan the driveway.

There is a car parked outside, but the snow is so pervasive that the vehicle is already shrouded in it, and the furious flakes in the sky, combined with the darkness, obscure her ability to discern make or color, even with the security lights from the barn illuminating parts of the driveway. All she can see is that it looks like a compact car of some sort. It's definitely not a squad car.

The doorbell rings again, followed by loud knocking. She puts on a robe, takes out Dan's Glock from the nightstand, and heads downstairs. Patton's barking reverberates through the halls of the old farmhouse as she cuts across the living room into the kitchen. She makes her way down the long hallway toward the front door at the west end of the house, and conceals the gun by holding it under her robe.

11

Patton's paws are balanced on the small ledge next to the doorway and he is barking ferociously. She looks out the side window and sees a shivering young woman standing in the porchlight. It's her sister, Kate. Unbelievable. Why would Kate be here at this hour? And why wouldn't she call first?

She darts into the library and puts the gun into a drawer and bounces back, opening the front door. "What are you doing here, Kate? You scared the hell out of me."

Patton immediately stops barking, probably because with Kate's scent, comes recognition. Instead, he licks Kate's right hand as soon as she removes her gloves. Kate stomps on the entry rug to dislodge the chunks of snow and ice from her boots. She is wearing a long red wool cape that covers her hair, and which is adorned with starry melting remnants of snowflakes. She looks down at the floor, so Cheney sees only her smooth forehead and the backs of her long eyelashes, and hears the muttering of an apology: "Sorry to come here so late."

When her sister looks up, and gracefully removes the hood of her cape, it is apparent that something is wrong: Kate's usually-remarkably clear blue eyes are bloodshot, her eyelids are swollen, and her creamy ivory complexion is blotted with patches of red. She is customarily a laughing creature, but Cheney has seen her cry on occasion, and her face bears all the telltale signs of recent sobbing.

"Jesus, Kate, what's wrong? What's going on?" Cheney takes Kate's cape and winces a bit when she does so. Even with the physical therapy sessions and the passage of time, there is still pain. Thankfully, the bullet hadn't caused any arterial or bone damage, but she is still recuperating nonetheless. When she pats Kate on her shoulder, she uses her left hand, instead of her right. She turns and hangs Kate's cape up in the hallway closet, but Kate seems too focused on herself to recognize that Cheney is still recovering from a bullet wound. Kate just stands in the hallway crying, tears streaming down her cheeks, gulping as if she cannot speak.

Cheney drapes her left arm over Kate's left shoulder, comforting her, and asks again, softer this time, "What is it, Kate? Tell me what's wrong."

Kate still doesn't answer; just shakes her head and continues crying. "Let me go get you some tissue," Cheney says and bolts into the nearby powder room, returning within seconds.

Kate has moved into the parlor, and is standing in front of the large bay window, staring out at the sky-fall of tumbling snowflakes. She is still crying, and when Cheney hands her the tissue, she says, "Thank you," before blowing her nose.

Cheney puts her left arm around her again, and says, "C'mon sit down with me," and she motions to the love seat, but Kate shakes her head, and insists, "No, no, I want to stand."

"Okay, okay," Cheney removes her arm from her sister's shoulder, and waits, awkwardly so, for her to speak. She really doesn't know how to approach this situation, for she has never really been that close to Kate. Sure, she loves her kid sister; but at the end of the day, there is such an emotional chasm between the two of them, that Kate has always seemed like a bit of a mystery to Cheney. In actuality, Cheney is much closer to several of her own friends, such as Lauren, than she is with her younger sister. This is probably, in part, due to the large age gap: at twenty-four, Kate is seven years younger than Cheney. Cheney lived most of the first decade of her life as an only child, and, in truth, she had liked being the sole object of her parents' affection, such that, when Kate came along, she was less than thrilled. Of course, over the years, she grew to be fond and even protective of her little sister, but there were also times where she was resentful and maybe even a bit envious of Kate. Some of those feelings from childhood linger still.

Even crying, evidenced by her beet-colored nose and splotchy skin, Kate looks radiantly beautiful, her reckless, violent-red hair coursing over her shoulders, and her pronounced jutting chin and high cheekbones staking out the room. At five-foot-ten, Kate is three inches taller than Cheney, and there is a graceful blend of a genteel and welcoming aura about her that is absent in Cheney's own standoffish and cynical personality.

Kate continues looking out the window, and Cheney asks her if she wants a cup of coffee, or some water or something to eat, but Kate just shakes her head, arms folded, tears streaming down her cheeks.

"I have some left-over pizza: sausage and mushroom," Cheney offers. "I could heat some up in the microwave."

"Oh, no, no, thank you," Kate says, wiping her nose politely and then finally moving away from the window and sitting down in the love seat. She is wearing a fitted-soft pink turtle neck sweater, a burgundy-satin skirt cut right above the knee, ebony tights, and low-heeled leather oxblood riding boots.

Cheney joins her on the opposite end of the burgundy and gold Victorian-era loveseat, waiting for her to speak. Patton lies down at Cheney's feet, and she folds over at the waist and pets him silently, waiting for her sister to tell her why she is here.

Kate looks like she can read Cheney's mind, and she begins: "I'm sorry to bother you so late."

"It's no bother. I was awake anyway," Cheney assures her, continuing petting Patton's bulky head. "But this guy," Cheney says referring to Patton, "he's another story. You've got some explaining to do to him. He was just on the verge of snoring when you rang the doorbell."

Kate smiles, but her eyes well up with tears, "I'm sorry. Really, I am. I just didn't know where else to go." She breaks down crying again.

"Geez, you know I was kidding about the dog," Cheney says, and gets up to retrieve more tissue and returns, handing her the entire box and patting her on the back. "I was just trying to make you laugh. It's okay, Kate. Really, it is. I've got to admit, though, you have me really worried here. You've got to tell me what's going on here."

"It has to do with Nic," Kate begins, choking on her words, and intermittently blowing her nose.

Nic, who's Nic? Kate brought some guy named Hal or Harry or something like that to Christmas; Cheney's never heard of a 'Nic'. Kate has had a lot of boyfriends over the years, and sometimes it's hard to get them straight; and, once in a while, some of them will even reappear years later, as a different, new-improved iteration. There was that guy she dated in high school, but his name was Todd, not Nic: Or was it?

At the risk of getting Kate more upset, she has to ask. She does so, gingerly. "Okay, Kate, who is Nic? Is this someone I've met before?"

"No, no; you've never met him. We've only been dating a month. I mean, we've been dating off and on for about six months, but we just started dating-dating in January."

"What happened to Hal?"

Kate looks confused.

"The guy you brought to Christmas."

"That was Harry."

"That was going to be my second guess," Cheney deadpans, but Kate doesn't laugh.

"Harry's just a friend. We weren't a couple or anything."

"Oh, okay," Cheney says. Maybe in Kate's mind they were just friends, but Harry had looked completely enraptured with Kate Costello, as most men are.

"I've never heard you mention the name Nic before," Cheney says.

Kate has stopped crying: the clarity needed to converse evidently forcing her to gain her composure. "Well, Cheney, I mean, really we don't talk that much these days. I mean, the only time I've seen you since Christmas was the play."

By 'these days' Kate must mean, 'since Dan was murdered.' It is true that Cheney has not had much contact with Kate, or anyone else for that matter, since early November. In the immediate weeks after Dan was murdered, Cheney had been obsessed with trying to learn the identity of his killer and bring him to justice. Still, it seems like yesterday that the two police officers showed up at the farmhouse to tell her that Dan had been gunned down in an alley while chasing a drug dealer. The discovery that Dan had been murdered was traumatic enough, let alone that her agony had been amplified when she had learned the identity of the person who had been accused of killing him: her former client, Solomon Wilson.

She had been so depressed it had been difficult to function. She had stayed home, isolated in her house, until she had learned that Solomon wanted to talk to her, and that he was insisting he was innocent. She had risked her law license by going to talk to Solomon in the jail, and he had told her that there had been a witness to the murder, a Latin King named Manuel Rodriguez. This is the part where things get hazy. It is hard for her to imagine what she did next. She cannot believe she had it in her to kidnap Manuel Rodriguez at gunpoint and cajole – No, let's face it, *force* - him into cooperating with her unofficial investigation into Dan's murder. This seems impossible that she actually did this, as fantastical as if she had flown across the Atlantic in a single-engine plane or had robbed a train on horseback.

Kate never brings up Manuel Rodriguez, and Cheney is relieved about that. She wonders how much Kate even knows about that situation: how much their mother actually divulged to Kate. Hopefully, not much. But it's true that Cheney hasn't been very communicative with anyone since Manuel was murdered in the Cook County Jail. She was released from the hospital only five days after she was shot by Derek Strozak, and she's been fairly isolated ever since. She spends most of her time either trying to sort through the memories of that fateful month or trying to figure out what she's going to do next, now that Dan is gone. In fairness, even if Kate had mentioned someone named Nic before - which, evidently, she had not - Cheney probably wouldn't have processed and stored the name anyway. It would have been as insubstantial as the snowflakes outside the bay window.

Cheney feels a tinge of guilt. She should be reaching out more to her family, despite her own grief and trauma. There are literally days that go by before she even returns a call from her mother or her sister. Recognizing this, Cheney apologizes to Kate: "I know. I'm sorry. I've been a bit preoccupied lately. I've just been dealing with a lot myself lately, so I guess I've just been kind of hiding out in my house away from civilization."

"No, no - no need to apologize," Kate says. "I get it. Really, I do. I didn't mean to make you feel bad or anything. It's just that I haven't wanted to trouble you either with what's going on in my personal life. I haven't wanted to burden you with my problems. I know you have enough going on right now as it is."

"Okay, so now that we've got that out of the way: What's up Kate?" Cheney asks her directly. "What's going on that led you to come way out here in the middle of the night in the midst of a raging blizzard?"

She suspects that it is some dramatic breakup between Kate and this Nic guy. When Kate was a senior in high school, she had called Cheney sobbing late one night, because the quarterback of the football team had dumped her only a week before prom. When Cheney had tried to comfort her by telling her that boys come and go, and that a much better guy would probably ask her to the dance in the morning, Kate had wailed: "But you can't understand. You're *you*. You don't care about boys like I do. Boys can't break your heart. They can't even get to it."

Kate had been right, of course. But only in part. It was true that Cheney didn't ever lose sleep or shed a tear over some guy not asking her out or breaking up with her: after all, there would always be another one right around the corner. But one man – no, actually *two* men - had been able to get into her heart: Dan Manning and Manuel Rodriguez. But they were both gone now and her heart was broken.

She prepared herself that Kate was going to tell her a sob story about how some fellow theater student had dumped her for one of her castmates in *Steel Magnolias*. She is accustomed to the dramatic ups and downs of Kate's love life, a roller-coaster of boys, from the athletic to the artistic. Kate knows no type, for she draws in and is seemingly attracted to a wide-array of men.

Kate breathes in, as if composing herself. She then stands up and pulls the turtleneck off over her head, baring her upper body. She holds up the backs of her arms to Cheney, almost defiantly, as if showing a disbeliever corroborating evidence. Patton seems to sense something serious is going on, and he looks up at Kate and sighs.

"This is what brought me here," Kate announces; and Cheney knows now why Kate came to her house at this hour.

# COMPLIMENT

*February 2nd*

There are visible, imperfect bruises like trails of brown river water above the backs of each of Kate's elbows and along the undersides of her forearms. Cheney has handled enough domestic battery cases to recognize that the marks have been inflicted by human hands, particularly the distinctive pinch marks on either side of Kate's slim arms.

Cheney remains outwardly calm, though inside she is furious at this Nic asshole who has harmed her little sister. "This guy did that to you?" she asks.

"Yes," Kate says. She has stopped crying, as if sharing her secret with her sister has empowered her in some way, and she pulls the turtleneck back on over her head. She sits down on one of the green-velvet winged-back chairs, facing Cheney.

"When did this happen?" Cheney asks, impassive, cloaking her outrage.

"Last night. We were out having dinner at his restaurant -"

"His restaurant?" Cheney interrupts her. She can hear the edge in her own voice.

"Yes. He owns two restaurants. One in Chicago and one in Loomisville. We were at the one in Loomisville." Her voice is no longer tremulous and she seems much more relaxed.

"Okay," Cheney says, waiting for her to continue.

"We had dinner and everything was okay, and then this guy came over to our table, a lawyer who is a politician of some sort. He came to introduce himself to Nic and to me. His name was - oh, I can't remember now, Mike or Miles or something like that. He knows you."

"He knows me?"

"Yes, he said you guys went to law school together and he knows you well. He's not very tall, maybe an inch or so shorter than me, and he kind of swaggers and he has dark hair, and these darling dimples. He has an east coast accent. He's from like New York or -"

"Boston. Matthew Brockton. He was just sworn in last November as the State's Attorney of Kent County."

"Yes, that's him: Matthew Brockton." Kate now sounds much more at ease, and the lilt of excited effervescence in her voice that is normally housed there is returning. "That's the guy. He came over to our table and we literally talked with him for less than five minutes. I guess he was having an event in the banquet room of the restaurant, and he wanted to just come over and introduce himself to Nic and let him know that the event was going great and invite us to stop by after we were finished with dinner if we felt like it. From the conversation between Nic and him I gathered that he was a lawyer and he was an elected official of some sort.

"When I heard he was an attorney, I told him that my sister was a public defender in Stickney County and he said, 'It's got to be Cheney

Manning,' and I asked, 'How did you guess?' and he said something like, 'Striking redhead. I can see the family resemblance.' And then he asked how you were doing with everything. And I said you were doing okay under the circumstances and he said he had gone to Dan's wake and that he had talked to you then, but that there were so many people there, that you were probably overwhelmed with everything, and that you may not even remember him being there."

"I do remember him being there," Cheney says definitively, though in truth, the memory of Matthew being at Dan's wake is kind of blurry. There were hundreds of faces, and hugs, and 'my condolences' from those who were familiar to her and some who were unfamiliar. Those days and weeks after Dan's murder all still seem like part of some kind of a foggy dream.

Kate continues, her exuberant personae kicking back into full gear. "Then he gave me his card with his cellphone number on it, and he said if you ever needed anything, feel free to give him a call - that he hadn't talked to you in years outside of Dan's wake - and it would be good to reconnect."

Cheney is wondering where this conversation is headed. Matthew Brockton was a guy she had liked years ago, back in law school. Long before she had met Dan, there was a time when she had been slightly curious whether Matthew Brockton would ask her out. He sat next to her in Criminal Procedure class in their second semester of their second year and they sometimes joked with each other in whispers or shared sarcastic comments penned along their brief margins, as though they were sixth-graders passing notes. She was taken in by those dimples along with the perfect white smile and the startling seafoam green eyes. He looked like a candidate for state's attorney even back then.

There was a night at the end of that semester when they had drunk a lot of beer at a local tavern celebrating completion of their final exams,

23

and he had walked her back to her apartment and had kissed her. It hadn't been just any kiss either. It was a memorable one. Followed by a series of other memorable ones. He had confessed to her that he had been waiting the entire semester to do that.

Still, she had not invited him inside, and nothing further had ever happened from there on out. They had gone their separate ways for the summer, and even though she had given him her cellphone number that night, he had never called. He left for Boston the next day. While they were friends on social media, he, like her, rarely posted anything. In fact, he didn't post anything at all the entire summer up until a week or so before the new semester started: A photo of him and an attractive brunette, announcing their engagement. At the time, Cheney had thought, 'No wonder I never heard from him,' but she hadn't been really surprised, nor was she particularly disappointed. She had figured a good-looking guy like him had to have some girl back home. When she had returned to law school, she learned from some of their mutual friends that the brunette was Matthew Brockton's college sweetheart, and that she was also a law student, but at some school out east.

In that last year of law school, Cheney seldom saw Matthew Brockton, and only exchanged small talk with him one or two times in passing. Besides, she had been busy with her internship at the public defender's office that year, as well as her trial advocacy team competition, so she rarely ran into him on campus. They didn't have any classes together, and on the few occasions when she would see him out at one of the local taverns, he would stick with his group of guy friends and not come over by her.

Once, only days before graduation, she had caught him looking at her across a popular bar and she allowed her gaze to stick with his for a few long seconds. He had smiled, his dimples reaching out to her from across the room, and he had kind of waved at her. But she had simply held up her beer bottle somewhat dismissively, like a sailor silently saying goodbye to a one-night stand before he goes off to sea. She had turned to one of her friends, and continued their conversation, as if engrossed in it, and she had not looked over in his direction again.

"And I'd give you his card, but I don't have it now," Kate says. "Nic took it and crumpled it up."

"What? In front of him?"

"No, later on," Kate says, and adds, "I'm sorry. He really sounded interested in talking to you."

"That's okay, Kate. Really. I don't have any use for Matthew Brockton's phone number anyway."

For some reason, Kate starts crying again. "I'm sorry," she says, tears streaming down her cheeks.

"Oh, Kate, please don't cry about me not having Matthew Brockton's cellphone number: the guy who blew me off in law school."

This last part seems to jerk Kate out of the throes of her sadness. She blows her nose, stops crying, and demands, "He blew you off in law school? Do tell!"

It is clear that Kate wants to deflect away from the difficult conversation that needs to take place. "C'mon, Kate. You're not here to listen to me talk about Matthew Brockton. Let's get back to the topic at hand here. Go back to where you left off. Tell me what happened."

Kate sighs. "So, after Matthew left our table, we finished our dinner but I could tell there was something wrong with Nic. He just seemed really distracted and he wasn't really talking to me, and he just kept looking down at his cellphone. He seemed like maybe he was angry about something, but I wasn't really sure. And then, when we got up to leave, I mentioned to him that maybe we could pop in to the fundraiser, just to see who was there and what it was about, and he took my arm, and said, 'No, we're not going to that,' and I could tell by the way he said it that he was mad about something.

Her eyes start to well up a little bit with tears again, and she dots at them with her tissue. "And then he kind of gripped me by my elbow and walked really close to me and said we needed to go to his office. His office is up on the second floor, so we took the stairs up there, and he was quiet the entire time, and I could sense he was angry about some-thing, but I wasn't sure what.

"And once we went into his office, that's when everything hap-pened. He kind of spun me around with his right hand, and then he used his left hand to slam the door shut. And he just-" she pauses, "- he just went off from there. He let go of my elbow and then he jerked on the strap on my shoulder bag and he pulled so hard that it literally broke open the clasp so that it was just hanging across my chest. And then he grabbed it off of me and he opened it up and took out Matthew's busi-ness card and crumpled it up and then shoved it into his own pocket, and said, 'You're not fucking calling this jagoff. Ever.'

"And I said, 'I wasn't going to call him anyway. It was for my sister,' and he said, 'Yeah, the fuck you weren't.' And then he let go of my elbow, but he was in my face, inches away, yelling at me, calling me a 'fucking whore', accusing me of flirting with Matthew. And I swear, Kate, I barely even talked to this Matthew guy. Really. I didn't do anything wrong at all. I was just being myself talking to him and there was nothing that I did where it would come off like I was flirting or anything. And I kept insisting to Nic that I wasn't flirting, that I wasn't interested in anyone but him, and that I only cared about him and no one else, but it just set him off even more. He just kept yelling in my face and calling me names. I couldn't believe that no one came into the room or that no one heard and called the police."

"But how did you get the bruises, Kate? What did he do to you?"

"I'm not really sure how it all happened. I was trying to leave and get around him, and he grabbed me above the elbow again and pinched down real hard like a vice. I'm pretty sure that's where I probably got some of the bruises. He kind of like pulled me over to the side of the room and then he pushed me into the wall, and then he pinned me - I guess you would call it - he *pinned* me up against the wall. At first, I held my arms up in front of my face because I was afraid he was going to hit me and he told me to 'put my fucking arms down' and 'not to worry – I don't hit women in the face.' But when I kept my arms up he jerked them down to my sides, and gripped them both down, hard. It hurt. So, I'm guessing that's where the other bruises came from.

"But then he pulled me again by the same arm, and he kind of threw me down on the floor and he just stood above me yelling, calling me a whore, calling me other things. I was actually cowering on the floor, holding my hands up across my face, hoping he wouldn't kick me."

Kate isn't crying anymore, and Cheney can tell that, while it is painful for her to recount the episode, it is kind of cathartic in a way. Kate seems more composed now that the story is reaching its conclusion.

"How did you get out of there?" Cheney asks.

"His cellphone started ringing. It was the banquet manager. Some business question. He was on the phone with him for a few minutes and it seemed to kind of cause him to snap out of it. I stood up while he was talking and I was waiting for him to get off the phone because I was afraid he would go at me again if I tried to leave, and then he said in a real calm voice to put on my coat, and that we were leaving. And I had left my coat upstairs in the office before we had gone to dinner, so I put it on, and then we left."

"You got into a car with him?" Cheney asks, astounded.

"Yes. I really didn't have a choice. I needed a ride back to DeKalb."

"You didn't let him stay at your apartment, did you?"

"No," Kate says, but Cheney can tell she is lying.

"C'mon, Kate."

"I'm serious. No. I didn't. He drove back to Loomisville that night."

"What happened in the car?"

"He was quiet and for some reason I felt like I should be the one to apologize, so I did."

"*You* apologized to *him*?"

"Yes. I know. I know it was stupid. But I was still kind of scared, or shaken, or something. I just wanted to keep him calm, you know? It seemed like the right thing to do at the time. And it worked. He was just quiet. He didn't say much the whole ride."

"Please tell me you didn't sleep with this guy when you came home," Cheney says.

"I didn't - I swear. Really, Cheney. I didn't."

Cheney just looks at her, and then Kate admits, "Okay, so he did stay over. I don't know why I let him, but I just felt bad letting him drive all the way back to Loomisville with ice on the roads. He slept on the couch though, Cheney. I swear."

"Okay, so what happened tonight, then? Why did you end up driving out here so late?"

"Well, we ended up hanging out during the day, and he seemed like he was fine, and then, all of a sudden after dinner, and after he had a few beers, he started back on the Matthew Brockton thing and accusing me of flirting with him, and calling me a 'striking redhead', and it just got worse from there on out. He picked up my smartphone and started scrolling through my contacts, and interrogating me as to who each guy was in my phone, and when the last time I talked to so-and-so was, and he was just getting angrier and angrier and he wouldn't listen to anything I said, and he just kept accusing me of lying, accusing me of cheating on him. And then all of a sudden, he just stopped talking and threw my phone so hard against the wall that it shattered and then he just put his coat on and left. And he didn't say anything to me.

"And, I didn't have any way to call you or anything, because my phone is broken, and I didn't have anywhere else to go. I didn't want to wake up Mom and Dad and worry them, but I was afraid to stay in my apartment, afraid that he would come back, so I just jumped in my car and drove here."

"Oh, man, Kate, what have you gotten yourself into? You're not going to go back to this asshole, are you?"

"No. No. I swear I won't, Cheney. I don't want anything to do with him ever again." Kate pauses. "Is it okay with you, if I stay here this weekend?"

"Of course," Cheney says without hesitation. "You don't even need to ask. My door is always open for you. You're the only kid sister I've got."

Although Kate has been composed for the recounting of the entire story, her eyes start to well up with tears again. "You're not going to tell mom and dad?"

"No," Cheney says. "This is your story to tell. Not mine."

"Thanks, Cheney," Kate says. "I appreciate all of this. I know you like to be alone, and I don't want to invade your private space."

It is true. Cheney usually does like to be by herself for long periods of time, reading or writing. But being alone is much different than being lonely, and lately she has experienced a desolation of sorts, particularly being in a remote area in the winter, with so many hours to mull over the events of the past few months.

It will be a comfort to have some company in the old farmhouse for a few days, particularly with the cold wind battering the windows and the snow covering the fields like the satin lining of a casket. February in Illinois can be a dreary enough month as it is; and, with the double-trauma of Dan's and Manuel's murders still affecting her, Cheney has a feeling that this particular February is going to be a challenging one to get through despite its brevity. It is a relief that she will not be alone in the house, at least for the next couple of nights.

# PHOTOGRAPH

*February 2nd*

Cheney was not prepared for the virtual phone conference at nine. She had stayed up with Kate until past three in the morning and even when Cheney finally went to bed she hadn't been able to sleep much. Kate had decided that a sausage and mushroom pizza sounded good after all. The two sisters ended up sitting in the living room, eating the entire large pizza, and talking. Cheney had finally suggested that they go to sleep, but she didn't tell Kate that she had a conference in the morning, because she didn't want Kate to feel bad about having kept her up so late.

Even though there was an additional bedroom on the second floor down the hallway from her own, Cheney decided she'd have Kate stay upstairs in the third-floor attic bedroom. The other bedroom on the second-floor was the one Cheney used primarily for her home office, and it contained the desktop computer that she was going to use for the video conference. She didn't want to wake Kate up in the morning, so she had opted to just have her sleep upstairs. Besides, the only bed in the office was a futon, whereas the room on the third floor had a queen-sized bed. The attic, however, was much colder than the second-floor, and Kate immediately complained about the temperature as soon as they went into the room.

"Do you have like a space heater that I could use or something? It's pretty chilly up here, Cheney," Kate had said, folding her arms, and saying "Brrrrrr…." under her breath. The cold was creeping in through the windows along the south wall, the wind continuing its relentless crusade against the old farmhouse.

"No," Cheney had said. "I swear you'll warm up though once you get under the covers. Underneath the quilt, there's a down comforter, and a blanket. But I have an extra pair of flannels if you want to wear those instead of these," she had said, gesturing to the t-shirt and shorts she had removed from her own dresser to give to her sister to wear.

"No, no. These are going to be fine," Kate had said, taking the clothes.

Cheney had sensed Kate's hesitancy, so she had offered, "You could sleep downstairs on the couch instead if you want?"

"No, no - that's okay," Kate had said. "You're right that once I get in bed, it will warm up. That wind, outside though, my gosh! It really sounds like it's howling. No wonder it's so cold in here."

"Is there anything else I can get you, Kate?" Cheney had asked. "I've really got to get some shut eye."

"No, nothing at all," Kate had said. "Thank you for everything. Really, I mean it. I don't know what I would have done without being able to come here." Kate had paused, looking reflective, and then, she had hesitated - almost as if she wasn't sure she should go there - but she did so anyway. She had asked Cheney, "Is this the room that that Manuel guy stayed in while he was here?"

That Manuel guy. "Yes, this is where *that Manuel guy* stayed," Cheney had said icily.

"Oh, I didn't mean any offense by that," Kate had said, evidently sensing Cheney's annoyance.

"None taken," Cheney had said, even though she was irritated by the way in which Kate had referred to Manuel. Cheney had not spoken to Kate at all about Manuel Rodriguez and she had no intention of doing so in the future. What happened between Manuel and her is really no one else's business.

She had wondered, though, how much Kate knew about Manuel, so she had asked her: "What did Mom say to you about Manuel?"

"Mom? She's said nothing," Kate had responded too quickly. And then, after evidently sensing Cheney's disbelief, Kate had added: "Really, Cheney. Mom and I have barely talked at all about that Manuel guy. Mom told me that some guy from Chicago had helped you find out who murdered Dan, and that he was arrested for something else, and then he was killed in the Cook County Jail. And I figured out that he was that hot guy that I had met in your house that one day I came over: the one who told me he was a policeman. That's all I know. The only ones who really told me anything about him were the police."

"The police?" Cheney was shocked. She had no idea that Kate had been interviewed by the police. "When did you talk to the police?"

"I don't know. Like a day or two after you had been shot. They showed up at my apartment to ask me questions."

"The Loomisville Police?"

"Yes, but I also talked to the Chicago Police like a few days after that."

Cheney tries to remain calm. Nevertheless, she hears the edge in her own voice: "What? You talked to the Loomisville Police and the Chicago Police?"

"Yes."

"And you didn't tell me?" Cheney had been interviewed by two Loomisville detectives a few days after she was released from the hospital, but she had refused to answer any questions pertaining to Manuel Rodriguez, other than to say that he had been a witness to Dan's murder and that he had identified Derek Strozak as Dan's killer. She had not been contacted by the Chicago Police at all, so this revelation that they had reached out to Kate and interviewed her was particularly disturbing.

"I didn't think I could," Kate had explained. "I was afraid I'd get in trouble or something or get you in trouble if I told you. But anyway, now it's been a few months, and I haven't heard back from them, so I guess it probably doesn't really matter if I tell you."

"Well, why did they go to talk to you in the first place?"

"Because when Mom had told me about that Manuel guy while you were in the hospital, she mentioned that the Loomisville Police had been asking her questions about him, and wondering if she had met him at your house, and Mom had told the police that she didn't know anything about him. Mom said the police told her that he had been staying at your house before you were shot, and then I realized it was the Mexican guy I had met in your library, so I told Mom. I told her that I thought he was a cop, and she told me he wasn't, but that's all she said. I guess Mom really didn't know what was going on with you – none of us did – actually, none of us still really know what was going on with you back then – but Mom must've thought it would help you if she told the police that I had met Manuel. I think that's why the police showed up at my apartment in DeKalb. At least, that's what they told me: that they had information that I had met Manuel Rodriguez at your house."

"They just showed up there without calling you?"

"Yes. Two detectives. Two men."

"Do you remember their names?"

"No. But I recognized one from the funeral. He was the guy who gave the eulogy."

"Jeff Cantoni."

"Yes. That was it."

"They didn't call you before they came to your apartment?"

"No."

"They just showed up?"

"That's right. I had actually just finished class for the day, and I literally was in my apartment for like thirty seconds and they rang the doorbell and there they were."

"What did they ask you?"

"Oh, gosh, Cheney, you know I had a lot on my mind then. My sister was lying in a hospital with a gunshot wound. My brother-in-law had been killed only a few weeks before that. I was just trying to hold it together for Mom and Dad at that point. They both had been through so much. It was kind of emotionally traumatic for all of us, you know?"

"How long were they there, at your apartment?"

"Oh, not that long from what I remember. A half an hour maybe."

"Do you remember, in general, what they were asking you about?"

"You. Manuel. How you knew him. How long you had known him. How you met him. How he ended up staying at your house. If you told me anything about him. I told them I didn't know anything about him other than having met him one time at the house and that he gave me some other name and that I assumed, and he confirmed, that he was a Loomisville police officer. And that was pretty much it. They wanted to know the name he gave me, and I told them it was George Morales."

"And how did you end up talking to the Chicago Police?"

"A detective called – maybe a day or two after I talked to Detective Cantoni and the other detective. The detective from Chicago asked if I could come downtown to the station to talk to him about Manuel Rodriguez, and so I drove there a day or two after that and met with two detectives."

"What did they ask you?"

"Same kind of questions as Jeff Cantoni had asked me. But they asked more about you than Manuel and they told me stuff about Manuel."

"Like what?" Cheney asks, her heart racing.

"What did they ask about you or what did they tell me about Manuel?"

"Both," Cheney says.

"About you, they wanted to know a lot about your personal life, like how your marriage with Dan was going before he was killed and names of your friends, and how long you had worked at the public defender's office; and, they asked a lot of questions about your personality - what you are like - and how you were acting after Dan was killed and whether I saw you much after the funeral: stuff like that. And about Manuel, they told me he was in a gang in Chicago and that they were trying to find out how you knew Manuel and how he ended up at your house. But the way they asked the questions, I started worrying that maybe you were in trouble for something and I asked them that, and they told me 'No,'; but, it seemed like maybe they were just saying that."

Cheney had tried to cloak her concern, but she could sense her own usually-inscrutable voice trembling. "Well, why would you think that I was in trouble for anything? It was my husband who was killed and I'm the one who was sitting in a hospital bed with a bullet wound."

"Because of the way they were asking questions, that's all," Kate had answered. "It just seemed like you were the one who was under investigation for something. They asked a lot of questions about you, but almost none about Manuel: except that they were asking how he was acting when I met him, if he seemed sad or scared or nervous, and I said, 'I wouldn't know because I didn't know him; I only met him that one time at your house, and he didn't seem like he was any of those things. He seemed like an easygoing kind of guy, with a nice smile, and he had just been sitting there reading a book in your library.' Oh, and they wanted to know what he was reading and I told them something by Tolstoy and they looked at each other and burst out laughing and one of them said, 'You got to be fucking kidding me? Tolstoy?' and I kind of was taken aback and I said, 'Isn't that Manuel guy dead? I mean, should you really be laughing at him?' and that kind of shut them up then."

When she went back down to her bedroom, Cheney had barely slept, worrying about the import of what her sister had said. After all, it was still possible that Cheney would be arrested for having kidnapped Manuel back in November. Unlikely, but possible. It would be a difficult case for the Chicago Police to solve, with Manuel dead and with the Latin Kings likely being uncooperative.

But there had been the girl in the room – Rachel - with Manuel during Cheney's criminal excursion. Cheney had forced Manuel at gunpoint to handcuff Rachel to the bed. It was possible that the Chicago Police would find out about Rachel and perhaps she would cooperate with their investigation and tell the detectives what Cheney did. The thought of getting arrested and sent to the Cook County Jail was enough to make Cheney restless, apprehensive, worried. Maybe she was reading too much into what Kate had said. Perhaps there was nothing to be concerned about at all. Besides, the Chicago Police had so many open murder investigations on their hands, the mere kidnapping of a Latin King would seem to be a very low priority, particularly when the suspect was the bereaved widow of a cop.

Still, this fear clings to her and distracts her during her visual conference with the non-profit that assists spouses of fallen police officers. There are four people on the computer screen along with her: two board members, the director, and a legal representative. The director, Garrett Simms, is a warm-faced man with a goatee and solemn eyes. He revisits the board's offer of paying off the mortgage on the farm, explaining that it is something that the organization typically does to assist families with the expenses and financial burden of having suffered the loss of a spouse.

Cheney is appreciative of the offer and she says as much. But she is hesitant to accept their offer, and she tells them so. She emphasizes that she is an attorney, without any children, and she should be able to swing the mortgage payments on her own, particularly with Dan's death benefits and life insurance proceeds. She does not share with them another reason for her rejecting such a gift: that she may possibly be charged with a series of felonies arising from her forcible abduction of Manuel Rodriguez.

Even though it is highly unlikely that she'll ever get charged for her criminal acts surrounding the night she kidnapped Manuel Rodriguez from the Latin King safehouse, *if* she were to ever get arrested, it could potentially bring unsavory publicity to the honorable organization. So, she is forceful this time when she declines the offer. She tells them that it would be impossible for her to accept such a generous benefit and she emphasizes that there are so many other families of fallen officers that are far more deserving. It takes a lot of convincing, but eventually, Mr. Simms ends the call by letting her know that they are there to assist her if she needs anything in the future, and to not hesitate to reach out if she changes her mind.

After the conference call ends, she sits in her chair for a minute, staring at the screensaver. It's a picture of Dan and her when they went to Santa Fe on vacation two years ago. They are standing in front of the Cathedral Basilica of St. Francis of Assisi, holding hands, smiling. Dan is wearing a pair of black tactical-gear pants and a plain gray t-shirt: with his broad-shoulders and crew cut he looks like the quintessential cop.

She remembers the lady who took their picture that day: a Navajo woman of advanced years who congenially had said 'Of course' when Dan asked her to do so. After the woman had taken their photo, she had told them that 'they would be together for the rest of their lifetimes.' No, that's not what she had said. She had directed her comment solely to Dan and had used the word 'lifetime', not 'lifetimes.' Cheney remembers it as clear as if it happened yesterday.

At the time, Cheney had thought the woman meant that they would be together for many years, but now, she wonders whether the lady had witnessed imminent death shadowing Dan. There had been that pensive, almost ominous, look when the woman had handed the smartphone back to Dan, and her voice had sounded heavy with sorrow when she said: "You will be together for the rest of your lifetime."

Dan had even mentioned it to Cheney later that evening, over drinks at a Mexican restaurant on the Square. "Didn't that old lady sound sad when she said we will be together for the rest of our lifetimes?"

At the time, Cheney had contemplated correcting him with: 'She said lifetime – not lifetimes.' But, she had thought better of it. She was always one for over-analyzing things, part of the curse of being a litigator, so she had just shrugged it off and said: "Oh, I'm guessing that she just was thinking about someone she loved once - a companion she lost, perhaps?"

That's not what the lady had been thinking though. Cheney is sure of it now. The Navajo woman had seen the death in Dan. But she shouldn't be surprised by this. After all, hadn't she seen it in him, too?

# RESIGNATION

*February 2nd*

It is nearly four in the afternoon when she receives a call back from her boss, Maria Calderon. She had called Maria earlier in the day, shortly after her morning videoconference call with the non-profit. When Maria had not answered, Cheney had left her a voicemail message letting her know that she wanted to talk about work, and asking if she could give her a return call.

It is snowing again outside, though Dax Hardy is nearly finished with plowing her driveway. Kate is outside helping him, which is unusual for her, since she is not usually one to engage in manual labor. Cheney had lent her a pair of Dan's sweatpants and a sweatshirt, along with Dan's black and white camouflage hip-length coat. Kate is also wearing a pair of Dan's boots, even though they are several sizes too big for her.

Kate had seemed eager to help out when she saw Dax come to the door to let Cheney know he was here. Dax is eighteen, though he looks older, and he is movie-star handsome, with black hair, a sparkling smile, and a quarterback-build. He's the son of the farmer who tends to Cheney's property and he drives one of his father's trucks with a plow in the winter months.

Kate practically leapt out of the loveseat in the parlor when she saw Dax exit his pickup and walk toward the house and she was the first to answer the door. Kate's beautiful face alighted with a bewitching glow, and her dimples were in full force when she introduced herself. As for his part, Dax looked absolutely smitten from the moment he laid eyes on the tall redhead and he did not hesitate in accepting her offer to help with the peripheral sidewalk areas, such as those around the garage and barn that could not be reached by the truck plow.

Prior to Maria calling, Cheney had sat on the loveseat, reading her next book assignment for the Spinach Omelet Book Nerds, Laura Ingalls Wilder's *The Long Winter*. However, Cheney would intermittently pause to watch the winter scene out the bay window: Dax looking over at Kate cautiously to make sure she was out of the way when he was backing up the truck, Kate playfully waving at him like a midwestern snow bunny on the low slopes of Alpine Valley, Patton prancing around on the white of the south lawn.

Observing Dax and Kate, brings back memories of Dan. They didn't own a snow blower, and instead enjoyed many mornings shoveling by hand the expansive driveway in the dead of winter. They had discussed buying a blower a few times in years' past; but they had jointly rejected the notion. They both had voiced to each other their preference for the physical labor of scraping the plastic to the concrete and heaving the bundles of snow, as opposed to easily pushing a gas-propelled piece of equipment. Staring out the bay window now, she thinks of Dan laughingly tossing loosely-packed snowballs at her that scattered into the air before contact and the dog, bounding between them, reveling in the feel of a fresh snowfall.

Cheney puts the book down and answers Maria's call, and she stands up for the conversation, watching Dax's truck push snow into banks along the perimeter of the concrete way. There is something relaxing about the sound of a snowplow, especially when snow is cascading downward, ready to pile up again.

She likes to pace when she's on the phone, particularly when it is a discussion that is uncomfortable or important. This conversation with Maria happens to be both. The Stickney County Public Defender's Office is the only place Cheney has worked since she graduated from law school. It is truly a job that she enjoyed, and, at one time in her life, prior to November of last year, she thought she would spend her entire legal career in the public defender's office.

Now, she can think of no attorney position that she would like to do less than being a public defender. It shouldn't be surprising, with everything she's been through over the course of the past several months, that she no longer wants to be a defense attorney. Still, though, she is amazed at her personal transformation: her role as a public defender, which she has always considered to be so important, has been her priority for years. Now, though, the job really doesn't seem to matter at all anymore. So much so, that she is ready to quit it without having another one lined up.

She has worked ever since she was fourteen. She used to detassel corn from July until mid-August in the summers and once she turned sixteen, she worked at a fast-food restaurant part-time on weekends and evenings. She worked all through college too: selling clothing at a specialty boutique a couple of nights a week, tutoring struggling students in English composition for an hourly fee, and writing freelance news and features articles for a local newspaper, *The Meskwaki Times*. During law school, she continued writing for the paper, but she also worked as a law clerk for a firm in Loomisville during her second and third years. Even during the summer when she was studying for the bar exam, she continued writing articles for the newspaper and performing legal research work for the firm.

Even though she really wants to quit her job, she is, quite frankly, scared. It is a bit unnerving to think about the prospect of being without a job, a paycheck, income. She wonders what her future holds, and whether it will even entail the practice of law. Still, she is certain that this is what she wants to do. But when she tells Maria that she is resigning and will not be returning to the office, there is a long pause and silence on the speaker phone, and Cheney can sense that her decision is not going over very well.

Cheney has a way of filling the void with words, so she does so: "I do thank you and Bob for being so understanding over these past few months. Please let Bob know that I appreciate that he gave me the leave of absence after Dan was killed and the patience and support everyone's shown to me after I was shot. I am grateful for everything you and Bob and everyone at the office has done for me. It's been a tough decision for me. I've really enjoyed working there and I am going to miss the job, the people."

"Are you sure this is what you really want to do?" Maria asks. "I could talk to Bob about extending your leave of absence for another month. I'm not sure if he'll go along with it, but I know he really wants you to stay, so maybe he would be amenable to that."

Cheney turns away from the bay window and heads down the long hallway toward the kitchen, thinking, talking. "I appreciate that. Really, I do. But, I'm sure. I just don't have it in me to come back. I hope you understand."

Again, a pause, but then Maria says, "I do. It's just that we were hoping you would come back. We really don't have anyone who's ready to move up from misdemeanors or juvie to felonies yet. We'll have to go to the outside and that, of course, will cause some consternation internally, I suppose. But that's nothing for you to worry about."

She does. She feels bad about pushing her caseload on to someone else, and she's felt guilty off and on over the past few months about the burden her absence has imposed on her co-workers. She feels particularly guilty now. "I'm really sorry. I know that I should have come to this decision sooner. I feel bad leaving you guys in a bind. Really, I do. It's not a decision that I came to lightly. I've given it a lot of thought though, believe me." She leans against the kitchen countertop against the east wall by the sink and continues talking into the cellphone on speaker. "It's just that, I can't even think about handling a criminal case right now, after everything I've been through. I'm just not ready to do it right now."

She hears a bump against the glass door next to the sink, and she turns around and heads over to let Patton in to the house. He is standing out on the porch, one of his giant paws pushing up against the outside handle of the door, as if trying to let himself inside. She puts the phone in her left hand, and then opens the door for the Rottweiler to charge through, while Maria tells her she understands her not wanting to return to the office right now, but asks whether she might reconsider in the future.

Cheney sets the phone down on the countertop, leans down to retrieve a can of dog food for Patton, and opens it while responding to Maria. "No. I won't change my mind about this, Maria. I'm ready to go."

"It's just that you were so dedicated to the job and to your clients," Maria says. "I understand that you're not ready to come back right now, like you just said, but, maybe in a month or two, you'll miss the job and want to come back. So, maybe you just want some more time to think about it before you resign."

Cheney finishes filling up Patton's food bowl and places it down on his spot across the room in a corner of the kitchen. "I know I was dedicated: Not so much now. Frankly, I would be doing a disservice to my clients if I were to return. Really, I would." She cuts back across the room and leans against the kitchen countertop again. "I just don't see myself being a defense attorney anymore. I don't have any passion for it. It's gone."

Another pause, and then: "What do you suppose you'll do? Are you going to go into solo practice or join a firm?"

"I'm not sure yet," she says, and she's not. She wants to write - plays or poetry or short stories - but she knows that sounds flakey to someone as dedicated to a legal career as Maria is. So, she doesn't say anything. Her words just hang there like a cloud deciding whether to rain or dissipate. She starts to walk toward the opposite end of the house again, back toward the parlor, leaving her dog behind in the kitchen with his bowl of food.

"Well, I'm sure that Bob would always hire you back if you ever want to return at some point," Maria says. Cheney's not so sure about that. Bob once told her that, if an assistant public defender leaves the office, he has a policy that he would not hire the person again. She doesn't mention this to Maria. She's not ever planning on returning to the Stickney County Public Defender's Office anyway, so what would be the point in correcting her?

Instead, she says, "That's good to know, Maria. Thank you. I appreciate it."

"Well, again, if there's anything you need from me, do not hesitate to reach out at any point," Maria says. "I'll always be happy to give you a reference. You're a great attorney, Cheney. One of the best."

"Thanks, Maria. That means a lot coming from you," Cheney says and makes her way back to the bay window. With the sky so overcast, dusk has come early.

Maria is talking, but Cheney does not process what she is saying. Instead, her brain is focused on what she is seeing out the window. It takes her a few seconds to recognize what actually is happening. It has stopped snowing and there is a black car with its headlights on down the driveway, not far from the garage. There is a man standing in front of the car, with his back to the house, but Cheney can see movement: the man is flailing his arms as if he is angry. Kate is facing him, only a foot or two away from him, and the shovel is on the ground near her feet. Cheney knows her sister well enough to tell, even from this distance, that she is in distress. The man grabs for Kate's right wrist and she wrests it away and looks like she is arguing with him.

The rear of Dax's truck is in view near the front of the house, and Dax emerges, walking quickly for a few steps and then breaking into a sprint toward the man and Kate. Even inside, Cheney can hear Dax call out something, though the sound is muffled.

"Oh my God," Cheney says.

"Cheney? What's wrong?" Maria asks. "Cheney?"

"I've got to go," Cheney says, and hits the red end-call button, dropping the phone down on the closest green-velvet chair. She doesn't bother to grab a hat or gloves; she just throws a pair of her boots on and she bolts out the door.

She runs past Dax's truck which is parked haphazardly outside close to the house, and she charges down the long driveway. The black car is backing up, rapidly, and a bit erratically, and it swerves out onto the roadway and heads out down the highway just as Cheney reaches Dax and Kate.

"Are you guys okay?" she asks.

47

"Yes," Kate answers at the same time, as Dax says, "Yeah, yeah; we're fine."

Kate doesn't appear visibly upset. Instead, she seems more like she has an adrenaline rush, but, nonetheless, Cheney goes over to her to make sure she's okay. She drapes her left arm over Kate's right shoulder and hugs her close. "Who the hell was that? What happened?" she asks.

Kate sighs. "Who do you think?"

"That jagoff Nic guy?"

"Yes," Kate says.

Cheney takes her arm off of her and looks at her. Dax is standing there, seeming as if he is uncertain whether he should leave them alone or stay.

"What was he doing here?" Cheney asks. "How would he even know how to find you here?"

"I don't know," Kate says.

"Kate, seriously, you didn't call him, did you?"

"No, I didn't call him," Kate insists. "You know I don't have a phone anyway. How would I possibly call him?"

Kate had used Cheney's computer earlier in the afternoon to check her emails and social media accounts, so Cheney point blank asks her: "You didn't email him or instant message him or anything when you were on my computer?"

Kate looks offended at Cheney's accusation, and seems embarrassed to be having the conversation in front of Dax. "Of course not." At the same time that Kate answers Cheney, Dax asks Cheney if she wants him to leave.

"No, no; please stay here for a minute, Dax. I want to hear what happened. Besides, I haven't paid you yet."

"Oh, that's okay," he says. "I can come back later or tomorrow to pick it up if that is easier."

"Just hold on a second, Dax," she says and then returns to questioning Kate. "How would he possibly know you were here then?"

"It's not that hard to figure out, Cheney," Kate says. "I mean, he knows I have sister. He knows your name is Cheney. You're my sister. Obviously, I've talked about you. He knows your husband was the officer who was murdered last year in Loomisville. If he went to my apartment and saw that my car was gone and that I wasn't there, he could've easily figured out that I would probably come here. It's possible to find out where anyone lives on the Internet."

It seems like Kate is telling the truth, so Cheney moves on to trying to figure out what just transpired. "Okay, so tell me what happened. I saw out the window that he looked like he grabbed you by the wrist."

"He did, but I'm not hurt or anything. He just kind of loosely grabbed it and I ripped my hand away from him. He was trying to get me to go into the car with him to talk and I kept saying, 'No.'"

"Are you sure you're okay?"

Yes, I'm sure," Kate insists.

"How long was here?"

"Literally, just like a minute or two. You must've seen most of it. I was over by the north side of the garage shoveling the sidewalk, and I didn't see or hear him pull in, so the first time I saw him he was like a couple of yards away from me. And I was shocked to see him standing there: like, really, my heart felt like it stopped. And he was calm at first, and he said he just wanted to talk to me and I said, 'No,' and I started heading back over toward the house and I just kind of walked by him, and then he grabbed my arm and kind of swung me around and I said, 'Don't touch me' and he said, 'I can touch you if I want to.' And then I kept walking and he walked in front of me and kind of blocked my way when I tried to get by and then he swatted the shovel out of my right hand and started raising his voice at me and I started telling him to leave me alone and to just go away; and that's probably when you saw him grab my wrist and I wrested it away and then that's when Dax came running over."

"Yeah, I was finished plowing right in front of the house," Dax says, "and I was backing up and I looked in my rear-view mirror and I could see right away that something was going on, so I jumped out of the truck and went over there. I could hear him kind of yelling at her or something, so I yelled out 'Hey', but as soon as I came over, he just went to his car, and opened the door and got inside."

"Thank you, by the way," Kate says politely. She always looks beautiful, but with the flush from shoveling in the cold and the recent brush with danger, her cheeks are even more aglow than usual and her blue eyes are particularly animated.

Dax smiles warmly and says, "No problem at all. I'm just glad I could help."

The flirtatious banter and eye-locking between Dax and Kate is a bit nauseating, since Cheney is trying to get to the bottom of what happened and make sure that this lunatic is not going to return with a firearm. "He didn't say anything to you then? He just drove off?"

"Well, he did say something to us before he left," Kate says.

"What?"

Both Kate and Dax look at each other, and Cheney can see that neither one of them wants to tell her what else this jerk said.

"What did he say, Kate?" Cheney repeats the question.

Kate doesn't answer, but Dax does. And the message in the words gives Cheney the feeling that for such a short month, February is going to be a long one.

"He said he'd be back," Dax says.

# CONNECTION

*February 2nd*

After paying Dax for plowing the driveway, Cheney had insisted that he stay for dinner. Kate had made a pot of chili earlier in the day and Kate told him that she would heat it up. Dax had not hesitated in agreeing, particularly when Kate smiled in her beguiling double-dimpled way.

Cheney felt bad that Dax had become embroiled in Kate's mess. Even though Cheney had encouraged Kate to file a police report, she had flatly refused to do so. Cheney had an ominous feeling about the whole situation, but there really wasn't anything more she could do. She just needed to accept that Kate was an adult and fully capable of making her own decisions – even if Cheney disagreed with some of them. Besides, Cheney's own decision-making had not been the best over the course of the past three months, so who was she to judge Kate?

Before they served dinner, Kate had asked Cheney if she could borrow something else to wear, besides sweats, and Cheney brought her up to her room to let her rummage through her closet and drawers. Ultimately, Kate settled on a knit burgundy sweater dress that fell right above Cheney's knees, but, on Kate's long legs, came to mid-thigh. Cheney had a pair of black boots that were a size too big for her, but which fit her sister snugly, so Kate put those on as well. For her part, Cheney threw on a black turtleneck, a pair of oversized boyfriend jeans with holes in each knee, and some comfy socks.

Kate was eyeing herself in Cheney's full-length Victorian-era mirror, when Cheney stood up from the edge of her sleigh-bed to return downstairs.

"Let's go, Kate," Cheney says. "We have a guest waiting downstairs."

"How does this dress look on me?" Kate asks.

The dress is fitted, and it emphasizes Kate's small waist and narrow hips, along with her regal shoulders and perfect posture. With her shiny red hair, jutting cheekbones, and smooth, pale skin, she looks striking.

"You look amazing, as always," Cheney answers.

"I left so quickly, I didn't grab my makeup bag from my apartment," Kate says, studying herself further. "All I have in my purse is some powder and a couple of lipsticks. I just need a little blush…"

"You look great," Cheney says, ignoring the hint to offer up any of her makeup to Kate.

"Don't you think I just need a smidgen of blush?" Kate asks.

"No," Cheney says definitively. "You look beautiful. You don't need to put any blush on."

"I do. I do. Just a little blush and some mascara. Maybe a bit of eyeshadow too. Even you have to have those basics here somewhere, right?"

Cheney usually eschews makeup, rarely putting anything on her bare face, though occasionally she puts on some lip gloss, or a light lip color, and a hint of mascara.

"We're not going out, Kate. We're staying in. I don't see what the point of putting on makeup is." But she does. Kate obviously is trying to impress Dax, so Cheney adds, "Dax already couldn't take his eyes off of you and that's when you were wearing Dan's oversized sweats and camouflage jacket. The poor guy's going to be bursting at the seams when he sees you in that dress."

"Oh, come on, Cheney. It will only take a second," Kate insists.

Cheney sighs. "Okay, come on. I've got some makeup in the bathroom."

The two of them head down the hall, beyond the staircase to the bathroom, where Cheney keeps a mid-century vintage makeup travel case containing various shades of nail polish, eyeshadow, and lipstick, along with makeup base, powder and blush. When she removes it from the vanity's cabinet underneath the sink, Kate exclaims: "I can't believe you have all of this!" Kate picks up the various tubes, compacts and brushes, and eyes the products with obvious amazement and delight. "You don't even wear makeup, and look at all of this! You've been holding out on me!"

"I keep it in case of a special occasion," Cheney says. Actually, she likes to purchase beauty products. She enjoys hoarding the inventory, even if she doesn't use it.

Cheney sits down on the small baby-blue chair in the corner next to the vanity, watching her sister put on eyeliner. Kate leans back slightly eyeing her handiwork in the mirror. With the rim of charcoal-colored eyeliner, her blue eyes become even more enhanced, more vibrant. She continues applying makeup, and asks Cheney: "Why do you buy all of this stuff, if you don't use it?"

"I don't know. Maybe I want to look my best in the event of a zombie apocalypse."

"Ha. Ha," Kate says, expertly contouring her lids with various shades of brown.

"You know he's only a senior in high school, don't you?" Cheney asks, nonchalantly.

"What?" Kate asks, seemingly surprised. "No, I didn't know that. I thought he was like around my age."

"No, actually he just turned eighteen around Christmas," Cheney says, amused by Kate's astonished reaction. "I'm friends with a mutual friend of his dad's on Facebook, and I remember when Dax had pictures up for his eighteenth birthday party not that long ago– some ice fishing excursion in Minnesota."

"Oh, my," Kate says, frowning, but still applying eyeshadow, seemingly undeterred. "That's disappointing - a high school student." Then as if thinking about it further, she says, "He's still adorable. Besides," she shrugs, "six years is not that big of a difference anyway. He seems much more mature for his age."

Cheney just shakes her head. "C'mon, Kate. Let's go. He's been waiting downstairs all this time for us. The poor guy's already been subjected to having to deal with your crazy boyfriend. Speaking of which, what is that lunatic's last name, anyway? In case he does come back here, I'd like to know with whom I'm dealing when I call 9-1-1."

"Zafeiropoulos."

"Oh, Geez. I'm not even going to try to take a stab at spelling that. Just write it down for me when you get a chance."

"His friends just call him 'Z'."

"Okay, well, again, just jot it down for me, so I know how to spell it if the need arises," Cheney says, standing up and heading out the door. "I'm going downstairs. It's rude to leave him down there by himself so long."

Dax is still sitting in the kitchen at the long barnwood table, waiting for them, when Cheney arrives downstairs. She had already put the pot of chili on the stove top before she had gone upstairs, and the cornbread was almost finished baking in the oven. When she starts to set the table, Dax offers to help, and Cheney tells him, "No; no, thank you, though. What can I get you to drink? Milk? A pop?"

"Milk's fine," Dax says, and Cheney goes to the refrigerator and pours herself and Dax each a glass of milk and then asks him about school. He says he's happy to be graduating in a few months, and that he's already taking a couple of classes at the Kent County Community College in Loomisville, but that he is planning on sticking with farming, like his dad. "I'm gonna keep on taking classes at KCC in the fall, but I'm gonna stay on the farm and help my dad and my little brother. I don't have any plans to leave anytime soon, and nothing really interests me other than farming."

Dax's dad, John, owns hundreds of acres of property, but he also farms other individuals' properties too, including Cheney's. Up until he was killed, Dan was the one who handled the crop share lease agreement with John Hardy, and Cheney knows she needs to get up to speed on the terms with spring approaching. Since Dan was the one who normally dealt with John Hardy, she really does not know Dax's father that well, though she has always sensed a kindness about him. Both John and Dax had come to Dan's wake, along with Dax's little brother, Canton, who is only about eight or nine, and who has Down's Syndrome. Over the years, Cheney has gathered, from bits and pieces of conversations, that Dax's mother died of breast cancer when Canton was an infant.

"No desire to be in an office, then?" she asks.

"Absolutely not," Dax says, grinning. "The open field is my office. I like working outdoors, working with my hands. I can't see it any other way."

Kate enters the room, and Dax stands up politely, gazing at her with a smile of awestruck admiration, as if he is in the presence of a movie star. Kate looks like one. Her vixen-red hair sways to mid-back and she wears it slung over on one side. Her high cheekbones are pronounced, and her ivory skin is radiant, such that when she gives a double-dimpled smile in the direction of Dax, Cheney can practically hear the young man's heart beating.

"What did I miss?" Kate asks joyfully.

Cheney pours Kate a glass of ice water, which is customarily Kate's beverage of choice. Cheney answers her sister's question. "We were just talking about Dax's plans when he graduates from high school in May." She is secretly enjoying tormenting Kate by taunting her with the mention of 'high school'.

The meal goes fine, and Cheney enjoys entertaining in the house again after so many months of not having done so. Dan and she used

58

to have so much fun hosting dinner parties or holiday events. It is nice to have laughter again in this place, shared around the barnwood table. The easy banter of Kate and Dax is fun and lighthearted, and there are so many jokes and stories shared, that the gnawing sense of loss and guilt that Cheney has felt for so many months, is finally thawing, albeit perhaps momentarily.

After the dishwasher has been filled and the leftovers have been put away, Dax says he has to head home, because his dad has been texting him reminding him that he has other driveways to plow early tomorrow morning that he did not get to today.

"It was a great dinner, really. Thank you both," he says politely, putting on his jacket, hat and gloves.

Cheney and Kate start to head down the hallway with him toward the front door to see him off when the doorbell rings, and all three of them stop in their tracks. It's past seven, and Cheney usually does not have unannounced visitors, so she immediately she thinks it's Kate's ex-boyfriend. Dax and Kate evidently think so too, for Kate turns to him wide-eyed and says, "It's him again, isn't it?" and Dax says, "I don't know. But I'll be ready for him if it is."

"Cheney, do you have your gun?" Kate asks in a whisper.

"Why are you whispering, Kate?" Cheney asks. "Whoever it is, is outside. They can't hear us."

"I don't know," Kate says, now in a normal tone. "But do you have your gun?"

"Actually, I have one in the desk in the library, but I'm not going to pick it up. It's there if we need it. I put it there when you came to the door in the dead of the night. At least this person is here at a respectable hour."

"We don't need a gun," Dax says definitely and Kate looks at him appreciatively.

"That's right," Cheney says, leading the way and continuing walking. "We've got Dax Hardy and General George S. Patton, the ferocious Rottweiler."

Patton is already at the door, paws balanced on the ridge of the side-window pane, barking. Even with Dax and Kate here, it is still a bit unsettling: a person showing up at the door in the dark unannounced. The farm is isolated, so it is always a bit unnerving whenever a doorbell rings out here. Besides, it could be that creep, Nic Zafeiropoulos, back to cause more trouble, and Kate is probably right to be concerned that he might pose another physical threat.

With apprehension, Cheney looks through the glass, but her concern quickly morphs to mild surprise.

"Is it him?" Kate asks.

"No," Cheney says.

"Who is it?" Kate asks.

There is probably no person that Cheney expects to see less than the woman who is at her door. "It's Cassandra Cantoni," Cheney replies, while opening the oak frame.

"Hello, Cassandra," Cheney says to her, trying to sound welcoming, and letting her in the door. "What a surprise." And it is. It really is.

Cheney and Cassandra have never been friends, and it is beyond bizarre that Cassandra Cantoni would show up on her doorstep on a Saturday night.

Even though Cheney cannot stand Cassandra, she tries her best to appear happy that she has stopped by the house. Cassandra looks a bit overwhelmed herself, taking in Kate and Dax, along with Patton, who has stopped barking and is sniffing her coat. Cassandra is wearing a long, hot-pink teddy-bear coat, silver leggings, a gray turtleneck, and calf-length faux-fur white snow boots. The outfit looks quite ridiculous on her five-foot tall, overweight frame, but somehow, Cassandra is able to make it work in a reality-show-star kind of way. It's her beautiful face which is always the focus, such that she could be wearing a fast-food uniform and she would still be a magnet to people with her gigantic wide-spaced brown eyes, markedly dramatic eyebrows, naturally full lips, and flawless cocoa-colored skin that draws people in to her chaotic, but attractive, aura.

Cassandra hands Cheney a bottle of wine, and says, "This is for you, Cheney. I was just checking in to see how you were doing. I was at my in-laws' farm and I just thought I would stop by on my way back to McNamee."

That's right: Jeff Cantoni's parents live only a mile or so down the road. But despite the close proximity of the two houses, Cheney's pretty sure that neither Jeff, nor Cassandra, has ever just popped in to Dan and Cheney's farm to say 'Hello'. Even though Jeff and Dan were close friends, Cheney can't remember a time when Jeff stopped by after visiting his parents. This whole thing is completely strange. There's something more to this visit. Cassandra must have a motive and it's not to perform a well-being check on Cheney.

Cheney makes introductions to Dax and Kate, and Cassandra says to Kate that she remembers meeting her at the gathering after Dan's funeral, and with Dax her eyes light up as if she is gauging his height, his build, his handsomeness. After Dax says, "Nice to meet you," to Cassandra he heads out the door, saying "Goodbye" and "Thanks again for everything." It is clear from the mutual parting glance between Kate and him that the two of them will be communicating in the future.

Once Dax leaves, Kate says she's going upstairs to go on the computer and heads down the hallway. Cheney asks Cassandra whether she may take her coat and hang it up, but Cassandra declines. "Honestly, I just stopped by to say "Hello" for a minute and make sure you were doing okay with this blizzard from yesterday. I wasn't sure if you were snowed in or not or if you needed anything. I don't intend to stay."

Cheney can tell she is lying. Even though she would normally not want Cassandra in her house, she is curious as to why she is here, so she presses. "Are you sure, you don't want to come back to the kitchen? We can crack open that bottle of wine, and I have some cheese and sausage if you'd like?"

"No, no, I've got to get back to McNamee," Cassandra insists. She seems uncomfortable and she adds, "Really, I knew I was coming to visit Paul and Ellen today and I thought I would just drop this off for you on the way back home and see how you are doing. I mean, with everything that has happened, I'm sure it must be tough."

For once, Cheney actually senses a bit of sincerity and compassion in Cassandra's voice and Cheney feels a stab of guilt for holding her in such contempt. Maybe Cassandra is telling the truth. Maybe she did just stop by to check on Cheney and bring her some good cheer.

"It has been tough," Cheney admits. "But things are getting better. I take it day by day. But I know it's never going to be the same now that Dan's gone."

"Well, Dan was a special man. One of a kind. A great cop. A great person." And again, her words seem kind and gentle, which surprises Cheney. As with any conversation with Cassandra, Cheney is always on edge, waiting for a backhanded compliment or overt hostility. Tonight, there seems like there's neither emanating from her. Cassandra seems genuinely concerned.

Cassandra looks at Cheney and her eyes are full of tears. "I'm really sorry, Cheney. I'm sorry for what you've been through. It's terrible, really. I know it must be awful for you." And then she adds, collecting herself a bit, "I'm glad your sister is here with you. I hate to think of you being out here so far away from everything on your own, particularly this time of year."

"Oh, well, actually she's only staying until Monday and then she's heading back to DeKalb. She's in school there: her last semester. She graduates in May."

"I see," Cassandra says, and she still looks a bit teary-eyed.

"Are you sure you don't want to come in for a drink, Cassandra? Or a pop or a cup of coffee or something?"

"Oh, no, no. I'm going to get going," Cassandra says and turns toward the door. When she reaches for the handle though, she turns back around and faces Cheney. Cheney is still waiting for a nasty remark from Cassandra, but instead there is simply kindness that emits. "You're really a strong person, Cheney," Cassandra says. "I admire that about you. I don't think I would be able to handle it if I had to go through what you've gone through."

"Thank you, Cassandra. That means a lot."

"I do have something to ask you, though," Cassandra says. Here it comes. There has to be a motive in her stopping by. It couldn't just be checking to make sure she is okay. "Would you mind grabbing a cup of coffee with me sometime next week?"

What is going on? This is the second person from the Loomisville Police Department that wants to meet with her next week. First, Brian Patterson and, now Cassandra Cantoni.

Cheney's curiosity to find out what Cassandra wants from her is not strong enough to overcome the negative feelings she still harbors for her from past conversations that went awry. She needs to punt this coffee clutch to a remote time that will never materialize. "I wish I could, but this upcoming week is actually really busy for me, Cassandra. I'm dealing with some final issues on Dan's estate and with filling out our tax returns, so I'm just not going to have time this month; but maybe next month?"

Her attempt to avoid a social event with Cassandra Cantoni does not work. Cassandra's appeal is simple: "Is there any way you could squeeze just a little bit of time in for me this week? It will only take a half an hour or maybe an hour. There's something I would really like to talk to you about. It kind of has to do with what you did after Dan was murdered – how you went about finding out that Derek Strozak was the one who killed him."

Now, her interest is piqued and not in a positive way. Does Cassandra know something about the police investigation into how it came to be that a Latin King helped her solve Dan's murder? Cassandra is married to Jeff Cantoni, who was the lead detective into Dan's homicide, so maybe Cassandra knows something and is willing to spill the beans. Cheney has always had a general disdain for Jeff Cantoni, even though he was one of Dan's closest friends, and she really despises

Cassandra. Yet, tonight, Cassandra seems sincere, congenial, even a tad bit repentant. Perhaps Cassandra is here to warn her that charges are coming down for her out of Cook County for aggravated kidnapping. While that scenario is so unlikely, it is still a possibility, and an unsettling one at that.

"Actually, I'm going to Meskwaki on Monday to meet a friend for lunch," Cheney says. She doesn't tell Cassandra that she is meeting Brian Patterson. It's none of her business, and besides, she'll probably read into it something that isn't there. "Why don't we meet somewhere afterwards, say, about one-thirty or two?"

"That's perfect," Cassandra says, and then suggests: "How about just coming to my house?"

Cassandra lives in McNamee on a bluff near the Fox River, less than a ten-minute drive from downtown Meskwaki. Cheney has been to her house in the past for get-togethers, so she knows it's an easy drive and won't take her long to get there. "Yes, that's fine. I'll see you then: weather permitting, of course. There's no forecast of another snowstorm anytime in the next few days, but, if one comes, I'm staying home."

"Understood," Cassandra says, and Cheney can see the relief and excitement on her face that she has been able to convince Cheney to meet with her. And then, as if she is afraid that Cheney will change her mind, she starts to head out the door. Before she opens the storm door, though, she turns to Cheney one final time and says, "Oh, before I go though, I wanted to mention to you something. It might be nothing; but I thought I would mention it anyway. When I pulled into your driveway tonight, a car pulled in behind me. But it was strange because it just stayed down by the entryway to your property; it didn't pull all the way down the driveway toward your house. When I got out, I turned and it was still sitting there, with its lights on; but it still didn't pull in all the way and I couldn't really see from that distance who was in the car. But it looked like it was a man: a man by himself, no passenger or anything. And then, when I reached your door, I turned around, and was backing up and he pulled away. It's probably nothing, but it just kind of gave me the creeps for some reason. I don't know why. Maybe it's because I'm a cop's wife and things like that which might seem normal to other people strike me as suspicious. You would know what I mean about that."

Yes, she would. Still, though, Cheney tries to seem unbothered when she asks, "What color was the car?"

And she tries to suppress the rattled feeling that comes when Cassandra answers: "It was black."

# VENGEANCE

*February 4*[th]

The drive from the farm to the town of Meskwaki on the Fox River takes less than thirty minutes. It is hard to find parking in the downtown area, but Cheney is able to squeeze her pickup truck into a space not far from the restaurant. It is a bitterly cold day, but not a snowy one, and the sun is centered in the sky like a warm yellow diamond, deceivingly bright on such a frigid afternoon.

Cheney is running a few minutes late. Her tardiness is due to having to jump Kate's car: Kate had been heading off to visit their parents for the day, but her car wouldn't start because the battery had died with the frigid overnight temperatures. It only took about fifteen minutes to jump the car, but long enough for Cheney to be delayed. Before Cheney had headed out to Meskwaki, she had texted Brian Patterson to tell him she had a late start, but that she would be there as fast as she could. Patterson had texted back with: "No prob. Don't speed. See you soon."

Cheney had been surprised, but somewhat relieved, when Kate had asked her on Sunday afternoon whether it would be okay to stay until Tuesday morning. Kate had explained that she didn't have class on Mondays and her first class of the week was on Tuesday afternoon. She also had explained that, even though she was scheduled to work all-day on Monday, she had already called her boss at her part-time job at the spa, and had told her that she was not feeling well, and that she would be unable to come in to work. Cheney had told her it was fine to stay an extra night, and, even though she had not conveyed it to Kate, she actually felt comforted having her kid sister around. It was kind of nice having someone else in the big farmhouse with whom to converse and stay up late laughing and playing board games or watching television. She'll be sad to see Kate go tomorrow.

To make up some of the time, Cheney walks at a fast clip, even though it is treacherously icy on the downtown sidewalk. She is wearing black low-heeled boots, a pair of faded blue jeans, an oversized cashmere camel-colored turtleneck, her black-leather below-the-hip-length car coat, and a black knit cap. She even swished on some strokes of mascara, and a coral-colored lip gloss, before she headed out for the day. Perhaps Kate is rubbing off on her just a bit.

When she walks into the restaurant, she tells the hostess that she is there to meet someone and starts to describe Patterson. "He's tall, dark hair with really blue eyes."

The hostess's eyes light up and she says, "Yes, I know who you are talking about. He *does* have really blue eyes!" She leads Cheney to a table way in the back of the restaurant, where Brian Patterson is sitting with his back to the rear wall.

Brian Patterson is good-looking, there is no doubt about that. With his lean, willowy frame, and robin's eggshell-colored eyes, there is a dreamy intelligence about him. He stands when Cheney approaches and greets her with a formal handshake and the sing-song lilt of his Irish brogue. "Hello, Cheney. It's good to see you. You look like you're healing well."

"I am. I am. Almost back to normal. Well, at least my shoulder is," Cheney says, gesturing with her left hand across her chest, and patting her right shoulder area.

"Yeah, I get it. You've been through a lot," he says.

Cheney has always been a bit uncomfortable around Brian Patterson, though she's not sure why. At first, she thought it was because he was with Dan on the night he was killed, and that maybe she subconsciously blames him for failing to protect her husband. But that's not it. She knows that Patterson could not have done anything to stop Dan from being shot. Patterson was just a rookie, only a short time on the job, and Dan was his field training officer. It's not Patterson's fault that Dan is dead. The sole responsibility for Dan's death falls on the man who killed him: Derek Strozak.

Cheney hasn't really pinpointed the reason for her anxiousness around Patterson, other than that he always seems guarded and suspicious of her. He's a person who makes her feel like maybe he knows something about her that will get her into trouble. He has a general restlessness, and a touch of mystery about him that spikes a heightened alert in her own senses. Because of this, the conversation between them has a lot of awkward pauses and there is a detached, bumpy rhythm to their discourse, which leads Cheney at times to stare off at another table, a server, a patron, or the wall.

They talk mostly about her physical therapy and his job. Last week was his final week with a field training officer, so he'll be out on his own tomorrow night. He says he is looking forward to having his own squad car, his own detail: but he admits he's a bit apprehensive at the same time. It is strange that he would want to meet for lunch simply to talk about his work and her shoulder injury. There must be some other reason he reached out to her, though she is fairly certain it is not a romantic one. She doesn't get a vibe that he has any personal interest in her other than a friendly and professional concern for his dead field training officer's widow.

To fill one of the prolonged silences, Cheney asks him if he is still writing poetry. He looks mildly surprised so she quickly reminds him, "Dan had once mentioned to me that you liked to write poems."

"No, I haven't written actually in quite a while," he replies. And then, as if pondering the notion, he says, "Actually, I haven't written a single poem since I started the police academy last summer. I don't get a lot of time to write now. The job presently takes up most of my energy. I don't feel much like writing poetry after dealing with what I see on the streets at night."

"Working in the criminal justice system is not conducive to one's creative space," Cheney says.

"That's right," he says, his face seeming to alight momentarily. "I forgot that you're a writer too. I can't remember, though: is it poetry or fiction?"

"I write poetry. Dabble with some short stories. Drama is where my interest mostly lies, though, and I like to incorporate poetry into my scripts."

"Ahhhhh…. I see," he says. "Have you been working on anything lately?"

"No," she says. "Just like you, I really haven't had much time to write, particularly with my former job. I haven't really written much at all since before I went to law school: Some poems here or there, and maybe a short story or two. But I really never have had time for writing because of my old job – the weight of it all. Even when I wasn't at work, I carried it home with me so that I was always thinking about the next case, the next client. It burdened me to a point of where it kind of snuffed out all of my creativity."

"I get that," he says. "Really, I do. It sounds just like how I feel. It's hard to go from the place of breaking up a bar fight or arresting a drug dealer to the space of writing a poem." And then, following up on something to which she had alluded, he asks: "You referenced your 'old job.' Aren't you working at the Public Defender's Office anymore?"

"Actually, I just resigned on Saturday."

"Wow," he says. "Where are you going next? A private firm?"

"No," she replies. "I'm not sure yet. I'm going to take some time before I jump back into the courtroom, some time to decompress. I'm going to take some 'me time' and use this creative desire that I have to produce... whatever - poetry, plays, maybe a novel. I'm just not sure yet what direction this will take me exactly."

He smiles. "That sounds great, actually. I get it. Really, I do."

The commonality of their affection for creative writing eases the tension going forward in the conversation and erases some of the prior awkwardness, so that it moves along at a more relaxed and unhindered pace. Toward the end of the lunch, after Patterson picks up the bill and, she thanks him, he says, "There's something I want to tell you before you go."

Here it comes: There has to be some point to this unusual lunch other than just a check on the status of her shoulder injury. She doesn't say anything; she waits for him to lead. He dives in, but she remains poker-faced, trying not to show any emotion. "The Chicago Police were looking in to how it came to be that Manuel Rodriguez ended up crashing through Derek Strozak's window and shooting him in the head," he explains. "Seems they were concerned as to how you and Manuel ended up working together. There were rumors circulating on the streets and in the jail that you had kidnapped Manuel Rodriguez at gunpoint and forced him to come out here to help you find out who killed your husband."

He stares at her with those extremely unsettlingly vibrant eyes, and she knows he is scanning her face for a reaction. She shows none.

"I'm probably telling you something you already know," he continues. "I'm sure Chicago has already interviewed you."

It's a statement that's really a question and she answers it. "Actually, no. I've never been contacted by the Chicago Police Department."

He looks a bit surprised, and his dark eyelashes flutter in a millisecond, and then he says, "Well, my understanding is that the investigation has been administratively closed: At least, that's what I've been told. No cooperative witnesses and a deceased victim."

She feels her heart, which felt constricted, relax with that disclosure, but still, she remains stone-faced. There is a very long and awkward silence, and she needs to fill it with a question. "Why are you telling me this?"

"I couldn't tell you before, because you were a suspect in an open investigation, and I didn't want to be accused of obstructing justice. But now that Chicago's investigation is closed, I felt you should know."

There must be more to this meeting than that disclosure. Surely, he wouldn't have contacted her to meet for lunch just to tell her that she had been a person of interest in a closed case. She waits for him to tell her what it is that is so imperative that he wanted her to meet for lunch on a day when it is only ten degrees outside.

He locks eyes with her, reeling her in with the gravity of his look. "The Latin Kings suspect that it was you who kidnapped Manuel Rodriguez from their safehouse in Chicago. They blame you for his death. They think that if you hadn't kidnapped Manuel Rodriguez he wouldn't have been locked up in the Cook County Jail on the witness warrant and then the Gangster Disciples wouldn't have had access to him."

The Latin Kings are right about that. Manuel would be alive if she hadn't kidnapped him. Her mouth feels dry and she drinks some of the dregs of the remaining glass of water. She catches herself nodding slowly as she bites into a piece of ice, crushing it in her molars. She stops moving her head, swallows the ice. "Is there anything else?" As soon as she says the words, she knows she sounds angry, hostile. Brian Patterson is obviously just trying to help her, and here she is lashing out at him. Once her question is released, she regrets it.

He looks grim. "I just thought you would want to know, so that you can exercise some caution. Be careful when you get out of your vehicle and when you go into your house at night, or even during the day. Pay attention to your surroundings."

"I always do," she says.

He continues talking. "You may want to get a security system of some sort if you don't have one."

"Good idea," she says. She's not getting a security system. She has a Rottweiler. She has a gun. She doesn't need some video surveillance equipment to make her feel safe in her own house.

He seems to sense that she only said 'Good idea' to appease him, because he adds: "I'm just saying, it may be worth it to invest in some kind of security system since you're out there all by yourself in such a rural area."

"Anything else?" she asks impatiently. She's ready to go. She really wants to be alone, in her truck, to process all of this.

"Just that, we're hearing some chatter in Loomisville that the Latin Kings may come after you. Nothing concrete. If it were, I wouldn't be the one reaching out to you. It would be the brass or the feds. Still, I felt you should know. I don't want you to be alarmed or anything; I just want you to watch yourself. I just thought you'd want to know."

"I appreciate the heads up," she says, trying not to sound overly concerned. The notion of the Latin Kings having a hit out on her is troubling, to say the least.

"Well, you can't really watch out for danger, unless you know it exists," he says soberly.

"I was married to a cop, remember? I know all about situational awareness." And then, tasting the backwash of the sting of her sarcasm, she adds, "I do appreciate your telling me. Really, I do. This isn't the first time you've stuck your neck out to help me. Thank you."

She really is grateful, and she wants Patterson to know that. When she had asked him back in November to give her booking photos shortly after Dan's murder, he had done so, even though she had concealed from him the reason she had been asking for the images. She had shown the photos to Manuel Rodriguez so he could try to identify the man whom he had seen shoot Dan in the alley. While the photos ultimately were not helpful in assisting Manuel in identifying the shooter, Cheney still appreciates the risk to his job that Patterson took in giving her unauthorized access to the images.

He's probably jeopardizing his job again in relaying the street chatter about the Latin Kings wanting to seek vengeance against her. He had shared with her once that he had wanted to be a police officer since he was a child, and she feels a slight tinge of guilt that she has once again put him in a position where he is risking his career in an effort to assist her. She almost hugs him when they say 'Goodbye' to each other in front of the restaurant, but she doesn't. Instead, she extends a gloved hand, shakes his, says "Thanks again," and heads down the sidewalk in the opposite direction from him.

Walking toward her truck, her thoughts, and fears, propel through her mind in rapid succession. Manuel had warned her that Corazon, the leader of the Latin Kings, would not forget what she had done and that he would come after her at some point. She had embarrassed and disrespected Corazon in his own home, by lying and claiming she was an attorney who was there to talk to Manuel. Instead, she was really there to force Manuel at gunpoint to come with her out to the farm and to help her prove that Solomon Wilson, her former client, had not been the one who had killed Dan. That night still seems so hazy, so surreal, that it is as if her criminal actions in kidnapping Manuel had been performed by someone else, not her. But she is indeed the person who lied her way into the Latin King safehouse, falsely claimed that she was wearing a suicide vest, and forced Manuel Rodriguez at gunpoint to drive her back to the farmhouse. That's probably not something that the Latin Kings are going to forget anytime soon. Still, it seems like so many weeks have passed by, so much has happened in the interim, that perhaps Corazon has moved on by now. Surely, Corazon must have more important scores to settle than going after some distraught widow.

Still, she texts Kate and asks her to let her know when she is heading back to the farm and Kate responds with a thumbs up. She's not going to tell Kate about Patterson's warning concerning the Latin Kings, but she is going to tell her to be aware of her surroundings when she comes back to the farm, in case Nic is lurking around. Kate is probably on heightened alert anyway after the incident on Saturday, but still, a warning to be cautious would be prudent under the circumstances.

Before she gets into her truck, she gulps in the severely cold air and feels her lungs take a beating with the inhalation. She holds her breath for a moment, trying to steady her nerves. The morning has already been full of enough disturbing information. She needs strength to take on her next meeting with Cassandra Cantoni. Even though Cassandra seemed civil enough when she stopped by the other night, she has a way of getting on Cheney's nerves with her not-so-subtle backhanded compliments or outright antagonistic remarks. Cheney is really not looking forward to going to her house, but her curiosity is getting the best of her. What news does Cassandra Cantoni want to share with her that so impelled her to come to her house with a bottle of wine on a Saturday night after a blizzard?

She lets out the air and expels it into the chill, into the unforgiving day.

# DAUGHTER

*February 4*[th]

Cassandra Cantoni's house is a two-story cantaloupe-colored Cape Cod situated on the bluff along the Fox River. When Cheney shows up at the door, Cassandra welcomes her inside and offers to get her something to drink or a fresh-baked oatmeal cookie, but Cheney declines, explaining that she just drank three large diet colas and she's full from lunch. In truth, she's not planning on staying long. She just wants to hear what Cassandra Cantoni has to say and then leave.

Cassandra invites her to sit down on the couch in the living room. The cool blue and ivory tones of the room invoke a summer feel, even in the dead of winter. There is an antique piano, painted with distressed white paint pleasingly stationed in the corner near the entryway, a stone fireplace along the far wall, and a giant bay window next to the front door that overlooks the Fox River. Cheney sits on one corner of the long gray couch in front of the window, while Cassandra excuses herself for a minute. When she returns, she is carrying a folio and a cup of coffee and she sits down in a chair beside the fireplace.

It is hard not to stare at Cassandra because she is wearing minimal makeup, which is unusual for her. Cheney doesn't think she has ever seen Cassandra without full facial coverage of base, mascara, eyeshadow and blush. She is still beautiful, if not more so, without it. She is also dressed casually, which is also uncommon for her, in a pair of wide-legged retro honey-colored velour pants, a matching cropped hoodie, and gym shoes.

"Are you sure I can't get you anything?" Cassandra asks seeming to detect that Cheney is gawking at her, and Cheney responds, "No – no, thank you. I can't stay long. My sister is still in town for an extra day. She decided to stay tonight and go back to school tomorrow morning." She's not even sure if Kate will be back from their parents' house by the time she gets home, but it's still a convenient excuse to restrict the amount of time she has to be here.

"Oh, sure, sure," Cassandra says. "I won't hold you up. I promise. I just wanted to ask you about something. It shouldn't take long. I need to leave here by two-forty-five to go pick up Miranda from school."

"I haven't seen Miranda in a couple of years," Cheney says. "How old is she now? Six?" The last time she can remember seeing Miranda was at a Fourth of July party at this house a few years ago, though time has speedily slipped away since then.

"Eight," Cassandra says.

"Eight. Wow. Time really goes by fast," Cheney says.

"It does," Cassandra replies, and then, adds, "So, you're probably wondering what the reason I asked you to come here is."

"I am."

"I need your help."

"You need *my* help?" Cheney asks, stunned. This is confusing. Why would Cassandra Cantoni ask her – of all people – for help, with anything? She has always believed the disdain she felt over the years for Cassandra was reciprocal, so it is staggering to hear Cassandra Cantoni ask her for a favor.

"Yes," Cassandra says. "It has to do with my mother."

"Your mother?" Cheney asks. She doesn't know anything about Cassandra Cantoni's mother and in fact, outside of Cassandra's husband, Jeff, and their daughter, Miranda, she has never met any of Cassandra's relatives. She has no idea for what reason Cassandra would need her assistance; though, she suspects it will be a request for legal advice of some sort.

Instead, Cassandra says, "I need your help finding out what happened with my mother. My mom -you see - she was killed years ago in Meskwaki."

"I must admit, I'm confused, Cassandra. I thought the reason you wanted to talk to me had something to do with Dan's murder and how I determined it was Derek Strozak who had killed him."

"Well, in a roundabout way it does. I'm coming to you because I believe that my mother was murdered years ago, but that the Meskwaki Police Department covered it up. You see, I know bits and pieces of what you did to find out who killed Dan. I know that you didn't trust the police version – my husband's version – and that you doubted that Solomon Wilson was the killer, and that you turned out to be right."

"Okay, well, I'm still not sure what my doubting that Solomon killed my husband in Loomisville last year has to do with your mother's death in Meskwaki years ago," Cheney says, confused. Cassandra's husband, Jeff, is a Loomisville police detective, so it's odd that Cassandra would come to a lawyer for help with a criminal investigation, as opposed to simply asking her own husband for assistance.

Cassandra pauses a moment before trying to explain why she is eliciting help from Cheney. "Because something inside of you told you that Solomon Wilson didn't do it and you didn't give up until you were able to find out who did. I have the same feeling about my mom – that she didn't die in the way that they say she did and I need your help in finding out what really happened to her. You see, I don't know everything you did after Dan was killed, only the parts that Jeff has told me, but I do know that you visited Jeff at work and that he was pissed off that you didn't believe that they had the right guy. He was so angry that night when he came home – actually, truthfully, I still think a part of him is angry at you – for doubting him, and for being right."

"Does Jeff know that you're discussing any of this with me?"

"No. And I'm not going to tell him either. There's no reason for him to know anyway. This has nothing to do with the Loomisville Police Department; it has to do with Meskwaki."

"It's just that, Jeff's a detective," Cheney points out. "I would think he could help you out with whatever it is you want to dig into. You know I'm not a police officer, nor a private detective for that matter. I'm just a lawyer, Cassandra. I can't help you with this."

Cassandra fixes her brown eyes on her, and Cheney can see she is not going to accept the 'I'm not a cop – I'm a lawyer' line. "I don't need a detective," Cassandra insists. "I need a lawyer: a lawyer who knows how to investigate a case, like how you did to find out what happened to Dan. I need you to use your legal skills and your instincts to find out who killed my mother."

This would be an opportune time to get up from the couch and leave. But, what is she going to do? Just stand up and announce, 'I've got to go,'? That would seem a little heartless, since Cassandra is clearly suffering emotionally. So, instead, Cheney asks, "I'm gathering from the little you've told me so far, that it's a cold case?"

80

"Yes and no. The coroner's inquest ruled my mother's death a suicide. It was in the paper back then. See."

Cassandra opens the file folder, removes a faded newspaper article from *The Meskwaki Times*, hands it to Cheney, and then returns to her chair. The headline reads: "Coroner's Inquest rules Dispatcher's Valentine's Day Gunshot Wound was Self-Inflicted." Cheney smiles wryly a bit when she sees the byline, and looks up from the article momentarily. "I know this reporter. Jack Stahl. He's an old timer. Boy, if he's still alive he's got to be in his late seventies now. I was a free-lancer at the *Times* when I was in undergrad and he was their main reporter then."

"Wow. I never knew you were a reporter," Cassandra says.

"Yeah," Cheney says, and then adds, more to herself out loud, than to Cassandra: "I wrote articles for the paper while I was in law school too, but Jack Stahl was retired by then."

"I never knew that about you," Cassandra repeats her thought, "-that you were a reporter. I don't remember Dan or Jeff ever mentioning that to me."

"Oh, well, it's something Dan probably didn't talk about. He liked reporters about as much as he liked lawyers." She smiles and returns to looking down at the paper, and then asks, though more of a comment than a question, "Your mother was a dispatcher, like you?"

"Yes," Cassandra says. "Except, of course, I'm in Loomisville and she was in Meskwaki."

"Is your mother the reason why you became a dispatcher?" Cheney asks.

"I don't know," Cassandra says. "Maybe. I've never really given it much thought. It's just kind of what I always knew I wanted to do."

Cheney nods slowly and skims through the article. She quickly surmises that Jazzie Gonzalez died of a gunshot wound to the chest on Valentine's Day. She was only nineteen-years-old on the date of death. According to the article, she shot herself at the residence she shared with her boyfriend, a thirty-four-year-old Meskwaki police lieutenant, Dennis Rausch.

"Your mom was only nineteen when she died?"

"Yes," Cassandra says. "She had me when she was fifteen."

"Were you at the house when-"

Before she can finish, Cassandra says, "No. My grandparents already had custody of me. I lived with them in McNamee." And then, Cassandra says, "You see, even though it was already publicized that it was a suicide, and it sounds like the case was closed years ago, the Meskwaki Police Department refuses to release any of the police reports to me; they make it sound like the investigation is ongoing and that's why they can't give me anything." Cassandra pauses, and she stares at Cheney, her eyes pleading with her to assist. "See, this is the kind of thing where I can use your help. I need a lawyer, not a cop. Cops don't handle FOIA appeals; lawyers do. I have the letter from the police department right here if you want to see it."

Cassandra starts opening the portfolio, but Cheney interrupts her movement with her words, "Look, I really don't know that I want to get involved in any of this, Cassandra. I'm not really practicing law right now. I actually just resigned from the public defender's office over the weekend, and I've decided I'm taking a break from the law for a while.

I've got so much going on right now, dealing with the loss of my husband and recovering from a bullet wound and everything else I've been through lately. I just don't think I have the time or wherewithal to help you. I've just got too much on my own plate."

"I get it. I get it. I was just hoping-" Cassandra breaks off and looks down at the portfolio, closing it without removing the paper and then clasping her hands. When she looks up, there are tears in her eyes. "It's been thirty years that have gone by. It will be thirty years to the day on Valentine's Day. That's when she was murdered - Valentine's Day."

It is clear Cassandra is in distress, and, even though Cheney really doesn't like her, she feels bad for her: saddened that someone has to carry such intense pain over so many years. It is almost like Cassandra, streetwise, strong and saucy, is transmuting into a child in the oversized gray chair. She suddenly doesn't look like a thirty-something conniving dispatcher, but instead, a lost little girl with horror and grief in her brown eyes.

Cassandra continues, "I was four when mi madre was murdered. Four. I've had to live with this burden my whole life, never knowing my own mother. I only have shadowy pieces of her left: memories that come sometimes - a scent, a laugh, a shade of lilac. That's all I have."

"I'm sorry, Cassandra. I wish I could help you. I really do. But I just can't right now. It's not a good time for me to be taking on something that I cannot devote the time and energy to complete."

Cassandra bites her bottom lip, and her tone is sincere, compelling. "I know I haven't always been kind to you, Cheney. I know that I've said some things in the past that I shouldn't have said. I'm sorry for that. I really am. Envy makes the tongue say bad things sometimes. I realize that. But I really need your help. Something tells me that you are the person who can help me with this - the only person. I don't know if it's

God or-" Her voice breaks off for a moment and she looks toward the backyard window as if wondering whether to say the next words, and then she does: "Sometimes I think it's mi madre talking to me, and she is telling me, 'Go to Cheney Manning. Ask for her help. She will be able to help you find out who killed me.'"

Cheney sighs. Cassandra's apology to her seems heartfelt and it is evident that she believes Cheney can assist her in some fashion. The public defender inside of Cheney will not let her say 'No' to a person in need of legal help. Against her better judgment, she asks, "Why don't you let me take a look at the declination letter?"

Cassandra's wide-set eyes go from sadness to joy in a microsecond and she swings open the portfolio and walks over to Cheney, taking a seat next to her on the couch. "Here is the letter where they denied my request for the police reports. I just received it last Wednesday."

Cheney scans through it quickly, and then says: "They're claiming two exemptions, essentially, which are both similar: subsection (i) which is where the release of information would interfere with pending or actually reasonably contemplated law enforcement proceedings and subsection (vii) which is where the release of the information would obstruct an ongoing law enforcement investigation." She looks up at Cassandra who is sitting close, with her eyes appearing to intensely wait for Cheney to say more.

Cheney continues, "Frankly, claiming both of these exemptions is absurd. First off, it's a thirty-year-old investigation that was deemed a suicide by the coroner. At this point, there's no pending or 'reasonably contemplated law enforcement proceeding'. Nor, for that matter, is there a good faith basis to claim that releasing this information to the victim's daughter would somehow 'obstruct an ongoing law enforcement investigation' thirty-years after the incident."

Cassandra's perfectly-shaped eyebrows lift with hope and her smooth cocoa-colored skin flushes with animation. "That sounds great. See: That's why I came to you! I knew you would be able to help me! What do I do now? Can you appeal this for me?"

The hope in Cassandra's voice and Cheney's irritation at the Meskwaki Police Department for having denied a FOIA request under these circumstances dissipates Cheney's initial hesitancy. "You have sixty days to file an appeal to the Public Access Counselor with the Attorney General's Office. But I don't think you'll have to do that. First, I think we should try drafting a letter back to the police department asking them to reconsider their exemptions and give them another chance to provide the materials before we appeal. Do you have your original request letter?"

"I do." Cassandra removes the letter from her folio and hands that to Cheney, keeping her eyes affixed to Cheney's face as she reviews it.

"You ask for the investigative reports relating to Jazzie Gonzalez's death and you provide her date of birth and her date of death, but nowhere in the letter do you mention that you're the daughter of Jazzie Gonzalez."

"I know," Cassandra says. "It didn't say anywhere that I had to mention that. Is that important? Should I have mentioned it?"

"Well, it could be. Keep in mind that my legal career has been limited to criminal law, so handling FOIA issues is not an area with which I am very familiar. And, I've never dealt with victims previously, other than cross-examining them on the witness stand, so this is outside of my normal wheelhouse. But I believe that victims of violent crimes may have rights under the law to certain information that otherwise is unavailable to the general public. At the very least, we should mention in a follow-up letter that you're the decedent's daughter. That might alter the FOIA officer's decision."

"You said: 'We'. Does that mean that you're going to help me?"

"Yes," Cheney says, but she puts a restriction on her offer to help. "I'll draft a letter and send it out under my signature. I'll represent you on this limited issue of trying to obtain the police reports. If the Meskwaki Police Department still declines to send you the requested information, I'll draft a request to review to the Public Access Counselor of the Attorney General's Office. That's all I'm willing to do though, Cassandra. I'm not willing to do anything beyond that."

"Understood, Cheney and thank you. Thank you so much."

"I'll need you to scan copies of what you have there – your initial request and Meskwaki's denial letter – and email them to me whenever you can."

"I'll do it as soon as you leave," Cassandra says excitedly.

"If you have a pen and a piece of paper, I'll write down my email address."

Cassandra opens the folio, removes a legal pad and a pen, and hands both to Cheney. As Cheney scribbles down her email address, Cassandra asks her how soon she thinks she could get a letter drafted to Meskwaki.

"I'll do it tomorrow," Cheney says.

"I can't tell you how much this means to me, Cheney. Thank you."

Cassandra leans over and hugs her. When Cassandra sits back, she wipes tears from her face and says, "Oh, and I want to pay you for your legal work, Cheney. How much will it cost for you to do this for me?"

"Nothing," Cheney says standing up. Cassandra stands up as well, and the two of them head for the door.

"But I've got to pay you something for your time, your work-"

"No, Cassandra. I wouldn't even know what to begin to charge you to do this anyway. I'm not in private practice. I don't have my own firm. Don't worry about it."

"Are you sure?"

"Yes, I'm sure," Cheney says.

But she really isn't. On the way home, she mulls over how significant of an undertaking this may turn out to be. The time that she'll spend resolving the FOIA issue is not what concerns her. She's fairly confident that they'll receive partial or full reports from the Meskwaki Police Department that will satisfy Cassandra. But she's worried about whether if, once Cassandra obtains the reports, she is going to ask Cheney to help her dig into the three-decades' old case. For some reason, she suspects that her involvement in this case will not end once she is finished with her legal work on the FOIA request. And, her instincts are usually correct.

# GRATITUDE

She stands out on the porch in her puffer jacket, snow boots, and hat, keeping a mindful eye on Patton on the south lawn, as Kate drives away. It is after sunrise, and the thick drifts of snow are twinkling in the rays' brilliance like oiled bodies sunbathing on the sands of Pensacola. Patton races toward Kate's car half-heartedly through the crests for a few yards, but then abandons his chase when her vehicle nears the fence line. He abruptly loses interest and starts sniffing around the spruce trees.

There is a loneliness that sinks into her stomach when she watches Kate turn onto the highway and drive away. Although she cherishes her solitude, she is sad to see Kate leave. It had been fun listening to her kid sister talk about school and her friends and her plans for the future. Cheney particularly had been uplifted by Kate's excitement and anticipation about finally graduating at the age of twenty-four this May with a bachelor of arts in theatre studies after so many years of indecision regarding her course of studies. But not only had Cheney enjoyed spending time with Kate during her visit, it had also been nice having the security of knowing that she had not been alone in the farmhouse, and that Kate had been sleeping upstairs on the third floor. It had been particularly comforting at night when the old house keened and wheezed from the blows of the harsh Illinois wind.

She hadn't told Kate about Corazon or the Latin Kings or what Patterson had told her. There really wasn't any reason to do so, particularly since Kate wasn't staying past Tuesday anyway. But she did tell her to be careful and to pay attention to her surroundings in the future now that Nic had shown up once at the house uninvited. Kate had seemed dismissive of the notion that she needed to be on heightened alert.

"Really, Cheney, I don't think Nic would hurt me or anything," Kate had said.

"Kate, he already has," Cheney had reminded her.

"Oh, those bruises are already gone," Kate had said. "Those were nothing, really."

"Oh, okay, so it was 'nothing' that made you drive to my house past midnight in the middle of a blizzard?" Cheney had asked sarcastically, and then, seriously she had questioned, "Tell me you're not going back to this asshole ever again, are you?"

"No," Kate had said, but Cheney had sensed some hesitancy in her voice.

"Kate, you don't sound so sure."

"I am sure, Cheney. Really, I am."

"What is it about this guy that's a positive? He sounds like the biggest asshole that's ever walked the face of the planet."

"He's not, really, Cheney. He's not that bad as I made him sound. He's a hard worker, very self-determined and confident. I mean, he started up both of those places with nothing really – all on his own – and within a couple of years he turned the one in Loomisville into the most popular restaurant in the area; and the one downtown in Chicago is doing well too. And it's just fun being around him, I guess, because he knows so many people: like when we're at his restaurant in the city, the politicians and the anchors and the professional athletes all come in and they'll stop by his table or his office and say 'Hello,' and it's fun, really, being with him."

"So, it's like a celebrity attraction?" Cheney had asked. She knew her tone sounded mocking or disgusted, or both.

"No, no. It's more than that. He's romantic, and charming, and sensitive-" Kate had paused and continued "-in fact, very sensitive."

"Yeah, he sounds like the real sensitive type," Cheney had said sarcastically and then, she had added, "Whatever, Kate. It's your life. I don't want to tell you how to run it. It's just that you have so much to offer. You're beautiful, you're smart, you're talented: practically every guy that lays eyes on you falls in love with you. I just can't see why you would be drawn to some piece of shit restauranteur who thinks it's okay to throw you around like a ragdoll."

After that conversation, when she had gone to bed last night, she hadn't been so sure that her sister was going to remain voluntarily detached from Nic Zafeiropoulos. It seemed like Kate was mulling over the possibility of hooking back up with him – the notion of which was simply staggering. Kate had always been a bit flighty at times, but how could she not have the good sense to understand the danger which being in an abusive relationship poses? The thought of Kate returning back to this idiot made Cheney's stomach turn.

Despite that she sat up in bed for an hour or so worrying about her sister's corrosive relationship with Nic, as well as mulling over the odds of Corazon showing up at the farmhouse in the dead of the night, Cheney had gone to sleep at a decent hour. In fact, she had slept well through the night. In the morning, though, she remained preoccupied with the thought of Kate returning to DeKalb. They were up early, as Kate was planning on heading to the cellphone store in DeKalb to buy a new device before returning to her apartment. Cheney had asked her to text her as soon as she was home, so that she would not worry about her. She had also admonished Kate to make sure that, if she saw or sensed anything unusual, to call her before going inside. Kate said she would do so.

After Kate had left, Cheney had made a pot of coffee and then headed upstairs to work on the FOIA issue on her computer. It didn't take her long to draft the correspondence requesting the Meskwaki Police Department to reconsider its FOIA denial. The draft of her email is direct, compelling and concise. She is confident that Meskwaki will send at least some, if not all, of the investigative reports. She proofreads the letter and then sends it out to Cassandra who responds almost immediately with a brief email response, "That looks great! Thnx!" Cheney then emails the correspondence out to the police department and just as she does so, her smartphone pings.

It's Kate letting her know that she's inside her apartment with her new phone, and, she is home safely. Cheney texts her back with a thumbs up and a blue heart, but when she looks up at her computer screen she is surprised by a new email in her inbox. It's from Solomon Wilson. She knows because part of the email address contains his gang name, Handler, and a bunch of other numbers and symbols that mean nothing to her. She has never received any communication from Solomon on her personal email account, nor has she heard from him since before she confronted Derek Strozak and was shot. But she had received email correspondence from his mother, Janetta, around the holidays in which Janetta had thanked her numerous times for risking her life to help Solomon. Cheney had also received a Christmas card from Janetta with a personal inscription, telling her how grateful she was for everything Cheney had done to help Solomon.

However, she has not heard anything from Solomon – until now. The last time she had received written correspondence from Solomon was in November. Back then, he had been confined in the Kent County Jail. Solomon had penned a letter to Cheney insisting that he had been wrongfully charged with Dan's murder and claiming he was aware of evidence that could prove his innocence. He had been telling the truth. The information Solomon had provided to Cheney led her to Manuel Rodriguez, who, in turn identified Derek Strozak – Solomon Wilson's criminal defense attorney - as Dan's killer. When Cheney had confronted Derek Strozak with her knowledge that he was the murderer, Strozak had shot her. Manuel had come to her defense and shot Strozak in the skull, killing him.

While Cheney was unsure exactly what Manuel had told the Loomisville detectives in the aftermath of Strozak's homicide, whatever he had said was enough for the State's Attorney to expeditiously dismiss the murder charges against Solomon and release him. Solomon still, however, had a Class X felony drug case pending at that time, but Cheney had heard through Maria Calderon that the State had ended up dropping that entire drug prosecution as well sometime late last year. Evidently, the prosecution had been concerned about due process issues with Derek Strozak having been Solomon's defense attorney on that case, and someone at the top ultimately decided to just forego prosecuting Solomon on those charges too.

On occasion, over the past few months, Cheney had wondered whether Solomon had been re-arrested on new charges, but since he's emailing her from a personal email account, that's a good sign that he hasn't. Well, at least, if he has, he must be out of custody. She opens the email and reads what Solomon has to say:

*Dear Ms. Manning: First off, I want to thank you for everything you done to help show that I did not murder your husband. You came to my aid at a time when I was in the worst spot in my life. No one else would've helped me the way you did and no one else could've helped the way you did either. I will never forget everything you done for me. I mean that.*

*I wanted to let you know that I am forever grateful that you did what you did. Some of what you did sounds like it was kind of crazy, but I guess you had to do what you had to do and I'm glad you did. The police told me what Manuel Rodriguez did to help too and that he saved your life. I guess he saved both of our lives in a way. Unless you think it would cause a problem, I would like to contact his family and thank them. I don't know anything about him, if he had a wife or kids or anything like that, but I suppose if you know, and if you think it wouldn't be a problem, I would like to talk or write to them just to tell them 'Thanks'. If you know any way for me to do that, I would appreciate it if you could let me know, unless you think it's a bad idea since I was a Disciple and he was a King. And I don't want to make a problem for you or anything. I mean, I already caused enough problems for you as it is. I am sorry.*

*Now on to some good news. You probably are going 'Hey, what do you mean -was- a GD?'" That's right. I'm not doing any of that gang shit anymore. I'm done with it. I know it sounds crazy, but, they let me go. I think mostly, because of all the shit I went through being set up for the murder. Part of it is, I think the gang just feels like they owe me or I've been through enough as it is, since they picked out Strozak for my lawyer and he turned out to be the one setting me up all along. Whatever it is, and believe me, I'm not pushing for an answer – I don't care why – all I care about is that they let me be out and I'm done for good now.*

*So, I'm back in school working on getting my G.E.D. and then in the fall, or at the latest next year, I'm going to work on getting my associates degree at Loomisville Community College. I'm actually taking a college level crim law class, and an English comp. class, at LCC right now. That's right. I'm going to college. I don't know what I'm going to focus on yet, but I've always been interested in the law, and I really like my crim law class, so maybe I'll end up doing something with lawyers or cops. Who knows?*

*I'm also working two jobs – both part-time- one at an animal shelter and the other at a call service center, but I'm looking for full-time. But the biggest news is that my daughter, Alveda Isaiah, was born two weeks ago and she's the best. She was born pretty early and she's real small and she has some stuff going on but the doctors say she's going to be fine. I still can't believe that I'm a father. It's pretty amazing, really.*

*And I have you to thank, Ms. Manning. Really, I do. I mean that. I have you to thank for believing in me and for giving me a chance to be with my little girl. If there's anything I can ever do for you to pay you back, please let me know. The way I see it is, I owe you big time, so if you ever need anything, you know where to find me. Take care of yourself.*
*Solomon Wilson*

She's not going to write back right now. It is nice that Solomon has reached out to her and that he has thanked her. It is great to learn that he has a new baby girl and that he's working on turning his life around. She is relieved that he sounds like he may finally be out of the grip of the Gangster Disciples. But still, she doesn't feel like responding. Reading Solomon's email just brings back that dark time in November, the bleak passage of days after Dan's death and her own erratic conduct that led her to hazardously confront Derek Strozak in his own home. If she had not done that, she wouldn't have been shot; but more importantly, if she had not done that, Manuel would still be alive.

The emotions from November swirl around her like an unstoppable blizzard and she really isn't prepared to deal with an overwhelming surge again. It was enough having to travel back to that tumultuous time during the meeting with Brian Patterson on Monday. She is still trying to process the grief that she carries over Dan's death and, Manuel's death. The conversation with Patterson renewed all of that pain, made it fresh like a recent snowfall.

She misses Kate throughout the day, wishes she was still around to cook meals for, to watch a 1980's movie with, to share family stories with and to laugh about silly things. Kate's lighthearted, vibrant personality is so infused with energy that she really brightened Cheney's spirits during the visit, despite the disconcerting circumstances that brought Kate to the farmhouse. With Kate having stayed at the house for only a few days, Cheney cannot believe that she misses her that much: but she does.

She is relieved when Kate calls her, even though it's past ten. While it is nice to hear Kate's voice, there is a feeling of isolation and remoteness that settles over her, knowing that Kate is some thirty-miles away in DeKalb. It is snowing out again, though not as hard as over the weekend, and Cheney watches the flakes spiral down as she talks to her sister. The conversation is not a lengthy one. She confirms that Kate is safe, that her afternoon classes were uneventful, and that she has not seen Nic anywhere around the apartment complex, nor at the campus. Kate apologizes for waiting so late to call: she explains that she ended up having to go grocery shopping after class and that she ran into one of her friends and ended up inviting her over for dinner. She apologizes to Cheney and says she lost track of the time entertaining her friend. Kate says that the friend is staying over, and Cheney draws some comfort in knowing that her sister won't be home alone – at least for the night – in her apartment.

After she gets off the phone, Cheney is struck how quiet the house sounds, for even though it is snowing outside, it is not windy, so the house is not aching from chilly blows. The flakes fall softly outside, like giant, ponderous marshmallows cascading downwards, appearing indecisive and insubstantial. Even though it is not as cold as it has been, and the house is still, Patton has joined her at the foot of the bed, instead of his normal resting place, the couch against the wall.

She contemplates going to sleep early tonight, but she has a book-club assignment to complete before Thursday. She has to read the first eight chapters of Laura Ingalls Wilder's *The Long Winter*. She only has three chapters to go, as she is gladly reading one of her favorite novels from childhood. She hasn't read this book in – what – No! It couldn't be that long, could it? Twenty-years?

She settles in for the night, under the covers, Patton curled up at the end of the comforter. And, as the snow tumbles down outside of her bedroom window, she immerses herself in the story of a pioneer winter on the Dakota plains.

# INQUEST

Ultimately, she is not surprised by the content of the Meskwaki Police Department response, granting the freedom of information request in part by agreeing to release redacted versions of the police reports. She had felt fairly confident that the police department would reply differently than its initial response, because she had pointed out the age of the case, the coroner's determination that the cause of death was suicide, and, that the requester is the daughter of the decedent.

Still, it is amazing how quickly the reply comes, such that when she first sees the email in her inbox Thursday morning, she momentarily doubts her initial confidence and is temporarily dismayed, thinking that the brief interval between the request and the response must be an indicator of another denial. Thankfully, she is wrong, and when she reads the email, she is thrilled that her legal efforts were successful. She immediately forwards to Cassandra the police department's response along with a brief explanatory note regarding its contents.

Cassandra replies immediately, but not by email, instead by phone. Her voice is rushed and infusive with joy. "Oh, thank you, thank you, Cheney. I can't tell you how much this means to me! I knew you'd get further than I could on this on my own!"

"No problem at all, Cassandra. I'm glad I could be of assistance. Now, keep in mind that you're going to have to contact the department directly to let them know if you wish the materials to be sent to you *via* a courier service or if you want to pick them up."

Practically before Cheney can finish, Cassandra chimes, "I want to pick them up."

"Okay, well, regardless of whether you pick them up or have them mailed to you it sounds from this response letter like the reports may be voluminous, so they may charge you a copy fee of some sort that you'll have to pay before they release them to you. If you do decide to have the documents delivered to you, they'll require that you pay for the courier service cost too in advance. Also, I just wanted to mention to you that you may want to email a FOIA request, similar to the one I drafted to Meskwaki, over to the Kent County Coroner's Office. The Coroner's Office may have documents, such as the inquest and the autopsy report, that may or may not be in the police department's possession."

"Oh, that's a good idea," she says. "I will do that."

"I just have to caution you, though, Cassandra, and I should have thought of this before, but I'll tell you now. Your FOIA request to the Meskwaki Police Department was fairly broad, and there are probably going to be copies of crime scene photos among the documents that they provide you. As for the Coroner's Office, be careful what you ask for. You may want to limit your request to exclude certain information. There may be things in that file, that you really don't want to subject yourself to seeing. Do you understand what I'm saying?"

"I do, Cheney. I get what you're saying, and I appreciate it. But I really want to see everything related to my mother's death. I really don't think it will bother me too much to look at the stuff, because it's been so many years and I was just a little girl when my mom died. And anyway,

I have to see it all. I won't be able to know what really happened unless I have everything that they had."

Cheney disagrees with her, but she doesn't say anything. She would not want to read the autopsy report or see crime scene photos concerning Dan's death. Ever. Regardless of the passage of time. But this is Cassandra Cantoni's life and it's her decision to make, and if she is comfortable viewing such things, that's entirely up to her. Cheney ends the conversation by reminding her that the documents from the Meskwaki Police Department will be redacted, and that the police department claimed various exemptions to support redaction. While she hesitates before doing so, she ends the call by offering to assist Cassandra if, for some reason, she's not satisfied with the completeness of the documents once she receives and reads through them. Cassandra thanks her again and reiterates her willingness to remunerate Cheney for her legal help, but Cheney again declines.

Cheney feels good about helping Cassandra. Even though she has never really liked her, and in fact, has loathed her in the past, she is seeing a different side of Cassandra. It is evident that Cassandra is trying. Clearly, Cassandra recognized that she has treated Cheney poorly over the years, and she apologized for it. It is impossible not to feel sympathy for Cassandra, particularly since losing her mother at such a young age and under such circumstances had to be traumatic. It probably is normal for a child to question whether their mother committed suicide. After all, what child wants to believe that their mother would prefer death to life?

Even though she has compassion for Cassandra, she is relieved that her involvement in the situation regarding Cassandra's mother is over. She really doesn't have the time, nor the energy, to take on any more legal work. She is happy that it worked out for Cassandra, and that Cassandra will be receiving the information she wants, but she is also relieved that there is no further action required on her part as an attorney. She has too much to do. Like shoveling.

It snowed again last night, and she didn't shovel yesterday, even though it had also snowed almost two inches on Tuesday night. Dax had texted her inquiring whether she wanted him to come with the plow, but she had declined and told him that she would just shovel herself. Still, she hadn't felt like going outside yesterday, and instead, had stayed indoors all day, letting Patton out the back-sliding glass door on occasion, but not venturing into the snow herself.

Today, it is relatively still outside, with no perceptible wind, and it's in the mid-thirties, so it is a perfect day for shoveling. This will be her first time shoveling since she was shot, and she doesn't know whether she'll be able to do it without physical distress. For the most part, her injury is healed, but she still feels jolts of pain on occasion if she strains herself by lifting something of significant weight or if she moves her shoulder too abruptly. She'll take it easy during the shoveling and if it becomes too much, she'll stop and text Dax to come over and finish the job.

She puts on a pair of leggings, sweatpants, a hooded sweatshirt, a three-quarter length jacket, a black hat, gloves and boots. The snow is light and insubstantial, as opposed to compact and heavy, so it is fairly easy going on her shoulder and she is without pain for the most part, outside of a slight twinge on occasion. There is satisfaction in the labor of pushing row upon row of the white fluffy stuff, hoisting it into her shovel, and tossing the flakes onto the rising banks along the lawn. Patton romps around outside in endless drifts of snow, as if he is prancing in sea foam, and, despite that the sky is overcast, it feels like a sunny day. It takes more than an hour to shovel the driveway, and occasionally, she glances over her shoulder whenever she hears a car pass by, to make sure it isn't turning into her driveway. She doesn't think that the Latin

Kings will show up during the day, if at all; but still, she is slightly wary, based on Patterson's warning.

After she is finished with the shoveling, she is re-energized after weeks of winter sluggishness, and she decides to take a run on the tread-mill. She changes into work-out gear, grabs a bottle of water, and heads to the home-gym in the barn. Running helps her process her thoughts, and she shifts between weighing the odds of Corazon showing up at the farm to musing whether her sister is going to reconcile with that asshole, Nic. She tries to put those twin concerns aside and focus on what she is going to do with her life now that Dan is gone and she has quit her job.

What she told Patterson is true; she really wants to spend some time on creative writing. Lately, she has been thinking of drafting a dramatic script. She even has her character's name selected – Hesperus Braun – and she has a plot worked out in her head as well as some bits of dialogue that she has started jotting down in her journal. But this run is particularly pro-ductive, because it shovels away the distracting drifts of heavy thoughts about Nic and Corazon, and instead, opens up her creative gateway to dreaming of fictional characters and conversations. And she is excited, really, and, moreover, optimistic, for the first time in weeks – no, actually, months. She is so lost in her artistic reverie, that she is surprised when she looks down and sees that she has completed four miles.

She spends the rest of the day with various indoor chores: cleaning the house, doing laundry, paying bills. When sundown comes, she real-izes she hasn't eaten all day, and she makes chicken linguini. But it's kind of sad eating alone at the big barnwood table in the kitchen, and she knows she'll have enough leftovers to last her for days. It would be nice if Kate were here.

She hasn't heard from Kate all day, and in fact, Kate didn't call or text her yesterday either. There is nothing particularly unusual about this. Prior to last weekend, Cheney would have thought nothing of it, for she and Kate only texted or spoke on the phone maybe once a week or so; and, there were even long stretches where they had gone two or more weeks without communicating at all. That had been the nature of their relationship for years really. But now, Cheney feels particularly close with Kate and even more protective of her than in the past, and she worries that this Nic guy might come after Kate or that Kate might willingly reunite with him. Cheney has handled enough domestic violence cases in the past to know how frequently either or both of those unfortunate scenarios happen.

So, after dinner, when she is curled up on the couch in the living room, watching television, she texts Kate asking her if she's okay. She doesn't get a response right away. In fact, more than an hour goes by before she gets a reply text: A thumbs up emoji, and a purple heart, followed by, "All is well. Busy with studying for mid-terms. No excitement here. I'll call you over the weekend." Cheney responds with a "Sounds good." Nothing about Kate's text message is particularly suspicious, but, for some reason, Cheney has a feeling that something is up between Kate and Nic. She doesn't press Kate on this though, and instead, lets Kate's response stand. She'll talk to Kate over the weekend and impart upon her again how unhealthy it would be for Kate to stay in such a toxic relationship. After all, she wouldn't be much of a big sister if she didn't try to give her advice that might protect her in the long run from emotional or physical harm.

The Spinach Omelet Book Nerds' meeting is at nine, but she goes upstairs a couple of hours prior to her videoconference. She relaxes in the second-floor office in a flame-orange wide-tufted club chair, with her feet stretched out on an ottoman, writing the first pages of her play script about Hesperus Braun. Hesperus is a disabled, former Chicago police detective, who was shot in the line of duty and is now trying to solve a cold case involving her own sister who went missing from the family farm in Hebron, Illinois twenty years earlier. Hesperus has returned to the small town in northern Illinois to review reports and interview people about her sister's disappearance. Cheney writes about ten pages of script before she realizes that the storyline would be much better suited for a novel. She begins converting the dialogue over into prose, ditching her journal for a spiral notebook, but she doesn't get very far. Her computer audio-prompt signals that Carmen is waiting for her to accept her invitation to join the club meeting.

The round face of the bespectacled nine-year-old pops up on her computer screen as soon as Cheney joins the conference. Cheney is not a fan of kids, and has always avowed that she would never have any of her own. She thinks the worst job in the world would be that of an elementary school teacher: she can't imagine how anyone could possibly find it rewarding to be around a bunch of obnoxious kids all day. She hasn't been around a lot of little kids herself - except for her own sister, Kate, since Kate is seven-years younger than her. Back when they were growing up, she oftentimes found her younger sister to be annoying, spoiled, and somewhat of a nuisance. Her experience with her own sibling probably influenced her desire to live a child-free existence and she seems to gravitate toward friends who share those views. Of her three closest friends - Lauren, Gunther and Carrie - none has any children.

Oddly, though, she looks forward to these Thursday evening virtual book club meetings with Carmen. Carmen is not annoying at all, and, moreover, she is far from spoiled: she lives in a tiny, but overly-crowded, two-bedroom bungalow with her mother, her two older brothers, her aunt and two younger cousins. Once in a while during their videoconference, one or both of Carmen's little cousins will photobomb behind or to the side of Carmen, making silly faces and laughing, or her brothers will stop by and tell her she needs to hurry up and finish, because they need the room. The weekly book club meeting is typically just a half an hour long, but Cheney can tell it's not easy for Carmen to be able to arrange to have any private time in that packed house-hold. So far, they have successfully been able to hold the club meeting every Thursday since the first week in December, which says more for Carmen's organizational skills and ambition, than Cheney's.

Once Cheney joins the meeting, Carmen knocks a gavel against her brothers' desk several times. It's a championship replica gavel from Cheney's law school moot court days that she had mailed to the child as a Christmas gift in December.

"Well, let's call to order our regularly scheduled meeting of the Spinach Omelet Book Nerds," Carmen announces officially. Clearly, she must watch a lot of public meetings on the Internet or cable, because she sure knows how to run one. "My name is Carmen Santo Vicente D'Avila-Rodriguez. I am the Chairman of the Spinach Omelet Book Nerds. This club is named in honor of my brother, Manuel D'Avila-Rodriguez." This is the same introduction that Carmen recites at the beginning of each meeting. Carmen insists on the title of 'Chairman', because she told Cheney at the inaugural meeting that she thinks that the term 'Chairperson' sounds "ridiculously stupid and grossly woke."

Carmen continues with the meeting's introduction: "Also present is First Member Cheney Manning. We are each appearing remotely. The time is 9:01 p.m.. We will now both stand for the Pledge of Allegiance."

The format of the meeting is Carmen's and Carmen's alone. She had insisted that their first meeting in December be one devoted to structure, and they ultimately agreed to lay out some ground rules for formatting future meetings. They did so; well, rather, Carmen did. Carmen drafted the bylaws of the Spinach Omelet Book Nerds, and Cheney voted to approve them. The first bylaw is that all members stand and recite the Pledge of Allegiance before each meeting. This necessitated Cheney removing Dan's American Flag from one of the walls in the barn and affixing it on a stand in the corner of the second-floor office in the house, since she didn't previously have an indoor flag. Carmen uses a small replica flag on her desk stand in her brothers' room to which to pledge, but Cheney has already decided that she is going to buy an American Flag for the child's imminent birthday in March and send it to her.

Cheney stands, puts her hand on her heart, and recites the Pledge of Allegiance solemnly, in concert with Carmen's remote voice. Cheney returns to her office chair and Carmen then announces, "Our first point of order is a discussion of the book, *The Long Winter*, by Laura Ingalls Wilder. First Member Manning, would you like to lead the discussion?"

"Sure," Cheney says.

"As a preliminary matter, did you fulfill the requirement of reading the first eight chapters?"

"Affirmative," Cheney answers.

"Proceed, then, First Member Manning," Carmen says.

"Well, I read *The Long Winter* many years ago, when I was about your age, maybe a little older, and it was one of my favorite novels back then. It's been a joy, really, reading it again, and I think people who read this book when they were children would enjoy revisiting it. For me, it's been fun sipping a cup of hot chocolate, bundled up in the bed upstairs of the farmhouse, snuggled next to my big dog, and reading this novel, while the snow is piling up outside. I love the flow of the book and the imagery, really. It's so beautifully written, so lyrical, I can understand why it is such an iconic piece of children's literature. What about you, Chairman?"

"I also really like it," Carmen says. "Even though I hate living here in Humboldt Park with all of the shootings and I am sometimes afraid to live here because of the violence and gangs, reading the first part of this book has made me think maybe I don't have it so bad as other people have had it in the past: you know what I mean? Maybe I should stop feeling sorry for myself and feel thankful because sometimes I get sad thinking of how my life is in this small house and with all these people – my aunt, and my cousins – living with us right now." Carmen pauses, and says, "I mean, my mattress is in my mom's closet. I don't know if I told you that before?"

"No," Cheney says quietly, attempting not to appear stunned by the child's revelation.

"It's a big closet though, but that's the only space we have for me to have my own light so that I can read at night and not keep my mom awake. My mom and my aunt sleep in the same bed, and there's room for me in there too if I want. I can sleep in there if I want to, but I like to stay up and read books and my mom likes to go sleep before ten, because she has to wake up at four in the morning to take the bus to get to work and she works so hard all day. I don't like the gang violence and going to school worrying - thinking about who might get in my face or grab my books or push me down. But I guess I should be thankful I have a warm house and a mattress to sleep on and a place of my own to read."

"And a library card," Cheney adds, trying to sound cheerful, even though she feels her eyes brimming up with tears after hearing Carmen's first-hand account of her living situation. She doesn't want the child to see her cry, because it may only tend to make Carmen feel worse.

"Yes, that's right!" Carmen says enthusiastically, her face lighting up. "I have books!"

Cheney tries to remain upbeat throughout the rest of the videoconference, but it's hard not to think of Carmen reading books at night in her mother's closet because that's the only space in the bungalow for her to do so. The meeting ends - as it always does according to the club's bylaws - with an announcement by the Chairman of the next reading assignment followed by a two-minute period for members' comments. This is an opportunity to talk about anything, as long as the member doesn't exceed two-minutes. Usually, Carmen talks about school or one of her friends. Tonight, she talks about Manuel; and, though her comments are brief, Cheney can tell the child is choked up with emotion. She talks about how he used to walk her to school sometimes, and how he used to read books to her when she was little, before she knew how to read, and how he took her on the log-ride at Great America last summer and that they went on it like four or five times until their clothes were soaked.

When Carmen concludes she says simply, "I miss him."

"I miss him, too," Cheney says. There is an uncomfortable silence, and the child appears to be waiting for Cheney to continue talking, but she doesn't. Despite her feelings, Cheney cannot share any thoughts other than those four words. It's as if any verbal expression of emotions she had felt – and still feels- for Manuel, are sealed in a vault in her throat. She is holding it together, but she fears she will start crying if she says anything beyond 'I miss him, too.'

"Meeting adjourned," Carmen announces, her voice quavering and her small face reflecting disappointment. She disappears from the screen.

# BEAUTY

*February 8*th

Cheney goes to sleep much earlier than usual on Friday night, and she is dozing when her phone pings. She only hears it in her subconscious and she does not rouse, merely incorporating the noise into her dream. But when the phone starts buzzing, that wakes her up. When she groggily moves across the room to her desk to retrieve her phone, she sees that it is a quarter after nine and that she has missed a text and a call from Kate. The text just says, "Call me" and Kate didn't leave a voicemail message. She has not heard from Kate all day and she doesn't have a good feeling when she calls her back.

When Kate answers she starts out by asking Cheney to promise not to be mad at her.

"About what, Kate?"

"I'm in the hospital."

"Where?"

"In Loomisville on Route 31."

It's the same hospital to which Cheney had been transported after Derek Strozak had shot her. "What happened?" Cheney asks; her voice, usually strong and measured, sounds slightly frantic.

111

"I'll tell you when you get here; but can you please come pick me up?"

Panic rises through her throat, making her words rush out. "What's wrong, Kate? Why are you in the hospital?"

Kate starts sobbing on the phone, and it's difficult to hear what she says but it sounds like, "I can't – I c-c-an't, do this. I can't- can't- t-t-tell you right now. C-c-an – can you please just pick me up?"

"Of course, I'll come get you. I'll leave right now."

Cheney gets ready in under five minutes. She throws on a pair of jeans, boots, a sweatshirt, puffer jacket, gloves and winter hat. She brings the dog outside briefly with her when she starts her pickup truck, because she's not sure how long she'll be gone. She lets Patton run around the south lawn while her truck warms up. She is both tired and anxious: so much so that she abandons all her self-admonishments to pay attention to her surroundings. Her yard could be crawling with Latin Kings hiding behind the spruce trees or the garage, and she wouldn't even notice.

She goes back inside, fills Patton's bowl with dry dog food in case she gets stuck at the hospital, puts fresh water in his other bowl, kisses him atop his head, and tells him she won't be too long. At least, that's what she hopes.

At this time of night, it's only about a forty-minute drive to Loomisville, and the roads are clear, so she does not hesitate to speed. The entire time she worries about what happened to Kate and why she is in the hospital. It could be anything - the flu, food poisoning, a car crash. But somehow, she knows it's none of those things. It has to be Nic Zafeiropoulos. It has something to do with that asshole. She's sure of it. He had to have hurt Kate and that's why she's in the hospital. There is no doubt about it.

Her instincts prove correct when she finds Kate lying on a hospital bed in a curtained- off section in the emergency room. Kate's head is wrapped along her forehead with a giant white bandage. Cheney tries not to react emotionally when she sees her, but it is impossible to do so. She covers her mouth and her voice is a blend of anguish and astonishment. "Oh, Kate. Oh my God. What did he do to you?"

"He hit me in the head with a beer bottle," Kate says and then starts crying. "Don't be mad at me, Cheney. Please don't."

"Oh, my God," Cheney repeats, hugging her. "I'm not mad at you, Kate. I'm not mad. I'm just glad you're going to be okay. You *are* going to be okay, right?"

Kate nods, sobbing. "Yes. I'll be fine," Kate says, and then, catching a glimpse of the emergency room physician who has entered the space, Kate asks him, "Won't I?"

Cheney stands up, releasing Kate from the hug, and steps back from the bed, folding her arms, while the doctor addresses Kate. "Yes, you'll be just fine." And then, to Cheney he asks, "Are you taking her home?"

"Yes. Well, I mean, she's going to come with me to my house," Cheney says. She hasn't discussed this with Kate, but, regardless, it's non-negotiable. She is not going to let Kate return to the apartment in DeKalb anytime soon.

"Good," the physician answers. He is a short, balding middle-eastern man with kind eyes and a direct, but sympathetic tone. "She shouldn't be alone tonight."

"Are the police coming to interview her?" Cheney asks him.

113

"They were already here," Kate answers.

"Yes," the doctor confirms. "They were here a couple of hours ago."

"When did this happen, Kate? How long have you been in here?"

"Um…it was after dinner. I don't know, Cheney, really. It's hard to think of time right now. I've kind of lost track of time."

"Yeah. Yeah. I get it. I'm sorry I asked." And then to the physician, Cheney says, "Well, she's coming home with me, so he won't be able to come after her again; but, if he does, I am well-armed and I have a dog."

"He's in jail, Cheney. They arrested him," Kate explains.

"Good," Cheney says.

The doctor addresses Cheney, clarifying his earlier comment. "I didn't mean that she shouldn't be alone because of her risk of harm from her attacker, which is a completely separate issue altogether. I meant that she shouldn't be alone because she has a concussion and she'll need someone with her over the next couple of days. She should take it easy at least for the next forty-eight hours: no physical or mental exertion. If she develops a headache or experiences dizziness, slurred speech-confusion, anything like that, you will need to bring her back in right away. They'll give you a sheet at the desk when you leave that will have the things to look out for. It will also have instructions on wound care for the lacerations."

Cheney looks at him inquisitively and he elaborates. "She has two lacerations, both of which are fairly deep: One on her scalp and the other at the top of her forehead right beneath the hairline. We've stitched them both up, but she'll have to follow up with her own physician in five days to have the stitches checked. They likely can be removed then,

114

but sometimes it takes a couple of days longer than that. In the mean-
time, she'll need to keep a close eye on the lacerations to make sure they
don't get infected. I've prescribed an anti-bacterial cream that you can
pick up at the front desk; and we'll give you directions, as I said, on how
to go about making sure that the wounds are properly cleaned and kept
free of infection."

It is unspoken, but clear: the stunning, unblemished face of her sister - that remarkable beauty - now may be disfigured in some way. This
notion is horrifying, maddening, shocking. Despite this, Cheney tries
her best not to show any reaction, and she remains stone-faced, though
she feels her bottom lip tremble a bit. This is a lot to take in, particularly
since she is still dealing with the emotional loss of Daniel, and Manuel.
She doesn't really know how much more she can take, though she must
just absorb this additional trauma, and move forward. She has to be here
for Kate. She must remain steady and strong for her sister.

On the ride home, Kate tells her what happened. They had been at
dinner at his restaurant in Loomisville and he had drunk a few beers.
Afterwards, they went upstairs to his office and he put on some music
and took out a beer from his mini-fridge; and then he started ridicul-
ing her, calling her names, accusing her of 'making eyes' at the waiter.
When she told him that it wasn't true, he became angry and swung the
beer bottle at her head at close range, cracking it across the top left side
of her skull and forehead. She said she knew immediately that she had
been badly cut and the blood just started pouring down into her eyes.
And he just stormed off and left her there, so she stumbled outside and
found a hostess, who called 9-1-1.

"Were you ever unconscious?" Cheney asks her, struggling to
focus on the road, trying to remain calm, feeling her heart race with
rage. She has never met Nic Zafeiropoulos, but nonetheless, she hates
him for what he has done to Kate.

"No," Kate says. "I never really even fell down. I was standing the whole time."

"So, the fucking coward just took off and fled?" Cheney asks, her voice shaking with barely-controlled anger.

"Yes. That's at least what I assume, because I never saw him after that," Kate says. "The amount of blood was unbelievable. I was in shock, and I mean, I even thought I might die. I had no idea how severe the cuts might have been, because I couldn't feel anything and there was so much blood pouring out. I wasn't sure how badly I had been cut. Lola, the hostess: she's the one who helped me. She was kind of in shock too, I think. She's just a little thing; can't be more than eighteen-years-old, but she knew to grab bar towels and put pressure on the wound to try to stem the bleeding. And the bar manager, Sal, he helped too. He just kept repeating, 'What a son of a bitch. I'm fucking quitting this place after this shit'."

"But the police found him after he fled and arrested him, right?" Cheney asks.

"That's what the officer told me at the hospital. Evidently, he came back to his restaurant after I had been taken away by ambulance, and someone at the restaurant, one of his staff members - maybe Lola or Sal, I'm guessing - called 9-1-1 when he showed up there. The officer arrested him in his office above the restaurant. At least, that's what the officer told me." Kate pauses. "He's going to stay locked up, right? He can't get out, can he?"

"He can get out," Cheney says. "He may be out already even as we speak."

"Oh, my God," Kate says softly. "How can that be? I mean, don't they have to keep someone locked up until trial for something like this?"

"No," Cheney says. "But chances are that a condition of his bond will be that he not have any contact with you."

"But, that's just a piece of paper," Kate says, seemingly horrified. "That's not the same as him being locked up in jail."

"You're right," Cheney says somberly. "It's not the same at all."

"I'm sorry, Cheney," Kate says and she starts crying. "I'm so sorry to have you put through this."

"Kate, you're the one who has stitches in your head, not me," Cheney replies. "Really, you shouldn't be apologizing to me. I'm concerned about you; it shouldn't be the other way around."

"But I *am* concerned about you," Kate wails. "You already have so much to deal with and now I'm just piling on with my own drama. I am so sorry, Cheney. I should never have gone back out with him."

"As I said, there's no need to apologize to me. Really there isn't," Cheney says firmly, and she believes this. "But while we're on the topic of this asshole, how did it come to be that you ended up going out with him again after everything you went through last weekend?"

"Ugh," Kate says, though she stops crying momentarily, wiping her eyes and blowing her nose. "I knew you were going to ask me that. I can't really explain it. It's just hard to explain, but, he started texting me when I got back to DeKalb and I ended up agreeing to see him that same night."

"By 'same night', you mean 'Tuesday night'?" Cheney asks, feeling herself slipping into litigator cross-examination mode.

"Yes," Kate says sheepishly.

"What?!" Cheney exclaims, gathering that Kate had lied to her earlier in the week. "He's the one that stayed over with you on Tuesday night, not 'your friend'?"

"Yes," Kate admits.

"Why did you lie to me?"

"Because I knew you'd react like this. I knew you'd be mad," she says.

"With damn good reason," Cheney says.

"I know. I know," Kate says, her eyes welling up with tears again. "I know it was stupid to get back together with him. I don't expect you to understand. I don't expect anybody to understand. It was really a terrible decision on my part and I'm paying the price for it."

That's true. Kate is paying the price. Cheney wants her sister to heal, emotionally and physically, and she certainly doesn't want to agitate Kate when she needs rest. So, she backs off. She lets it go. Even though a part of her is grossly disappointed, and even angry, at Kate for having subjected herself to further damage by this idiot, she bites her tongue and changes the topic.

"I'd like you to stay with me for the rest of the semester, Kate. You said you're only taking three classes this semester to graduate in May, and I'm sure if you talk to your dean, that she'll let you finish the term remotely under the circumstances."

"I have my job, though, at the salon," Kate says.

"Kate, you're a shampoo girl," Cheney says. "I think they can handle you quitting with no notice."

"I'm also a receptionist there," Kate corrects her. "They depend on me to be there."

"Your safety is more important than that job, Kate. It's certainly not one to die over."

Kate nods as if thinking and then asks, "But what about my lease?"

"Isn't it up in May?" Cheney asks.

"Yes," Kate says. "Actually, May 31st."

"I think you should try to get the landlord to release you from the lease. Let him know that you are a dom batt victim and that you don't feel safe living in the apartment. In the worse-case scenario, we may need to just pay a penalty in order to get you out of the lease, even if that's paying the remaining three months' rent."

Kate is quiet and Cheney asks her, "What you are thinking, Kate?"

"I'm thinking about that phrase you used," she says.

"What phrase?"

"'Dom Batt victim'. I don't like it. I don't like those words being applied to me." Kate pauses, and then adds, "And this has nothing to do with you, Cheney. I know you're just using your legal slang when you say that phrase. Don't think I'm upset with you for calling me a Dom Batt victim. I know that's how you lawyers refer to people like me."

Before Cheney can apologize, or clarify or defend, Kate says, "It's just that it's not anything I've ever thought I would be called. And it's not anything I ever want to be called again. And this has nothing to do with you, Cheney: It has to do with me."

For the first time since Cheney heard the name Nic Zafeiropoulos, she is convinced that it is unlikely that Kate will reunite with him. It is possible, though, that she is wrong and Kate may inexplicably go back to him, even with the wounds Kate has suffered as a result of his rage. That possibility exists, and Cheney silently reminds herself that it's better to be prepared for it, then to believe it is never going to happen.

# ACQUIESCENCE

*February 9*th

It's still dark outside when Cheney's cellphone pings with an incoming text message. Unfuckingbelievable. Who would be texting at this hour? It's a Saturday and it can't even be seven o'clock yet, because the sun isn't up. Maybe she should just ignore it and look at it later when she's out of bed. She rolls over; but there it is – another annoying ping.

Patton is lying on his couch and he lifts his big head and watches Cheney make her way over to the desk. She is half-asleep and when she looks down at her phone, she sees it's six-thirty and that the message is from Cassandra Cantoni. It reads: "I'm sorry for texting you so early, but I need to talk to you right away."

Cheney thinks about just turning the phone off altogether and calling her later. She is exhausted after last night. Kate went to bed as soon as they arrived home: probably a result of the trauma, the adrenaline dump, and the pain killers. Cheney, however, had been wide awake worrying about her, and had gone upstairs to the third-floor bedroom a couple of times to check on her while she was sleeping. When Cheney finally dozed off herself, it was past two.

"Four and a half hours of sleep, God? Really? That's all you're giving me?" She speaks out loud, while looking up at the ceiling. She really just wants to go back to sleep, but now that she's awake, what's the point? It will take her a good half an hour, if not longer, to fall asleep anyway, so she may as well call Cassandra and get this over with.

"Buenos dias," Cheney says when Cassandra answers her call.

"I am sorry for texting you so early," Cassandra says in Spanish, and at a pace that Cheney understands. Although Cheney minored in Spanish in undergrad, her Spanish-speaking and comprehension abilities are somewhat limited; however, she understands quite a bit if the speaker enunciates slowly. Cassandra oftentimes slips between Spanish and English, but when she speaks too quickly, it is usually lost on Cheney.

"No problema," Cheney responds. "Qué pasa?"

Cassandra switches to English. "I got the reports yesterday – including the documents from the Coroner's Office too – I had FOIAd those separately on Thursday after we talked, and the Coroner responded right away by email that I could pick them up at his office on Friday. And I talked to Cindy, the records clerk, over at the Meskwaki Police Department on Thursday after you and I spoke, and she told me the redacted documents would be ready for me Friday afternoon. So, I spent yesterday afternoon and evening reading through everything, and I haven't even slept, because I just kept pouring over everything and taking notes and I just need to tell someone – and I can't tell Jeff because he wouldn't understand and he'd tell me I was wrong, like he told you that you were wrong about Solomon Wilson – But, I'm telling you, I am certain in looking at these reports that my mother did not kill herself."

"Okay." Cheney is wide-awake now and she turns on the lamp on her nightstand. "Well, who do you believe killed her then? The lieutenant?"

"Well, I don't want to tell you because I don't want to taint your opinion," Cassandra says. "I would like you to review the materials and see if you reach the same conclusion as I did."

"Oh, Cassandra, I really can't-"

"Please, Cheney. I really need your help again. I'm sorry to bother you with everything you're going through."

Boy, if she only knew. "Listen, Cassandra, it's just really not a good time for me right now. I mean, I didn't mind helping you out in obtaining the documents, and I am glad it worked out for you, but I don't have time to review them."

"I'll pay you," Cassandra offers and Cheney can tell by her voice that she is desperate. "I'll pay you three hundred dollars an hour to review them or whatever amount you think is fair."

"No, no," Cheney says. "It's not about the money, Cassandra. Really. It's about the time. I just don't have the time to take on anything else right now." She focuses on time, but she's also concerned about emotion. She doesn't have it in her to review a homicide case right now. It is the furthest thing from her mind. She doesn't want anything to do with reading through police reports regarding a violent death of anyone, even if it happened to a stranger thirty years ago. She doesn't want to absorb the pain.

"Please," Cassandra says. "I really don't have anyone else I can ask. I really believe that you're the only person who can help me."

People stuck their necks out for Cheney when she needed assistance with finding out who had killed Dan. Both Brian Patterson and Manuel Rodriguez had assisted her; and Manuel ultimately paid dearly for it. She has been where Cassandra is right now: a person begging someone to help her find out the truth about a loved one who died a violent death. She knows what's going through Cassandra's mind and heart, and she knows it is incredibly painful and confusing.

"I'll do it," Cheney says resignedly. "I'll pick up the reports at your house on Monday."

"Thank you! Thank you, Cheney! I can't tell you how much this means to me and my family," Cassandra says. "You don't have to drive all the way out to my house though. I can actually drop the reports off to you today. I'm heading out to visit my in-laws anyway and I'll be right by your place around eleven this morning."

"That's fine," Cheney says. "I'll see you then."

"Thank you, Cheney," Cassandra says. "You don't know how much this means to me."

"Actually, I do," Cheney says, and Cassandra says nothing in response to that comment other than to thank her again and then a quick, "Hasta luego!"

Since she's up anyway, Cheney goes upstairs and checks on Kate. She moves up the stairs as quietly as possible, even though they tend to squeak. Her sister is sound asleep, curled up on her side, the bandage wrapped around the top of her head like a cocoon. When she returns to the second-floor, Patton is waiting for her in the hallway, as if wanting to be let out early for his morning rounds. Sunlight is starting to meekly make its way into the hallway from the southern room windows.

"Let's go back to bed," she whispers to the dog, but he looks at her imploringly, and she reluctantly heads down the stairs. She lets him out the back-sliding glass doors and contemplates making a pot of coffee. She decides against it. She really needs to get some sleep, and Cassandra is not coming until eleven anyway. If Kate doesn't wake up early, she should be able to get several hours of sleep during that window.

Her phone starts pinging again from all the way upstairs on the second-floor. It's got to be Cassandra again. Maybe she's calling to push the time back to the afternoon. She tries to go up the stairs as quickly, but quietly, as possible, but the floorboards of the old farmhouse groan with each misplaced step. She would ignore the incoming texts altogether if she wasn't concerned that the pinging might wake up her sister.

She snatches the phone off of the bed, and looks out the window in the early morning twilight to see if Patton is running around the south lawn, but he isn't. He's probably ready to come in, and is likely waiting outside by the sliding glass doors. She looks down at the phone as she heads back downstairs, and sees that it is not Cassandra who has texted her, but, rather, Dan's brother, Dale. Dale is a Chicago cop, but even though he and Dan had shared occupations, they had been estranged at the time of Dan's death. Cheney had never even met Dale, but they had talked on the phone several times over the past few months, mostly about Dan's estate, since he had died intestate. Cheney intended on giving some of Dan's family photographs and police memorabilia to Dale, even though she had not yet arranged a day to meet him. It is strange that Dale is reaching out to her at this early hour.

Dale's text reads, "Call me when you get this." Pretty direct for a man she has never met and who was estranged from her husband.

Patton is indeed waiting for her outside and she lets him back into the house and fills his water bowl in the kitchen. She heads toward the parlor in the front of the house and calls Dale as she walks down the hallway.

"Hey, I'm sorry for texting you this early," he begins. "I'm sorry if I woke you up."

"Actually, no. Believe it or not, you're not my first texter this morning," she says. "That honor belongs to someone else."

"Hey, as I said, I'm really sorry, but I wanted to ask you something."

"Okay," she says, standing in front of the bay window, watching the day awaken. "Shoot." She has no idea why Dan's brother would be contacting her at this hour, but she figures it must be something important.

"I know this sounds like kind of a strange question, but are you in some kind of a book club with some Latin Kings?"

Even though she is stunned by his question, she suspects immediately that this must have something to do with what Patterson had told her about the Latin Kings. She tries to sound nonchalant and unrattled. "*Kind* of a strange question? That *is* a really strange question and the answer is 'No'; I am not in a book club with Latin Kings," she says definitively, "though I wish I was. That sounds kind of entertaining actually."

"I'm really not joking," he says dryly. "Are you sure you're not in some kind of a book club where there might be a couple of Latin Kings in Chicago involved?"

It's early in the morning, and her brain is still a bit sluggish, particularly after the harrowing night and only three hours of restless sleep, but now she gets it. The Spinach Omelet Book Nerds. Carmen's brothers: Elias and Miguel. They must be Latin Kings like their brother, Manuel, was.

126

"Oh," she says. She paces across the hallway to the library and back, looping between both rooms as she talks. "I know what you're talking about. I *am* in a book club, but there are no Latin Kings in it. A member of the Club appears remotely from a bedroom in Chicago in which one or two Latin Kings might reside. Is this to what you are referring?"

"I don't know," he says. "You tell me."

She really wishes she had a cup of coffee. She stops pacing and stands looking out the bay window again. "I'm in a virtual book club with a nine-year-old girl who lives in Humboldt Park. Her brother, Manuel Rodriguez, was the Latin King who helped me prove that Derek Strozak had killed Dan. Her brother saved my life when Strozak shot me. But then he was arrested on a failure to appear warrant for a subpoena for Grand Jury out of Cook County on a completely unrelated homicide case where he was an eyewitness: the one where the head of the GDs killed a train conductor in Blue Island."

"Where is he now?"

"He's dead," she says emotionless, and starts walking again, this time down the hall toward the kitchen. "The GDs ended up killing him in the Cook County Jail not long after he was picked up on the witness warrant."

"Then, what's this you mentioned about a Latin King bedroom? If he's dead, I'm not understanding what you mean?"

"Yeah, so the little girl, Carmen, with whom I am in the virtual book club, has two other brothers: Elias and Miguel. I suspect they may be in the Latin Kings like their brother was."

"What do you base that on?"

She turns around and paces back toward the parlor. "Instinct. Visible tattoos. Mannerisms."

"You know them?"

"Only met them once." She's answered a lot of questions for him, and now it's time for him to answer some questions for her. "What's this all about, Dale? Why are you calling me to ask me all of these questions? Am I in some trouble or something for discussing Laura Ingalls Wilder books with a little sister of some Kings? Is this the New World Order I keep hearing about? Has the government resorted to surveilling virtual book club meetings now?"

"No, no, nothing like that. We're just getting some intel about you and I have permission from my Captain to disclose it to you. We're hearing some chatter: You may be in some danger from the Latin Kings. We're not quite sure though, nothing solid. Just talk on the streets and we're not clear what to make of it yet."

She stops in front of the bay window again. "What does this have to do with the Spinach Omelet Book Nerds?"

"What are you talking about?" he asks.

"That's our book club. The Spinach Omelet Book Nerds. What do the street rumors have to do with the book club?"

"Just that we're hearing that you are in a book club with some Latin Kings and that the ones who are in the club with you don't want the gang to take any action against you. Evidently, there's some internal dispute within the gang, where the leadership wants you dead but a couple of the members are intervening on your behalf, trying to persuade them to leave you alone. Obviously, we must've got the first part wrong. It's that you're in a book club with a sister of two Latin Kings - not that you're in a book club *with* two Latin Kings."

"How concerned should I be about any of this, Dale?"

"I don't know," Dale says, but she can tell by his voice, even though she hardly knows him, that she should be very concerned.

The sun has not even fully risen yet, and she has already taken on too much for one day.

# SETTING

When her mom calls to ask if she's heard from Kate over the past couple of days, Cheney isn't really sure what to say. It's nine o'clock at night, and Kate's already upstairs sleeping. Cheney is sitting up in bed, with police reports and copies of crime scene photographs strewn atop the comforter. She's read through everything; she's taken notes and, she's just about to call Cassandra. When her cellphone starts buzzing and she sees that it's her mom calling, she prepares herself to speak in accordance with the discussion that she had with Kate in the afternoon.

Kate had slept most of the day, and didn't get up until past noon. Cheney had been concerned that Cassandra would wake Kate up by ringing the doorbell, and she had wanted Kate to be able to continue sleeping as the doctor had recommended. Additionally, she really didn't want to get into a three-way conversation among Kate, Cassandra and her regarding the cause of Kate's injury. Cheney was certain that Kate really wouldn't be up to someone gawking at her head dressing and asking a lot of painful questions, which Cassandra probably would have posited.

With the goal of protecting Kate's health and privacy in mind, Cheney had waited for Cassandra in the front parlor to head her off at the pass. As soon as Cassandra had pulled up in the driveway, Cheney had opened the front door to greet her, but had not invited her inside. Instead, Cheney had just taken the box of documents from her and then fired off some rapid-fire pleasantries to get her moving on her way. Cheney had been successful in sending a message *via* mostly non-verbal cues that she had no time for small talk and that she had things to do. Even though Cheney had sensed that Cassandra was dying to come in to talk to her about her mother's case, Cassandra just thanked her again, said she really valued Cheney's opinion, and then left without further conversation.

While it had been surprisingly easy to protect Kate from having to deal with what would have likely been Cassandra's shocked face and stream of questions, fending their mother off is going to be a challenging task. Cheney doesn't want to lie to her own mother, but she really feels that the situation is Kate's story to tell, not hers. She had discussed this with Kate in the afternoon, a couple of hours after Kate had woken up from her long slumber, and after Cheney had applied antibacterial ointment to her wounds and replaced her bandages. Kate had still seemed a bit groggy, but she had been fairly alert and in good spirits. Unfortunately, though, the conversation had quickly unraveled without resolution.

"What am I supposed to tell Mom or Dad if either of them calls?" Cheney had asked her.

"Oh, I don't know," Kate had replied. "I don't want either of them to worry about me. I don't want them to know what happened."

Cheney is a big proponent of telling the truth, even where it is painful to do so. With that in mind, she had tried to influence Kate to do the right thing. "But we have to tell them the truth, Kate. We can't lie to our own parents. They'll find the truth out eventually anyway. We can't keep it from them."

"Like I said, I just really don't want to get into it with them right now," Kate had said definitively. "It's just too painful. Besides, after everything they've been through lately, I really don't think they could handle the stress right now – particularly dad. I'm worried about his heart."

Their father had suffered a heart attack - what was it? Two? No, three - years ago now. He was a stoic, inscrutable man, who shouldered the burdens of life silently, to a point of where his arteries paid dearly. He has never expressed a lot of emotion, but he had been visibly torn up by Dan's murder, to a point of where his love for Cheney, along with his personal agony of her suffering, had been evident. He had also been distraught over Cheney's subsequent injury and hospitalization, and he looked like he had aged a decade over the course of the past three months. Kate was right. Their dad couldn't take on any more stress right now.

"I get that about Dad," Cheney had agreed. "You're right. He probably can't take on much more than he has. But what is it you want me to say? I mean, I really don't want to lie to either of them and Mom will know something is up anyway if I were to lie. You know I'm the worst person to try to tell a lie. I suck at it."

"Do you really think one of them is going to call?" Kate had asked.

"Not Dad," Cheney said. "You know that he doesn't usually call to talk on the phone. But, Mom: I'm sure she'll be calling sometime tomorrow or Sunday, if not tonight."

"I don't know what you should say when Mom calls. I just know that I don't want you to tell her anything about what Nic did or anything about my face having to be stitched up. She'll be hysterical, and Dad will get all worried about me, and about her and I'm afraid it will kill him. I really am." Kate had seemed like she was getting tired, the pace of her words slowing down. Her face became very pale and her eyelids seemed like they were drooping a bit. She had yawned, loudly and then had stood up, in effect ending the conversation. "I don't know what you should tell them, Cheney. You'll just have to think of something. You're the word-smith of the family. I know that you'll be able to come up with something to cover for me." She had yawned again and then said, "I've got to go back to bed. I'm sorry. All of a sudden it just hit me. I'm so tired."

Cheney had been hoping that she would have an opportunity to talk to Kate again in order to attempt to convince her to have a can-did conversation with their parents before their mother called Cheney. Unfortunately, that did not pan out. So, when her mother asks early on in the call as to whether she's heard from her sister in the past few days, Cheney freezes for a moment, and then goes with the truth: Well, par-tially so. "Actually, she's here tonight."

"She's at your house? Well, why didn't she tell me she was going there?"

"I don't know, Mom. Maybe because she's twenty-four. And, she's Kate."

"Well, when I'm through talking to you, can you give the phone to her? I'd like to talk to my youngest child, too."

"Actually, she's sleeping, Mom," Cheney says.

"Sleeping? Well, I didn't know it was that late."

"Well, it's not really that late. We just had a long day and she turned in early."

"Oh. Well, is she going to be there all weekend? Maybe Dad and I will stop by or, even better than that, maybe the two of you could come over here on Sunday. I could make a pot roast. I haven't talked to her since Monday when she came over here to visit. I was starting to get worried about her, because she said she broke her cell phone and she was going to call me once she got a new phone, and all I received was a text from her on Tuesday saying she had a new phone and a few texts from her Thursday in the afternoon. I tried calling her a couple of times this week, but she hasn't called me back"

"Oh, yeah, well, I think she's been pretty busy with school, being that she is actually graduating in May."

"Yes! Isn't that wonderful? I am so proud of her. It took her a while to find her stride, unlike you. You always knew what you wanted to do and would zero in on it and complete whatever you set your mind to do. But Kate does a bit of a zig zag at times on her journey, though she always ends up getting there at the end of the day: just takes a little more time with her. Dad and I are so proud of her; but I must admit, we have no idea what she is going to do with a degree in theatre."

"I don't think she does either," Cheney says, relieved that the conversation is going in this direction instead of an inquiry as to why Kate is staying at her house for the weekend.

"But, you don't know what you're going to be doing now either do you?" her mom asks, and Cheney can tell she is a bit concerned. Cheney had broken the news to her parents earlier in the week that she had resigned from the Public Defender's Office.

"Actually, I'm writing a novel," Cheney says.

Her mother kind of glosses over that, and asks, "Are you looking for a job at a law firm?"

"No, Mom," Cheney says. "I'm not looking for a job right now. Like I told you and Dad already, I'm taking a break from the practice of law for a while. I'm writing a book."

"Uh huh," her mom says.

"Aren't you even going to ask me what the book is about, Mom?"

"Sure, Cheney," her mom says, "What's the book about?"

After Cheney rattles off a sketch of the plot of the novel, her mom says, "Oh, it sounds interesting, Cheney. Really interesting. I really like murder mysteries. But, I just don't know if I like that name though: Hesperus Braun. Can't you come up with a different name than that?"

"What's wrong with the name, Mom?"

"It's not a very romantic-sounding name," her mom says.

"It's not a romance novel, Mom. It's a murder mystery."

"Hesperus: It just sounds funny, that's all. I don't think I like it. But, it's your book, Cheney; so, name your character anything you want. Maybe if you write it as a play script, Kate could play the lead role if it's ever produced."

"Perhaps," Cheney says. Her mother has a way of generally steering conversations back to Kate. "But only if I change the character's name from Hesperus to something more romantic."

"Yes; that's right!" her mother says good-naturedly, evidently not catching on to Cheney's sarcasm. "And getting back to Kate, she's talking about moving back here with Dad and me when she graduates in May, so that she can look for a job and find out where she is going in life. It's just that - twenty-four? Geesh, I was already married by the time I was twenty-four and had been teaching for three years by then." She sighs heavily. "Hopefully, she'll figure out what she wants to do between now and May."

That's unlikely. Kate is indecisive about a career path as it is, let alone having to deal with the physical and mental fall-out of an abusive relationship. It would be good for Kate to go live with their parents though after graduation; she'll be safe there in Dostam Heights. Their parents live in a townhouse in a gated community not far from the police station. There are so many people around in that area, unlike the remoteness of Cheney's farmhouse. It's unlikely that Nic Zafeiropoulos would get past the security guard and, even if he did, her parents have a top-notch video-surveillance security system set up. Comparatively, Cheney's security system is simply her dog and a Glock.

Cheney is able to get through the remainder of the conversation without any direct questions from her mother about Kate, so she is relieved that she is not put into a position of having to either disappoint Kate or having to be deceitful to their mother. She does, however, tell her mother, vaguely so, that they have too much going on over the weekend already, so that a Sunday visit will not work out. She doesn't, however, explain what it is that is preoccupying their time: Kate has to rest and recuperate from the head injury and Cheney has to monitor her to make sure she is okay. She's not going to go into any of that with her mother, and, thankfully, her mother doesn't press her. The ambiguous, 'we've got too much going on' line is sufficient and her mother cheerfully asks her to pass along to Kate to give her a call sometime over the weekend. Cheney assures her that she will give Kate the message.

As soon as the call is finished, Cheney hits Cassandra's number on her cell. It only rings one time, and she picks up. Cassandra doesn't even say hello; instead, questions rush from her. "So, what did you think? Did you read through everything already? Do you believe my mother killed herself?"

"Well, 'Hello', to you, too," Cheney says sarcastically. She continues, "And, 'Yes', I read through everything, and, 'No,' I do not believe your mother killed herself."

"I knew you would see that too!" Cassandra exclaims. "That's exactly what I think! And my grandparents and my uncles – none of us ever believed my mom killed herself! This is such a relief to hear someone else – someone who is not related to my mom – who has looked at this objectively and now confirms what we believe." It is evident that Cassandra cannot suppress her zeal and relief. "Jazzie Gonzalez - my mother, Jazzie Gonzalez – did not kill herself. It's true. You believe it, too."

"I do."

"I can't wait to hear what you have to say. Hold on just a second."

Cheney can hear Cassandra, in Spanish, saying some words of comfort to her daughter and then telling the child to go back to bed. The voice of the child in distress protests softly, Cassandra says into the phone, "Un momento," and there is silence for almost a full five minutes she returns. When she does, she apologizes, and explains quickly that her daughter was having a nightmare and she went to go tuck her back into bed.

Cassandra then dives in with a direct question. "What makes you think that my mom was murdered?"

Cheney pictures the lifeless body of the beautiful woman sprawled out on her back, her arms splayed above her head as if she had been frozen while making snow angels, white glistening ice-flakes adorning her long, black hair, her eyes open with a doll-like startled, mystified look. Jazzie Gonzalez had been wearing a long, dark wool coat and a red velvet mid-thigh v-neck dress. There had been a heart-shaped ruby-colored pendant necklace adorning her décolletage. Her heels were department-store black stilettos, and her feet had slipped out from them when she had collapsed backward from the fatal wound. The look in her eyes was particularly haunting: her presence, her gaze, captured by the crime scene technician's lens, displayed an unsettling self-determination, as if she was confident she could will herself to continue breathing, despite the gravity of the injury.

When she answers Cassandra, Cheney chooses her words carefully. "A lot of things. I don't want to be too graphic here, and I'm sorry-"

"No, no; don't worry, at all. Just lay it out for me. Please. Don't be concerned about my feelings. Remember, I read through it all too. I looked at the crime scene photos, the autopsy report, everything. I'm okay. Really, I am. Just tell me what you think. Don't hold back."

The photos of the crime scene were not particularly gruesome: the wound to the chest was evident, since her coat was open and draped on either side of her body, but there was an absence of blood or gore. Still, the images had intruded Cheney's dreams throughout the night, and she had woken up when she had taken a brief nap in the afternoon after having a disturbing nightmare of herself having been shot by Derek Strozak. In her dream, she had been dressed up for a Valentine's Day date with Derek Strozak, but when he had appeared on the porch he had simply laughed at her and shot her in the chest. She had felt herself dying, lying on her back under a falling snow. But then the scene had shifted, and it was actually Kate lying in the snow, with a gash to her skull, blood dripping down her crown, covering her eyes. Cheney had rushed to her aid, screaming in horror, but then had woken up. Her heart had been racing, and Patton had been staring at her from across the room on his couch, looking alarmed and concerned by her distress. She had been able to fall back asleep, but it had taken her a few minutes to convince herself that it had all just been a nightmare.

She shudders at the thought of that nightmare before she answers Cassandra: "The place of the wound: a single bullet to the chest. That seems strange to me for a suicide: I would think it would be more likely to be a shot to the head. But I think I've read or heard before that with women, they're less likely to shoot themselves in the face, so maybe it's not that strange after all. But still, I think it's an odd way to kill oneself: shooting yourself in the chest. And then also, I'm not seeing anything in the reports about any gunshot residue being found around the wound. There would typically be soot with a contact wound, which is usually the case with a self-inflicted injury."

"So that means the gun was fired at a further range than a self-inflicted injury, right?"

"Yes," Cheney says, "but I caution, that's not always the case. It's also possible that there was gunshot residue near the wound, and the Meskwaki Police and the Coroner just failed to denote it in their reports, or maybe it was brushed off inadvertently when the body was being handled. It's impossible to tell. But also, the reports say that it was snowing pretty heavily outside and, from the photos, it appears that your mom was wearing a long coat over a dress. I can't tell from the reports though whether the coat was buttoned or unbuttoned when she was shot. The reports note that, prior to ambulance personnel arriving, Rausch had tried unsuccessfully to resuscitate her, so it's possible that either he or a paramedic unbuttoned her coat at some point."

"I'm confused. Why is that important?" Cassandra asks.

"It may not be. But I am guessing that if a person is wearing a thick winter coat over the area where they are shot, that there wouldn't be any soot left on the body anyway, because the soot would have been left on the exterior of the coat instead of the body."

"Well, if they found soot on my mom's coat wouldn't they have written that down somewhere in the reports?"

"Not necessarily," Cheney says. "Particularly back then: I mean, we're talking about thirty years ago."

Cassandra sounds disappointed, but dogged. "Well, what else is it that makes you think it was murder and not suicide?"

"No suicide note. No indication that she was depressed," Cheney says. "There didn't seem to be anything that would have caused her to kill herself other than-" Cheney hesitates, not sure she wants to go further, but Cassandra helps her out.

"Me," Cassandra says softly. "It's okay, Cheney. I read the reports too, so I knew what you were going to say. The State was going to move forward with terminating my mom's parental rights, and she had given up and signed the papers voluntarily surrendering guardianship to DCFS earlier that day. I hadn't known about that until I read the reports yesterday."

"I'm sorry," Cheney says.

"It's okay, Cheney. Really it is. I don't really even remember ever living with my mom, or I should say, barely remember it. I was two when I went to live with my grandparents. My mom would come over and visit me and take me places before she died, but I knew from the time I was very little that it was my grandparents who were taking care of me, and would always be there for me. They're the ones who raised me. I knew that they had adopted me and all, but I never knew that my mom had given me up-" She breaks off for a second, and some of her earlier enthusiasm in her voice dims, "- that she had surrendered me to the courts. I thought that all that legal stuff had happened after my mom had died. Learning that she gave me up - it hurts. I'm not going to kid you. It hurts really bad. But, I'm okay. Really, I am. I needed to know all of this. It's good that I'm finding it all out now. It's all good, really."

Cassandra pauses again, and then continues, the animation in her voice returning a bit. "Until I read the reports the other day, I never had heard before that my mom had been in court that morning of her death, signing those papers. But you see, I know my mom was not perfect. It doesn't change how I feel about her. She still was my mom. And I love her still. And I need to know what happened to her. I need to do this for her."

"I get it," Cheney says and then continues, "So, surrendering parental rights would definitely be a significant, triggering event, under most circumstances. But, in this case, your mother was aware that her parents would be the ones adopting you. Your mother lived less than a mile away from her parents, and, from what the interviews of your grandparents say, she had a great, though at times strained, relation-ship with them. Your grandfather and grandmother both averred that they had discussed the termination of parental rights with your mom at length and that she was at peace with it, because she knew they would allow her to be an active participant in your upbringing, she could come visit you anytime she wished, and, she had an open invitation to come live with you in their house as well."

"These are all the things I've thought of, too, after reading through the reports," Cassandra says. "It's just such a relief to hear someone else think the same thing that I do, especially someone like you, with your legal background."

"Well, and, of course, the most obvious thing pointing to homicide, is that there's some suggestion in the reports that the relationship between Denny Rausch and your mother was less than rosy at times, though that certainly wasn't fleshed out much in the investigation. It's clear that they lived together in his house, but it was an on-again-off-again relationship. I wish there was more in these reports exploring that angle."

"Don't you think that was intentional on Meskwaki's part?" Cassandra asks.

"Maybe," Cheney says. "Or again, it might just be poor police work. They might have just thought it was a suicide from the get-go and had tunnel vision going forward."

"My grandparents have always said he was very controlling," Cassandra interjects. "They were scared that he would do something to my mother."

"None of that's in the reports," Cheney observes.

"I know," Cassandra says. "Maybe the Meskwaki police didn't ask them about what they thought of Denny. I don't know: or maybe they did ask and they didn't put it in the reports. I've asked my grandparents and neither of them remembers much about being interviewed by the police back then. It's too long ago, and it was too traumatic for them."

Cheney nods, says "That's understandable," and then continues with her impressions of the police investigation. "Also, your mom was wearing a red-dress, high heels, and jewelry. This doesn't sound like someone who was dressed to take her own life; instead, it sounds like someone who was planning on heading out to celebrate Valentine's Day. It's also strange that she was standing outside on the second-floor back porch of Rausch's house when it was only about thirty-five degrees out and snowing that night. It just seems like a strange environment to kill oneself, though I suppose anything is possible."

Cheney pauses, and continues. "Also, I saw from the evidence logs that there were three cigarette butts found in the snow outside on the porch, so maybe she was outside smoking. I don't know what to make of that or whether it is significant, but again, it just seems like an odd setting to take one's own life. According to Dennis Rausch, he and your mother had dinner plans for that evening, but when he came home from working his shift, he found her body on the second-floor back porch. Combined with everything else, the circumstances seem to suggest homicide, rather than suicide. There was no signed of forced entry, so it would seem that whoever killed her was let into the house."

"And who is it that you think murdered my mother?" Cassandra asks.

Cheney answers without hesitation. "Lieutenant Dennis Rausch."

# STAY

*February 10*<sup>th</sup>

Over the course of the night, it had snowed heavily again, so that when Cheney looks out of her bedroom window, she is amazed. She can't remember when the last time it was that it had snowed so much in a single winter: perhaps, when she was in fourth or fifth grade? It seems like a long time ago, whenever it was. She really doesn't feel like shoveling again today, and, it looks like a heavy snow, so she texts Dax and he replies within minutes saying he'll stop by between eleven and noon.

She goes downstairs and is surprised that Kate is already awake and lying on the couch, watching TV, in Cheney's favorite spot closest to the room's southern wall, with Patton dozing on the other part of the L-shaped sectional that faces the west. Kate is wearing a pair of Dan's gray sweatpants, an oversized oatmeal-colored cable-knit sweater of Cheney's, and a pair of Cheney's slouchy socks. It appears that she is making herself at home, and it is good to see that she is relaxing, and appears unstressed, even though it has been less than forty-eight hours since she was viciously attacked.

The dog gets up when he sees Cheney and approaches her, tail wagging and she bends over to hug him. The blinds to the sliding glass doors are rolled up, so that standing in the living room seems like being on the observation deck of an expansive winter snow globe. She walks over toward the doors, stretches, and with her back to Kate asks her what time she got up.

"Oh, I've been up since around eight-ish. I already let him out," Kate says. "This is late for you, isn't it? It's almost ten o'clock."

"Yeah, well, I didn't get much sleep the night before," she says, heading over to the opposite end of the sectional facing westward, with her back to the sliding-glass doors. Patton jumps back up and lies down next to her in the spot from which he had just departed. "I didn't even hear you," Cheney adds.

"I'm sorry," Kate says. "That's my fault."

"No, not really," Cheney says. "I had two texts come in early on Saturday morning that woke me up."

"Really? I thought you quit the public defender's office?"

"I did," Cheney says. "They weren't work-related texts."

"Oh," Kate says, and she doesn't ask anything further, though she looks as though she might be mildly curious as to who might have been texting Cheney so early on a Saturday morning.

"Do you want anything for breakfast?" Cheney asks. "I could make you an omelet. I have eggs, cheese, bacon. After you went back to sleep yesterday afternoon, I went grocery shopping and I also stocked up on a bunch of veggies and fruits for you. I even bought you almond milk for your smoothies."

"I saw that," Kate says. "Thank you. I actually already made a blueberry, avocado and banana smoothie this morning. You shouldn't have gone to all that trouble."

"I had to go out anyway to get your medicine and more gauze," Cheney says, "which, by the way, we should change this morning."

"Why don't you get something to eat first? You don't have to worry about me right now. You just woke up. I'm fine, Cheney. Really."

Cheney stands up, acquiescing and heading toward the kitchen, Patton padding behind her. "Can I get you anything? A cup of coffee? Some hot tea?"

"No, Cheney. Really, I'm fine. But thank you. I've got water here, and I don't need anything else right now."

While she's making a pot of coffee and some wheat toast, she calls out to Kate that Dax is coming over to do the driveway between eleven and noon.

As expected, Kate freaks out at this news. "Oh, God, Cheney, he can't see me like this! Please don't tell him I'm here!"

"That's fine, Kate," Cheney says. She doesn't want Kate to get stressed out about anything, but the driveway has to get plowed and she is not up to doing it today with everything else on her plate. Besides, her shoulder is still kind of sore from shoveling the driveway on Thursday.

"You won't let him in the house, will you?" Kate asks, appearing in the threshold of the kitchen, arms crossed.

"He usually doesn't come in at all. He just comes to the door when he's finished; I hand him his money and he leaves," Cheney says. "The only reason he came inside last time is because we wanted him to stay for dinner after all the drama we put him through with Nic Zafeiropoulos."

"Not all the drama *we* put him through: you mean, all the drama *I* put him through," Kate says, sitting down in one of the chairs at the barnwood table.

Cheney spreads peanut butter on her toast and grabs a banana. "I didn't want to make you feel bad by using 'I', so I used 'we' instead."

"That's nice of you," Kate says.

"Just trying to be a good big sister," Cheney says.

"You're a great big sister," Kate corrects her. "Not just a good one: Putting up with me and all of this nonsense with Nic. I have so much to thank you for - doing all of this for me. I don't know how I can ever repay you."

"I do. You can promise me you'll never talk to that bastard again." Even though she has never met Nic Zafeiropoulos, she hates him for what he has done to her sister. When Cheney had first removed the bandage from Kate's head yesterday to clean out the wounds, she had been horrified, though she had attempted to remain inscrutable. The lacerations were much longer and gorier in appearance than she had imagined. Her soul literally writhed in agony when she saw the sizable patch of exposed scalp on the top left side of Kate's head where the medical staff had shorn her beautiful red locks, and, where black-raised stitches protruded like the backside of a first baseman's mitt. There was an additional set of stitches along the laceration on Kate's hitherto flawless forehead just beneath the hairline: though, thankfully, the one on her exposed skin was only about two centimeters in length.

Kate smiles. "Well, that's a promise I can definitely keep. That's already a done deal, Cheney. I told you that I'll never go back to him."

"Yeah," Cheney says. "I just like to hear you say it out loud, because I think doing so serves to reinforce your own resolve," Cheney says.

Kate seemingly recoils a bit at Cheney's comment. "You really don't think I would go back to him, do you? After what he's done to me? I mean, he's scarred me for life, Cheney."

Kate's eyes begin welling up with tears. The last thing that Cheney wants is for Kate to get distressed, so she says, "No. No. I don't think that at all, Kate. I know you'd never go back to him." But she's not so sure. After all, she didn't think Kate would ever return to that asshole after what he did to her last weekend: but yet, here they are, with Kate wearing a bandage around her head like a combat soldier.

Her words seem to mollify Kate. Cheney pours herself a cup of coffee, and asks Kate if she wants one.

Kate says, "Sure."

"Do you want some almond milk too?"

"Yes, but I can get it," Kate says, standing up.

"No. No. Sit down. I'll get it for you," Cheney says and goes to the refrigerator, pulling out the carton.

Kate sits back down, and smiles. "You don't have to do all this for me, Cheney."

"Hey, I'm your big sister. This is what big sisters do." She sets the almond milk down on the table in front of Kate and then brings her over a cup of coffee.

"Well, thank you, Cheney. I appreciate all of this," Kate says.

"Are you going to take me up on my offer and stay here with me and finish off your semester remotely?" Cheney asks her, sitting down at the table with her toast, banana and cup of coffee.

"Yes. I thought about it yesterday, and, if the school agrees to let me finish my classes remotely, then 'Yes', I would prefer to stay here, rather than go back to stay in the apartment," Kate says. "I'm going to email Kathy over at the salon today and let her know I'm not coming back."

"Good," Cheney says. This news comes as a relief. She won't worry about Kate as much if Kate really stays here for the next few months and doesn't go back to live in the apartment.

Kate continues, "And then I'm going to email my dean and try to explain the circumstances and see if it's possible for me to finish my classes remotely. If she tells me it's okay, then I'll definitely stay with you for a while. I mean, I'll still have to go back to DeKalb sometime this week though to get all of my stuff: my clothes, my computer, my furniture. I don't know what I'm going to do with all of that. And I'll still have to try to contact my landlord and see if he's going to let me out of the lease."

"Let's take it one step at a time," Cheney says, sensing that Kate is getting overwhelmed. "Start with your job and then the dean and then we'll go from there. There's plenty of storage for your stuff out here. There's a ton of empty space toward the back of the barn, and there's space in the loft above the garage too. Besides, most of what you have is clothes anyway. That apartment of yours is small, so you don't have much furniture to begin with."

"Well, I have that dining room set that was Grandma's, and I also have my bedroom set that I bought down there, and I have some other furniture too."

"Like I said: Don't worry about it. There's plenty of storage space here," Cheney says.

"I hate to impose on you like this, Cheney," Kate says.

"It's no imposition, whatsoever," Cheney says. And it isn't. Surprisingly, she likes having her kid sister around. The isolation of the farmhouse in her first winter without Dan has been dreadful and there have been so many nights where she has laid in bed thinking about him, tears streaming down her face. Not only has sadness kept her awake at night, but, so too, has her sleep been disturbed by the eerie blizzard winds that scratch against the sides of the old farmhouse like icy-phantom fingers.

Cheney has a mouthful of peanut butter and wheat toast, when Kate abruptly jumps up at the unmistakable sound of a plow scraping against cement. "Oh, my God, he's here, isn't he?" Kate asks, touching the dressing on her head. "I'm going upstairs!"

"I'm going to be up there in a minute!" Cheney calls out to her as Kate bolts out of the room and runs up the stairwell. "We need to change that bandage!"

As soon as Kate flees, Cheney's phone pings, and she sees that it is Cassandra asking if she has time for a phone call. Cheney texts back, "Not now. I'll call you later." The response text is a single word,

"When?" and Cheney replies, "Not sure when I'll have time. I have a guest. Probably this evening after six, but if I get a chance to call earlier, I will." She doesn't receive a response right away, but, after a few minutes, a thumbs up emoji with "Thx" arrives.

Once she finishes eating, she loads the dishwasher, and then goes upstairs to help Kate. The attic bathroom is tiny, so they have been using the bathroom on the second floor for cleaning the wounds and changing the dressing. Cheney has been faithfully adhering to the doctor's verbal instructions and the written directions. Even though she is not a nurse, when she removes Kate's bandages she can tell that the wounds are healing well and that there is no sign of infection. It's a fairly long process though, between unwrapping the bandage, dabbing the antibacterial ointment along the wounds and then reapplying the dressing around Kate's head. This is the part that Cheney has not yet mastered, and Kate either complains that the dressing is too tight, or that Cheney wraps it so loose that it falls down across her eyebrows. It takes Cheney multiple attempts before she gets it just right.

"You're getting better at this," Kate says approvingly, eyeing Cheney's handiwork in the mirror.

"Just when I get the hang of it, it will be time for stitches to come out," Cheney says. "I'm going to head downstairs to write for a bit. I take it you want to stay up here until he leaves?"

Kate nods. "Actually, I'm just going to play around on the computer a bit and then I'm going to call Mom."

"Good deal," Cheney says, relieved that Kate will be talking directly to their mother. "What are you going to tell her?"

"I don't know yet," Kate says. "I think I'm just going to tell her that I was dating a guy and he became abusive and that I don't really want to talk about it, but that I'm hoping to stay here until the semester is over."

"Well, that's a start at least," Cheney says. She doubts that their mother will let it go at that without probing for details, but at least it's a gateway for Kate to begin sharing with their parents some information about her situation. This will hopefully take away some of the pressure that Cheney has been shouldering with having to dodge questions from their mother, while at the same time carrying the responsibility to tend to Kate's health and safety.

Cheney heads downstairs, and settles on the parlor loveseat, writing her novel. She only finishes two pages, before she is interrupted by Dax's knocking. She opens the door and pays him, but does not invite him inside, even though she can see by his face that he is eager to know whether Kate is around. Yet, he doesn't inquire about her; instead, he looks disappointed and walks away sullen-shouldered, seemingly dejected at having gone without a glimpse of the red-haired beauty.

Cheney watches him drive away. She goes to the bottom of the stairwell and calls out to Kate, "He's gone! The coast is clear!"

Cheney sits down on the L-shaped sectional side that faces the staircase within the west wall. Patton jumps up next to her, but Kate doesn't come back downstairs right away. After a few minutes, Cheney turns the TV on mute and she can hear Kate's voice drifting downstairs from the office room on the second floor. Good. She must be talking to their mother. After about fifteen minutes, Kate comes downstairs; she looks somber or worried, or both.

"Did you talk to Mom?" Cheney asks.

"I did," Kate answers, plopping down on the sectional sofa along the south wall and curling up next to a pillow.

"How did it go?"

"Good, really. I talked to both of them actually: Mom and Dad. They seemed to take it well. I told them everything."

"Everything?"

"Yeah," Kate says.

Cheney doesn't believe her. "You mean, you told them that a guy sliced your head open with a beer bottle and that you ended up in the hospital?"

"Well, no - I didn't go into that much detail. I just told them what I said I was going to tell them: that I had been dating some guy that became abusive and that I broke it off with him and that I'm going to be staying here until I graduate."

"They didn't press you for details?"

"Not really. Mom asked a few questions like what did I mean by 'abusive', and Dad wanted to know what the guy's name was and whether they had ever met him before."

"What did you tell Mom when she asked you about what you meant by 'abusive'?"

"I just told her that he had a drinking problem, and that he would get jealous and angry and that he would shove me around sometimes when he had too much to drink. She wanted to know if he ever hurt me, and I told her 'Yes', but when she started asking me what he did to me and whether I was okay, I just told her that I was fine and that I didn't want to go into all of it right now. She seemed like she got it and let it go. At least for now."

"Was she upset that you hadn't called her earlier and told her?"

"No," Kate says. "She didn't seem mad at me or anything. She was just mad at you for not having told her last night when you spoke to her on the phone. She said that she knew something was wrong, and that she couldn't believe that you didn't tell her."

Of course. The oldest sibling always gets the blame. "Great," Cheney says. "I'll have to smooth that over with her later."

"Oh, no, you won't, Cheney. Don't worry about it. I told her that I'm the one who told you not to say anything. I told her not to be mad at you, because you were only doing what I asked you to do. She got it. Really, she did. You know how Mom is. She never stays mad for long anyway."

"She's not just going to show up here out of the blue to check on how you are doing, is she?" Cheney asks.

"I don't think so," Kate says. "She did offer to bring food by, but I said, 'No.' I made it pretty clear to her that I wasn't up to seeing anyone and that I just really need to sleep."

"I heard you talking on the phone, but I didn't want to bother you. I figured you were talking to Mom."

"Actually, I finished talking to Mom about a half an hour ago." Kate says, frowning. "When you heard me talking on the phone, I was actually on a call with the State's Attorney's Office." She pauses. "He posted bond last night. He's out of custody. They were calling to notify me. They said that the judge entered a no-contact order though and that they'll email it to me. Do you know what those typically say?"

Cheney starts to answer. "Yes, I do. They usually-"

But her sentence is broken off by Kate's mortified look. With her back to the sliding glass doors, Cheney doesn't know what Kate is looking at, but Kate's eyebrows are raised and she is holding her hand across her mouth staring outside.

Evidently reading Kate's body language, Patton jumps off of the couch and makes a U-turn toward the door barking. At the same time, Cheney turns around and she is surprised at what she sees: Dax is standing behind the glass, pointing to the handle of the door, as if requesting to be let inside the house.

# JOHN

*February 10th*

It is too late for Kate to hide, and Cheney feels for her; she really does. But there is nothing else she can do but let Dax into her house. He's standing outside in the freezing cold and clearly something is wrong or else he wouldn't be back here, and he wouldn't be showing up on the back porch of the house unannounced.

As soon as she lets him inside, Patton stops barking and sniffs him in recognition, with Dax patting the big dog on the head. Kate stands up and hovers by the entrance to the stairwell, as if she is contemplating running upstairs. But it's no use, for Kate had been directly facing the doors, and Dax would have had an unobstructed view of her when he was looking through the glass.

He apologizes right away. "I'm sorry to be a bother, and I hope I didn't scare you guys, but my truck engine overheated about a quarter mile away and I forgot my cellphone at home this morning. I need to call my dad and have him pick me up." His eyes shift from Cheney to Kate, "I should've gone to the front door. I'm sorry; but my truck is down the road in this direction and I could see you guys sitting in here from the roadway when I walked up; so rather than go all the way to the front of the house, I just came up to this door instead."

"It's no problem at all," Cheney says. "My cellphone is in the kitchen, so let's go in there and you can call your dad."

Dax starts to follow Cheney into the kitchen, but he stops midway and looks over at Kate who is still standing over by the stairs, as if she is frozen, or trying to be invisible and he says, "Hi, Kate."

She says "Hello" back, sheepishly for her, and then he asks, "What happened to your head? Were you in an accident?"

Cheney has stopped too, now in the threshold of the kitchen, and she literally feels her heart freeze up with concern for her sister at having to be in this position. She isn't sure what Kate is going to say, and she feels terrible for Kate having to be in this awkward situation, when all Kate is trying to do is heal out here in the farmhouse.

She is proud of her sister when she answers, her fierce chin nobly stationed with indelible defiance and she says, "I was hit in the head with a beer bottle."

Dax's jaw noticeably clenches and his dark eyes flash. "Was it that dude that came here last weekend?"

"Yes," Kate says and Cheney admires her for telling the truth and for not making up some story about a car crash or a fall from a ladder. There is no reason for Kate to run from the truth. She should not be the one who is ashamed: asshole Nic Zafeiropoulos should be the one who is embarrassed – not Kate.

Dax doesn't say anything for a few seconds, even though he continues making eye contact with Kate. "I hope he's in jail?"

"No," Kate says. "He's out."

He looks over at Cheney. "Are you guys going to be okay out here by yourselves?"

"Yes," Cheney says. "We've got Patton and I've got a bunch of guns."

He nods and then looks over at Kate. "Well, if you guys need anything, just let me know. If he shows up or something, you could always call me. I'm not even a mile away. It literally would take me a couple of minutes to get here."

"Thanks, Dax," Cheney says at the same time as Kate says, "Thank you, Dax."

Cheney walks into the kitchen with Dax behind her, and she hears Kate's footsteps go up the stairwell. As she hands him her cellphone she asks if he wants anything to drink and he says he'll take a glass of water, so she goes to pour him one. She doesn't want to eavesdrop on his conversation, but she catches it in its entirety, for it is brief, and he talks to his dad on speaker phone. When he explains to his dad that his truck overheated and where it is parked, his dad tells him that he can't get there for another hour and a half or so: that he is with Canton plowing a commercial property in Hanley.

"I can give you a ride home if you want," Cheney interrupts the conversation.

"Hold on, Dad," Dax says into the phone and then addresses Cheney. "Well, once I get home, I'd just have to come back this way anyway, because my dad's going to have to fix that truck for me or we'll have to get a tow. We can't leave it where I parked it overnight. Would it be okay if I just stay here until my dad picks me up? It should only be an hour and a half."

"Actually, maybe even sooner than that," John Hardy pipes in over the speaker phone. "Canton and I are making pretty good time on this job. Aren't we Canton?"

"Yes!" Canton says enthusiastically in the background.

"That's fine if you want to stay here and wait for your dad," Cheney says to Dax. "I don't have any problem with that. I just thought you might want a ride home, but if you'd rather stay here, that would be okay with me."

"Did you hear that, Dad?" Dax asks.

"You're going to stay at Mrs. Manning's until I get there?" John Hardy asks.

"Yes," Dax says.

"Got it. We'll see you in a while."

This day is not turning out how she had planned. She had hoped she could complete writing three or four chapters of her novel and get a four-mile run in on the treadmill. At this point, it doesn't look like she will accomplish either of those things. Now she's going to have to entertain Dax for at least the next hour: but maybe not. She hears Kate gliding down the stairs and then she comes into the kitchen smiling. She looks radiant, even with the thick dressing about her head, and Dax's face lights up with apparent admiration when she enters the room. It's good to see her happy, and confident, despite what she has been through over the past week. Kate clearly enjoys Dax's company and seems comfortable enough around him to tell him the truth about Friday night. Cheney's been afraid to leave Kate alone since Friday night, because she is concerned that Kate might get dizzy and fall or might need something, so she has kept close to her. But now, with Dax here for a while, she may actually be able to sneak out to the barn and get a run in before his dad comes.

"Dax is going to be staying for a little while, until his dad picks him up. Would the two of you mind if I go out for a run in the barn? I should be back before his dad comes."

"Not at all," Kate says, at the same time as Dax says, "No". They both seem enthused that Cheney is leaving the two of them alone to talk privately.

She gets in an entire four-mile run on the treadmill before she calls Cassandra. She is still in the barn when she decides to place the call to Cassandra, sitting on one of the barstools, drinking water and cooling down. The conversation is short, but, at the end, she commits to doing something she swore to herself that she wouldn't do: more work into the death of Jazzie Gonzalez. Cassandra starts out the phone call by relating that she has spoken with all three of her mother's brothers - as well as her grandparents – and they all confirmed that Jazzie was not a smoker and that they had never seen Jazzie smoke a cigarette.

"There were cigarette butts found on the deck, so someone must have been smoking out there and it was not mi madre," Cassandra says, her voice reflecting her excitement. "Someone else was out on that deck with her and that's the person who killed her, see? We have to get the DNA off of those cigarettes somehow. I guarantee that it will come back as Dennis Rausch's DNA."

"Well, we don't even know that the cigarettes are still in evidence, Cassandra," Cheney says patiently, toweling the sweat off her brow with a hand towel. "All that evidence might have been destroyed years ago. The coroner determined it was a suicide, so it wasn't like there's been an open homicide investigation all of these years. I'd be surprised if those cigarette butts are even still around. Someone may have tossed them long ago."

"You can check, though, right, Cheney? You could check with the police for me, right? They might tell you if the cigarettes are still around or if they were destroyed."

"I can check," Cheney confirms.

"Couldn't you go into court and do like a motion for DNA testing or something like that? My family would pay for the DNA testing if you could get access to the evidence. Isn't that something you could do?"

"Probably not," Cheney explains. "As I said before, this is a case that was already deemed a suicide by the coroner. There is no open criminal investigation, nor was anyone ever charged and convicted of a crime. It would be an uphill battle to file a freestanding civil action trying to convince a judge to permit DNA testing in a thirty-year old suicide. I just don't see it happening."

Cassandra sounds disappointed. "Isn't there anything else we could do?"

Here it goes: that cursed public defender desire within her to help others kicks in again. Despite her reluctance to help Cassandra more than she already has, she feels impelled to do so. "I know the State's Attorney," she says. "I went to law school with him. I could call him and see if he would be willing to do an agreed order to permit DNA testing of the cigarette butts."

Cassandra's joy is palpable over the speaker. It is evident that Cassandra is ecstatic, and she is profuse with her praise for Cheney. She repeats over and over again that she and her family cannot thank Cheney enough. The words of gratitude are nice, but, after Cheney disconnects the phone, she wonders what the hell she is doing getting further involved in this case when she has so much else on her plate.

After all, why is she getting so wrapped up in a thirty-year old death investigation to help out someone who has been such an obnoxious asshole to her all these years? Why does she have so much compassion for Cassandra Cantoni? Does she already miss being a public defender so much that she feels obligated to use her legal knowledge free of charge to assist someone even though all she really wants to do right now is focus on creative writing? Maybe she should just call Maria and tell her she was wrong to quit and that she wants her job back. Perhaps being a public defender is her true calling.

She is putting on her coat and hat to head back to the house when she hears a vehicle pull into the driveway. She is a bit apprehensive when she walks out the side door, because she is still concerned over Patterson's warning about the Latin Kings, Dale's street intel, and Nic Zafeiropoulos' release from custody. But there is a safety in daylight, and it is unlikely that either the Kings or Nic Zafeiropoulos would be approaching her farm at this hour. It's most certainly going to be Dax's father who has pulled in to the driveway, since this would be the time he is expected here.

She's right. It's a black pick-up truck with a plow, and John Hardy is already on the porch and Dax is behind the glass of the storm-door about to come outside. Cheney can see Canton in the front passenger seat of the truck, which is still running, so Cheney walks over to say "Hello" to him, and he lowers the window to talk to her.

"Hello, Mrs. Manning," he says. "We're here to pick up my brother. His truck broke down. My dad and I were in Hanley plowing snow."

"Well, that's nice you guys came to get him. I am sure he appreciates it. Do you have other jobs lined-up today, too?"

"Yes, we have two driveways to plow over in the new subdivision off of Route 47, but we're going to have to get to those later. Dad has to fix Dax's truck first. If Dad can't fix Dax's truck, we'll have to get a tow."

John and Dax are walking back toward the truck, so Cheney says "Goodbye" to Canton. She loops around the front of the vehicle, passing by Dax, who says, "Thanks again, Mrs. Manning", and then he jumps into the back of the truck behind his brother.

John approaches and shakes her hand. "Thanks for letting Dax stay here while we finished up that job in Hanley. I appreciate it."

"No problem, at all," Cheney says. "He's a great kid."

"Well, thanks again," John says. "I heard you had an uninvited visitor here the last time he plowed." His voice sounds concerned.

"Oh, yeah, yeah. It was a guy my sister was dating. He just showed up out of nowhere."

"It sounds like he was giving her a hard time."

"Yes, until Dax walked over by him. That's all it took and then he drove off."

"Yeah, Dax has that effect on people, I suppose. A man would have to be soft in the head to tangle with Dax," he says. "Anyway, I hope whoever the guy is, he doesn't come back to bother you again. Dax had mentioned last weekend that your sister was visiting for a few days?"

"Yeah, actually, she's going to be staying with me for a while. Didn't you just meet her at the door?"

"Oh, no. Dax came out right away. I didn't meet her." He then lowers his voice, as if Dax might hear. "Between you and me, my son seems a bit smitten with your sister. I told him no college girl is going to be interested in a high school boy."

You never know with Kate. Quite frankly, Dax Hardy's 'smitten' feeling seemed to be reciprocal. But Cheney doesn't correct John Hardy. She just smiles, nods and says, "Probably so."

John Hardy is a slim-built man in his mid-forties, and his fair-skinned face bears the look of a person who has suffered the loss of his spouse to cancer and has spent many years in open fields under a pelting sun. He looks nothing like his son Dax: he is a couple of inches shorter than Dax, significantly narrower in build, and, in contrast to Dax's dark hair and olive-toned complexion, John has red hair, a beard, and a splay of freckles across his cheeks. Cheney has always thought him to be handsome in a way, mostly because of his unassuming and sincere demeanor; there is a reticent, self-effacing modesty about him that is rare and refreshing to encounter in this millennium.

He looks at her directly and she can see the branches of friendly smile lines around the sides of his compassionate eyes. "Anyway, it's good to see you, Cheney. How are you doing?"

"I'm doing okay," Cheney says. Well, it's mostly true: some days she's doing okay, and others, not so much.

And almost as if he can read her mind, he asks, "Are you sure?"

"Yeah, yeah, I am," she says. "Well, at least right now at this moment I'm okay. I just ran four miles on the treadmill and the sun's out and the sky's taking a pause from snowing. So those are all good things. If you ask me another day, I won't be so sure." She smiles.

His brown eyes twinkle with compassion and a comforting mirth. "Nothing beats a sunny day in February."

"That's true," she says.

"Well, if you ever need anything, you can always call us. You have my number and you have Dax's number. We're right down the road."

"I appreciate that," Cheney says. And she does.

He looks at her for a moment, holding her eyes steady, as if he is trying to read her face or assure her or something and then he nods, and says, "Well, we've got to head out and check out what's happening with Dax's truck."

She watches from the front porch as he maneuvers the truck around and then she waves at all of them as they drive off. Though she does not know him well, there is a feeling of security that John Hardy gives her, and there is a comfort in knowing that he lives just down the road. And there is a feeling that drifts to her even after he drives away, a thought that she may need to call upon him for assistance in the future, though she is not quite sure why.

# DNA

*February 11*th

She forgot how strikingly good-looking Matthew Brockton was, but she is reminded when he greets her with a smile and a handshake. He is as trim as his law school days, and he is wearing a solid-gray suit, a baby-blue dress shirt, and a navy tie with thin gray stripes. All she really takes in though is the seafoam green of his eyes, the sparkling smile, and the dimples. He looks the same as when he used to write wisecracks in the margins of her notebook during class.

"Cheney, it's so good to see you. How are you doing?" he asks. "May I take your coat?"

"No, that's okay. I'll just set it here," she says, laying her long wool coat and fur hat onto an office chair in front of his desk, and then sitting down in the chair beside it.

"I'm doing well," she says. She notices he's not wearing a wedding ring - nor are there any pictures of a wife or kids in his office.

"You look great," he says, sitting down behind the desk. She had actually woken up early, washed and blow-dried her hair, and flicked on mascara along with some vixen-red lipstick. She had even worn a suit: scarlet wool fitted-flared pants and a matching cropped jacket, combined with a white-oxford blouse. Dan would have told her she looked beautiful, and she can sense that Matthew Brockton is thinking that identical sentiment now.

"How's your shoulder healing?" he asks.

"Actually, it's feeling pretty good," she says. "I even shoveled the other day for the first time this year."

"Oh, that's great. That's good to hear." He pauses. It's evident that, even though he is glad to see her, that he has a lot to do and he doesn't want to waste time with small talk. It's a Monday morning in a State's Attorney's Office. She knows how busy Mondays generally are in the criminal justice system. This is about the worst time she could've possibly picked to have seen him, so she was surprised when she had texted him yesterday to ask to meet with him and he had texted back immediately that eight a.m. Monday morning would work.

"So, what's up, Cheney? You picked one of the coldest days of the year to come here, so it must be important. Your text was pretty cryptic but you said you wanted to meet with me about a case. I wasn't sure what case you would have as a public defender in Stickney County that would have anything to do with Kent County, but I have to admit, it piqued my interest."

"Actually, I'm not a public defender anymore," she says.

He looks surprised. "Oh. Where are you working now?"

"Nowhere really," she says.

He smiles. "Do you want a job? I've got two openings for ASAs right now."

Cheney laughs. "No. No. Thank you, though. I'm trying to just take some time off and work on my creative writing."

"Oh, that's right. I recall that you were a playwright. Poetry too, right?"

"Yes," she says. "But I'm working on a novel right now."

"I really want to hear what that's about," he says, "but I have Grand Jury at eight-thirty and I want to get to what you're here to see me about. If it's not a public defender case, what is it?"

"It's for a friend of mine, Cassandra Cantoni. You might know her. She's a dispatcher in Loomisville and her husband is Detective Jeff Cantoni."

"I don't know her. I know Jeff, though. So, what kind of case is this?"

"It's an old death investigation: a thirty-year-old case. Cassandra's mother, Jazzie Gonzalez, was found shot in the chest on a second-floor back porch of a residence in Meskwaki. The coroner's inquest determined her death was a suicide. But I've looked at the reports and there's a number of factors that point to a homicide, not a suicide."

"Let's take a step back for a minute: How did you get involved in this case?"

"Originally, Cassandra reached out to ask me to help her with a FOIA to the police department and then, once she received the reports, she asked me to read through them to see what I thought of the investigation. I guess the family has long suspected it was a homicide, not a suicide; and, when I read through everything, I reached the same conclusion."

"And who is it that you think killed Ms. Gonzalez?"

"The man with whom she lived in the residence: a then-Meskwaki police lieutenant, Dennis Rausch."

He looks stunned. "Okay, so are you asking for my office to review the case to see if murder charges are warranted against a law enforcement officer from thirty years ago?"

"No," she says. "Not at this point. You see, there were several cigarette butts found at the scene and the family is saying that Jazzie Gonzalez did not smoke. I called the Meskwaki Police Department yesterday, and I spoke with a detective and I asked him whether the cigarette butts were still in existence. He texted me back later in the day and indicated that the three cigarette butts collected at the scene are contained in separate sealed envelopes. After I received that confirmation from him, I texted you. What I'm asking for is simply to ascertain whether you would agree to ship those samples to a lab for DNA testing. The family has said they are willing to pay for the expense of testing."

He asks her if she can give him a five-minute summary of why she thinks this is a homicide and not a suicide and she does so. At the end of her explanation, he looks intrigued, but he says, "Listen, Cheney, the circumstances do sound a bit bizarre, and I can see where you are coming from – really, I can – but I just don't think there's enough there for me to start allowing you to dig around into some thirty-year-old death investigation. So, at this point, I'm going to say, 'No'. If something, however, turns up in the future - if you come up with something more - I would be open to reconsidering my position."

This is disappointing, but expected. Still, she persists. "But, it wouldn't even cost the State a penny to send them in for DNA testing.

The family will pay for the whole thing. I don't see what the harm is in sending the evidence in to be tested."

"The system relies on finality of judgments," he says. "And here, as you mentioned, there's a coroner's inquest that determined the cause of death was suicide. There is nothing you have told me that casts any significant doubt on that finding. We can't open up and re-litigate cases from thirty years ago, just because the family takes issue with the death determination. We have enough pending prosecutions as well as unsolved cases as it is. We just don't have the time or the resources to be going back into the past just because of curiosity or doubt by some family members."

She disagrees with this, but she understands. "I get it," she says. "I do. I'm sorry to have bothered you with this, but I thank you for taking the time to meet with me. I do appreciate it."

They both stand up contemporaneously and he says, "No bother at all. Any time." He hesitates for a second and she can tell that he is weighing whether to say his next words, and he does: "I thought when you texted me about a case this morning that it may have been something to do with the prosecution of Nic Zafeiropoulos. I just want you to know that my office is going to vigorously prosecute him for what he did to Kate. How is your sister doing?"

"First off, 'Thank you' for that. I appreciate your telling me that and for asking about her. And actually, she's doing okay. She's pretty tough" she says. So tough, it has surprised her, but she doesn't say that.

"Kind of like her big sister, I suppose," he says and his eyes twinkle. "The two of you have both been through a lot over the past few months."

"Yeah, that's true. We have been through a lot. Actually, she's staying with me on the farm for the next couple of months. I'm kind of getting used to having her around."

"Well, that's good for the two of you to stick together. When times get tough, it's nice to have your family around you," he says. And as he walks her to the door, he adds, "And that offer remains open for you to join my staff. At any time. If you feel like coming back to the courtroom, let me know. I'd love to have you on my team."

"Thanks," Cheney says. She can't imagine ever wanting to be a prosecutor, after having been such a dedicated public defender, so she will likely never take him up on his offer. Still, it's nice to have options. Besides, there's something kind of alluring about the thought of working with Matthew Brockton every day.

Before she exits his office, she adds, "You have my number if you change your mind about the DNA testing." Assuming he's not in a relationship, she kind of half-hopes that he calls her 'just-because'. It would be nice to have a drink and some laughs with him sometime, but she doesn't suggest or encourage it. Instead, she frames it in professional terms, simply says "Goodbye", and leaves.

On her ride back toward home she thinks about what Matthew Brockton had to say and she can't really take issue with it. He's right, after all. She can't just expect the State to agree to allow items to be tested three decades later after a death investigation has been closed. If he were to allow that to happen in this situation, then what of the next case where a family member comes forward and wants evidence tested from years ago simply because of doubts as to the determination of the authorities? It would set a dangerous precedent and open up the floodgates to such requests, depleting precious resources that need to be devoted to open cases.

She puts on some rap music, super loud, and drives toward Route 47. But what if she could change Matthew Brockton's mind? What if she could come up with some evidence to provide a sufficient basis to convince him that DNA testing is warranted? She may be able to prove that Jazzie Gonzalez did not take her own life, which would be of significant solace to Jazzie's parents, siblings, and daughter. Perhaps with a little digging she can find out more information to convince Matthew Brockton to allow the family to pursue DNA testing.

She pulls over on the side of the road, turns the music off, and scrolls through her contacts until she finds a number for Jack Stahl. Jack was the reporter who wrote the story about the coroner's inquest thirty years ago. Cheney hasn't spoken to him in years – since her days as a freelance reporter when she was in college – but she still has his number in her cellphone. She's not sure it's even a good number anymore; Jack Stahl retired from the paper and he could be dead for all she knows. Hell, if he's still around, he's got to be upwards of seventy by now.

He picks up after only one ring, and there is the crisp, cocky voice of an old Chicago newsman. "Jack Stahl here."

"Uh…hello, Mr. Stahl. I don't know if you remember me, but my name is Cheney Manning. I used to go by Cheney Costello back then, before I was married. I was a freelance reporter for *The Meskwaki Times* some years ago and I don't know if you remember me…"

He cuts her off. "Good looking redhead? Of course, I remember you."

"Well, thank you…I guess," Cheney says.

"You're an attorney, right?"

"Yes."

"I remember you were planning on going to law school back when you freelanced at the paper. Once in a while, you would stop by the newsroom and you and I would have a healthy debate about the law or politics."

"Yes. That's right." He definitely remembers who she is: no doubt about it.

"You were in the news not that long ago," he continues, as if he is impressed by his own ability to recall and recite facts. "Your husband was the police officer who was killed in Loomisville."

"Yes," she says. Sometimes it seems like someone else suffered that loss, and not her. Right now, is one of those times.

"Well, I'm sorry to hear about that. And then there was some hulla-baloo about your client having been charged with your husband's mur-der and you went out on your own and proved it was someone else who killed him: that defense lawyer, Derek Strozak. I never liked that guy. A cocky s.o.b. if I have ever seen one. Not surprised he turned out to be a killer." He finally takes a pause. "So, what's up with you, Cheney Manning? What leads you to call an old retired newsman on a Monday morning?"

She can hear the excitement in his voice after she explains to him that she is researching the death of Jazzie Gonzalez and that she's won-dering if he remembers the case and if he would be willing to talk to her about it.

"Of course, I remember that case," he says, not masking his enthu-siasm. "How could I forget that one? A young dispatcher found shot in the home of a Meskwaki police sergeant. Things like that don't happen every day."

"Lieutenant," she corrects him.

"Yes. That's right. Lieutenant. When do you want to meet to talk about it?"

Within seconds of getting his address and ending the call, she is turning around and heading east toward Meskwaki. If there is a barrier to getting to the science, she's going to navigate around the blockade with a little intellectual excavation work.

# RETIREMENT

Jack Stahl looks exactly the same as the last time Cheney saw him: a cap of thinning silver hair, black wiry high-arched eyebrows, protruding earlobes, a face full of wrinkles from too much coffee, late nights, and cigarettes. He is wearing a plaid sports-coat with faux-leather tan patches on the elbows. He's probably had that jacket since the 1970s.

His house is a small, Chicago-style bungalow, only a few blocks from the Fox River. It is full of Bears memorabilia, including an autographed picture of Mike Ditka in the front hallway, that Cheney stops to gawk at for a few seconds.

"I saw him once," she remarks.

"Who's that?" Stahl asks, still walking down a dark, short hallway, covered with gaudy goldish wallpaper and various tilted photographs, most of which feature Stahl displaying fish of varying lengths.

She follows him into a messy living room area, crowded with a couple of recliners, a sad- looking sofa, and well-worn lime green carpet littered with leaning piles of newspapers and magazines, that look to be in some odd, yet intentional, order.

"Mike Ditka," she says.

He sits down in one of the recliners, and gestures to her to sit down on the sofa. There is a very large, almost feral looking, black cat lying on one of the armrests, and Jack tells her, "Don't worry. Loretta doesn't bite." He returns to the topic of the picture of the former coach. "My son got that autograph for me. He used to work for the Bears back in the Eighties. Where'd you meet Ditka?"

"Oh, I've never met him. Just saw him once a couple of years ago. Driving around Galena."

"Galena, huh? That's one of my favorite places. Did you talk to him?"

"Oh, no. My husband I were just driving down the main drag and there he was walking along on the sidewalk."

"How do you know it was Mike Ditka?"

"C'mon," she says. "It's Mike Ditka. You know him when you see him."

He smiles and she sees that his teeth are yellowed with nicotine and age. "I suppose that would be true. Anyway, you want to know about the Jazzie Gonzalez case, huh? That's a name I hadn't heard in years until you called me this morning. Terrible shame entire way around."

"Yes. So, I'm just kind of curious if you could tell me what you remember about the death investigation, but also what you were hearing in the newsroom back then: what the people of the county were saying – the word on the street, so to speak. I'm looking for any insight you may have into whether it was really a suicide or whether it could have been a homicide."

Like the reporter he once was, he asks a question before he answers any. "So, what's your interest in the case? You're a young woman. You probably weren't even alive yet when she was killed. What are you: twenty-eight, twenty-nine?"

"Actually, I'm thirty-one."

"Okay, well you're thirty-one. Let me see here, what year was she killed?" He looks across the room as if thinking. "So, it was about thirty years ago, if I recall correctly. So, you would have been an infant. Actually, thirty years ago in just a few days. It happened on Valentine's Day. So, you're a writer and a lawyer; you must be writing a book about the case?"

"No," she says. "Actually, I am friends with Jazzie Gonzalez's daughter, Cassandra. She asked me to help her look into the case. She and the rest of her family do not believe that Jazzie took her own life."

"Well, a lot of folks around here believe that, so they're not the only ones," he says, literally licking his chapped lips as if loosening up to chat. He leans down in his chair like a collegiate coach, clasping his gnarled hands together loosely and he opens up. "Let's see, Jazzie Gonzalez. She was from McNamee if I recall correctly, came from an immigrant family from Mexico. Before she was a dispatcher, she worked at a bar in downtown McNamee on the river. It's still there, but it's got a different name now. Back then, it was called like Hijinks or something like that, kind of a seedy joint. Lots of drugs passing in and out of there in those days, at least those were the rumors. Powder cocaine, thin girls wearing white-skinny flares; they all looked like California models hanging out on the deck overlooking the river. Anyway, this Jazzie, she was a real looker. Beautiful smile, big brown eyes, and what we used to describe as a 'Nice rack' back then, but I'm not allowed to say that now, right? I'm sure that phrase is banned as part of this goddamn Me-Too-cancel-culture crap.

"So, where was I? Yes, Jazzie Gonzalez turns up dead, single bullet wound to the chest I believe, on the back porch of her boyfriend's house. The rumors start flying right away. Everybody thought that her boyfriend killed her."

"Why was that?" she asks, hoping she hasn't interrupted the free-flow of his narrative.

"Her boyfriend was a police officer. His name was Dennis Schultz."

"Rausch," she corrects him, still concerned that she'll miss a nugget if she derails his train of thought.

"Rausch - that's right. Anyway, he was known as having a hair-trigger temper. One of those cops who you wouldn't want to be pulled over by because if you questioned why he pulled you over, he would make sure to not only issue you a speeding ticket but he would also pile on a bunch of equipment violations. Anyway, he supposedly met Jazzie at the bar and made her quit. Didn't like the men gawking at her tits. I'm probably not allowed to say 'tits' either anymore, am I?"

She shrugs. "It doesn't offend me. I just want to hear what happened."

He laughs and she sees a glint in his eyes that she really doesn't like. He had not seemed so crass when she had worked with him at the paper – at least that's not how she remembered him being back then. Maybe his filter has dissipated with age. Regardless of how boorish she finds his comments, she can endure a little salty talk in order to get some information about Jazzie Gonzalez and Dennis Rausch, and he sure seems to be a wellspring of rumors from back then.

He continues, unfettered. "Denny Rausch punched at least one patron in the face for hitting on her. I know that's true, because I know the guy he punched. He was my neighbor: Jack Cummings. He sold insurance. Great golfer. Great guy all around. He's dead now. Must've been dead at least ten – no thirteen – has it been that long? Jesus, it has. Jack Cummings has been dead thirteen years. Holy shit. Well, anyway, from what Jack said all he did was pinch Jazzie in the ass when she walked by with a tray, and then this Rausch guy comes swinging around with a right hook and knocked him right off his barstool. And then Rausch had enough with Jazzie working at the bar with her tits hanging out from those skimpy little shirts that the girls used to wear at that place. So, he forced her to quit and got her a job at the department. She went to stay with him in his house here in Meskwaki, not far from the river.

"He was a lot older than her, maybe by like twenty years or something. I can't remember how old she was, but she was serving alcohol, so she had to be like twenty-one or twenty-two, or something around there?"

"Nineteen," she corrects him. "And he was fifteen years older than her."

"Oh, okay. Really? I didn't remember her being that young. Well, like I said, that Hijinks was known for some illegal activity, so the owner probably didn't even care that she was serving liquor underage. Besides, her boyfriend was a lieutenant on the force, so the owner probably figured he was insulated – nothing was going to happen to him for having a cop's girlfriend tend bar there." He seems to be searching for something to say next and then he asks, "So what else is it that you want to know?"

"Well, you mentioned that some people thought it was a homicide, not a suicide: Why did they think that?"

"Oh, I suppose, just because of the age difference between them and that he was known as being the jealous type. But I never heard he hit her or anything like that. From what I heard, they had one of those on-again, off-again relationships. She supposedly would break up with him or he would break up with her and she would go stay with friends."

"Why wouldn't she stay with her parents? They lived such a short distance away – in McNamee."

"That's a good question. I don't know the answer to that. Maybe she didn't want her parents to know she was having trouble with him. Maybe she was protecting him because she knew she would end up back in his bed again at some point. Who knows what broads in those situations think?"

Broads. There's that icky feeling again. She bristles, defensively, at the thought of what he would say about her own sister, Kate. If she told him about Kate's situation he would probably react by saying, "What the hell is that dumb broad thinking hanging out with that guy? She deserves to get hit in the head with a beer bottle! Maybe that will knock some sense in to her!"

One thing is certain: This guy is a real tool. How did this guy work at the paper all those years and not get fired? It would be humorous to look him in the eye and state, "Hey, you're a jagoff. Am I allowed to say that?" She feels her lips curl up inadvertently at her own inward sarcasm.

He evidently catches on to her not-so-subtle wry smile and asks, "Did I say something funny?"

"No, nothing," she deadpans. "I just was thinking of something unrelated. Anyway, getting back to this case, did you form any opinion back then when you were covering the investigation as to whether Jazzie Gonzalez had been murdered?"

"Oh, I remember thinking that maybe he killed her, but I was never sure, so don't quote me on that. This is all off- the-record, anyway, right? You said you're just doing this to help out your friend. None of this is going on the Internet or anything, right? I don't need Dennis Schultz suing me or showing up at my house with a shotgun one night or anything like that."

"Rausch," she reminds him again.

"Right. Dennis Rausch," he says, and he seems annoyed at her correction.

"And yes," she assures him. "None of this is going on the Internet or in any book or anything like that. I'm just trying to find out the truth to help out Jazzie's daughter, Cassandra. What you're telling me is helpful, because it provides insight into the personalities of Jazzie and Denny and some background into their relationship."

"Good. That's good to hear. Anyway, I didn't know this Rausch guy from Adam. All I know is that there was a lot of talk back then that he killed her, that he was the jealous type and that they would argue a lot. I don't know if any of it is true, but that's what people said back then. Hell, those who were alive back then still say it now. There's a lot of people still think that he's the one who shot her.

"But you know, from what I recall about the investigation, the cop had somewhat of an alibi. He was on his way home from work or something. Stopped by a convenient store about ten minutes away from his house. Neighbors heard the shot at a particular time, but disregarded it: just thought it was a car backfiring. But a couple of them were consistent on the precise time they heard the sound because they had either looked at a clock or were watching something particular on tv at a specific time. Anyway, the shot would've been around the time Schultz – I mean, Rausch - was either at the convenient store or still on his way home from there. When he came home, he went through the house, couldn't find her. They were supposed to be going out that evening for Valentine's Day. He ended finding her dead on the back porch of the second floor and he's the one who called 9-1-1."

"Yes, you're remembering correctly," she says. "All of that is in the reports."

"But I also remember that it was kind of an alibi, but not a perfect one," he continues. "Even with the neighbors saying that they were sure of the time when they heard the car backfire, Rausch could never really prove that he was at the convenient store at a particular time. The store had one of those warning signs on its front door that people were under surveillance, but in reality, the store didn't have any tape in the video-recorder. There was a clerk at the store who knew Rausch, and Rausch evidently used to stop there habitually on his way home from work, and the clerk recalled having seen him there and could give a time frame which would have provided Rausch with an alibi. But, if I remember correctly, the clerk wasn't one-hundred percent sure of the precise time that Rausch was in the store. He was a little bit ambivalent. That's why I say it was 'kind of an alibi.'"

"You're remembering it right. That's what's in the reports," she says, impressed at his memory of the details, except for his persistent confusion between 'Schultz' and 'Rausch.'

"And that always kind of gave me the impression that maybe he did kill her – that he might have had the opportunity to do so," Stahl says. "Being that he worked for the Meskwaki Police Department, they sure weren't going to look too hard at that angle. I think they just kind of hoped it was a suicide, and didn't put a lot of effort into trying to figure out if it was anything other than that. Lots of people still think it was a cover-up and maybe it was. Who knows?

"Other than what I've said, I really don't remember much else about the investigation. It's been a long time ago now." He seems like he is getting tired or bored or both and that he wants her to leave. He stands up, and she does the same. Evidently the conversation is over.

"I don't know if I've been of much help to you, Cheney Manning," he says, walking toward his front door, with her right behind him.

"Oh, you have," she says. "I appreciate your taking the time to talk to me today."

"I'll give you an old reporter's tip. If you want to know the truth, go directly to the subject."

"You mean, Dennis Rausch?"

"Yes."

"He still lives around here?"

"Oh, of course. He was born and raised here. He's a river rat, like me. I thought you knew that already."

"No, I guess I assumed that he would've left town."

"Nope. Lives in the same house where Jazzie was killed."

This is shocking. She had assumed, wrongly, that he would've moved. "Is he retired?"

"Yes. He's been retired for a long time now. I see him around town now and then, but he pretty much keeps to himself. He still drinks in that little dive bar down by the river in Meskwaki: the one with the funny name. I can't think of the name of it. He's friends with the owner. It's got kind of a strange name – a body part."

"Knee's Joint," she says. She knows the place. It's probably not something to brag about, but she knows every dive bar in the Fox River Valley.

"Yes, that's it. Knee's Joint. If you want to find Denny Rausch, that's where I'd look first."

She knows where she's going tomorrow night. She just has to make a plan before she goes there.

# VELVET

*February 11*th

When Cheney gets home, she finds Kate curled up sleeping on the sectional sofa, in Cheney's favorite spot, a game show on television. Patton is on the other side of the sectional, though he jumps up when Cheney walks in and greets her. "Hello, you," she says, patting the big dog on the head.

"How is sleeping beauty over there?" she asks Kate, as her sister coils upward, yawning and stretching.

"Wow! You're the beauty," Kate croons. "Look at you. Red lipstick even. You look gorgeous."

"Thanks," Cheney says. "Getting back to you, how are you feeling?"

"Still tired for some reason," Kate answers. "I was up for a couple of hours this morning, but then I fell back asleep. I can't believe how tired I still am. I feel like all I do is sleep now."

"It's your body fighting off infection," Cheney says. "It has a way of draining you. Let me make you something to eat."

Kate seemed to be unusually tired yesterday, more so than on Saturday, and that is a bit worrisome. When Cheney had gone into the house after the Hardys had left, Kate was nowhere to be found on the first two floors. Cheney had found her in the attic bedroom, wrapped up in a blanket, comforter and quilt, sound asleep. Kate had roused a few hours later and Cheney had been able to convince her to have a cup of soup and some bread, but after that she had gone right back to sleep.

Kate had only come downstairs once more, groggily so, after sunset, to have her bandage changed and to eat a banana and drink some almond milk. It was then that Cheney had told her that she would be gone in the morning and that she had a meeting at the Kent County Courthouse at eight. Though Kate was usually an inquisitive person, she hadn't even bothered to ask Cheney with whom she was meeting or why. Instead, she had just nodded her head and asked her listlessly what time she thought she would be back. Cheney had told her she thought she would be back no later than ten. Now it was past noon, but Kate didn't seem to be curious in the very least as to why Cheney had been gone for so long or what the purpose of her meeting was. Instead, she was uncharacteristically disinterested, seeming to be in a post-concussive fog.

Kate stands up, and stretches her arms up high above her head, standing on her tippy toes, but she says, "I'm not really hungry."

"Did you eat anything yet this morning?"

"Some blueberries. That's it."

"Let me make you some comfort food. How about a chicken pot pie?"

"No, no. That's alright. As I said, I'm not very hungry."

"Can I at least make you a sandwich? I bought turkey over the weekend - swiss cheese, tomatoes, your favorite honey mustard."

"Are you going to have one, too?"

"Sure," Cheney says.

"Okay, well, I guess I'll have one then."

"I'm just going to go upstairs and change," Cheney says. "I'll be down in a sec." She trots upstairs, Patton following her, kicks off her pumps, and switches out of the red suit into a pair of sweats, a t-shirt, green-plaid flannel and slouchy socks.

When she goes back downstairs, Kate is at the kitchen table, scanning her smartphone. "Do you need any help?" she asks Cheney, without looking up from her device.

"Nope," Cheney says. "I take it you want water with your meal?"

"I can get it," Kate says, and starts to stand up.

"No, just stay down," Cheney says. "Relax."

Cheney pours her a glass of water, and a glass of diet pop for herself, setting them down on the table. She goes to the refrigerator, takes out a carton of potato salad as a side dish, plops a big serving spoon in the container and sets it on the table. She starts making two sandwiches: one for herself and one for Kate.

"Did you know Lauren is in Florida?" Kate asks, looking up from her smartphone.

"Yes," Cheney says. "She went down there with some friends of hers from work. Miami Beach, I believe."

"Ryan didn't go with her?" Kate asks.

Ryan is Lauren's new beau, and even though they have only been dating for a couple of months, they are already living together. "I think he may have," Cheney answers. "I don't know. You want the honey mustard, right? No mayo?"

"Correct," Kate says. "Well, he's not in any of these pictures." She continues studying her smartphone. "Looks like they're having a lot of fun," she says dreamily.

"Well, it's a good time of year to be down there," Cheney says. "Actually, now that you asked about Ryan, she did tell me it was just a girls' trip and he was staying home."

"She didn't ask you to go?" Kate asks.

"She did, but I didn't want to right now. I've got too much to do here."

"You should've gone," Kate says. "It would've been good for you to spend some time laughing out in the sun."

"Well, if I had gone, then I wouldn't have been here to spend time with you now, would I have?" she asks, setting the plates down on the table and sitting down across from Kate. "So, everything works out in the end, right?"

"I think it would have been a lot more fun for you to have been out on a beach drinking a margarita, than changing my icky bandage and sitting around cooped up in this house with me all day," Kate says. "And thanks for the sandwich." She takes a bite and gestures to Cheney with the sandwich before setting it down on her plate.

"Actually, it's nice having you around here, Kate," Cheney says. "I mean that. I wouldn't have it any other way."

"Oh, speaking of which, I did get an email back from the Dean today asking me to call her, and I spoke with her at length, and she agreed that, as long as my individual professors don't have any issue with it, I can attend my classes remotely. I already sent out an email to each of them this morning before I fell back asleep."

"Well, that's good news," Cheney says.

"But I would really like to head out to DeKalb tomorrow to go get some of my stuff: some clothes, some books, my laptop, my makeup kit. I'd like to get my car and bring it back here, too."

"I don't think you should be driving, Kate," Cheney says.

"Why? I stopped taking the pain pills yesterday. All I'm on now is an antibiotic. I looked at the bottle, and it doesn't say anything about not driving. Besides, I won't be driving until Thursday, because I'm going to stay over tomorrow and Wednesday night."

"Kate, I can't stay over in DeKalb tomorrow, or Wednesday, for that matter. I don't have anyone to watch Patton for me, with Lauren in Florida."

"Oh, I'm not asking you to come with me. I already have someone to drive me down there."

"Who is that?"

"Dax Hardy."

"Oh, come on. Seriously? Doesn't he have to be in school?"

"No, he's free all day. He takes an AP course on Tuesday at nights at Loomisville Community College. So, he's going to drive me to DeKalb in the afternoon and I'm going to treat him to an early dinner and then he's going to head up to Loomisville."

"Kate – he's only in high school."

"I know. I know. But he won't be in three months." And then Kate laughs. "I'm just kidding, Cheney. He's a handsome young man – a really, really, handsome young man - but I am not romantically interested in him."

"Does he know that, though? I mean, the way he looks at you, I can tell he has a massive crush on you."

"I don't know what he thinks, but all I can tell you is that I'm not interested in him in that way. We're just friends."

"Just don't lead him on, Kate. I have to live here, remember? He and his dad are my one-mile neighbors. His dad and I have a business relationship. He farms our property every year. It would be a bit awkward if my kid sister breaks his son's heart."

"Oh, I won't do that, Cheney," Kate says. "I promise."

She doesn't believe her, but she moves on to the topic of Kate's safety. "So, I'm going to have to worry about you staying down in DeKalb for two nights by yourself? I don't think it's a good idea to stay there when that maniac is out on bond."

"I won't be alone. Taleeka is staying with me both nights. And actually, Taleeka *and* Ashley are both staying with me on Wednesday night."

The last time Kate told her that a friend was staying over at her apartment with her, the friend turned out to be Nic Zafeiropoulos. She chews silently, just watching Kate. Kate is daintily eating a spoonful of potato salad, and looks at her with her wide eyes as if trying to discern what Cheney is thinking, and then, when she finishes swallowing, Kate says, "And no, it's not Nic Zafeiropoulos who is coming over. I can't believe you would think that after everything he's done to me."

"I didn't say anything," Cheney says.

"You didn't have to. I know you were thinking it," Kate says.

"What about your doctor's appointment to get your stitches out?" Cheney asks, ignoring Kate's comment. "That's Wednesday morning."

"I already canceled it and made an appointment with a doctor in DeKalb for Wednesday. He's been my regular doctor anyway now for years, so I'd rather go to him. Taleeka is going to go with me. I also want to be down there in case any of my professors give me any push-back about attending class remotely for the next few months. If any of them are reluctant to do so, I figure I could try to meet with them while I still have this big bandage on my head. Maybe they'll feel sorry for me and capitulate."

Cheney is already finished with her sandwich, as this conversation with Kate is driving her to eat quickly from anxiousness. She stands up and goes over to the sink to clean off her plate and load the dishwasher.

Just when she thinks that Kate has no interest in anything she is doing presently, her sister asks, "So, what are you going to do now that you quit being a public defender? You said something about writing?"

"Yes. As I mentioned to you before, I'm just going to take some time off and do some creative writing."

"For how long?"

"I don't know. We'll see how it goes. Maybe I won't go back to practicing law at all again."

"But you went to court this morning, so you must be taking some cases, right?"

"No," Cheney says, continuing loading the dishwasher, her back to Kate. "I went to the courthouse, not court. I was just helping out a friend with something."

"Oh," Kate says, and there is a long pause as if she expects Cheney to provide a further explanation. Cheney doesn't.

Cheney turns around, walks over to the table and picks up the carton of potato salad. "Are you finished with this?"

Kate still has nearly a half of a sandwich left. "Yes. Yes. This is all great - thanks."

Cheney puts the potato salad away, drops the spoon in the sink, then returns to pick up Kate's glass. She is filling it with more water and ice, when Kate asks her, "So, what are you writing then?" Cheney can tell Kate's inquiry is half-hearted, because Kate's attention is focused on her smartphone and she is text messaging someone.

"I'm writing a novel, actually." Cheney sets the glass of water down in front of Kate and returns to the sink. "It started out as a screenplay, but now it's going to be a novel."

"Really? What's it about?"

"A Chicago police detective who returns to her hometown of Hebron, Illinois to try to solve the mystery of her older sister's disappearance."

"Wow. That sounds interesting." Not that interesting evidently, because Cheney can hear the soft rapid clicks of Kate intensely text messaging.

"What's the detective's name?" Kate asks.

"Hesperus Braun." Cheney turns around, leaning her butt against the counter, folding her arms, looking at Kate who appears aghast.

"Hesperus Braun?" Kate laughs out loud. "What kind of name is that?"

"What do you mean?" Cheney asks.

"I mean that's a terrible sounding name: Hesperus. I've never heard that name before but it is certainly not romantic sounding. You need a name like Chloe or Valencia or Pamela, you know something that sounds light and airy and inviting – not Hesperus for Godssake."

"It's not a romance novel, Kate. It's a murder mystery. Truthfully, you sound just like, Mom. She doesn't like the name Hesperus either."

"With good reason. I'm just telling you, as an actress, I would not be disappointed if I was passed over for the role of Hesperus Braun. Just saying."

And then, as if sensing that Cheney might be a bit annoyed, Kate asks, "How far along are you?" Kate's attention quickly reverts to an incoming text, and she is smiling while reading it.

"I haven't even finished writing the first chapter yet."

Still studying the text message and still grinning, Kate says, "Good. Then there's time for you to convert Hesperus Braun over to a more sonorous-sounding name."

"Are you finished?" Cheney asks walking over toward her and Kate nods, "Yes, it was great; thank you."

Cheney starts clearing the table and Kate offers to help, but Cheney tells her to just sit back and relax.

As Cheney works, Kate asks her, "You're not mad at me about staying in DeKalb; are you?"

Cheney's not angry, and in fact, she is a bit relieved. After all, she is intending on going under-cover tomorrow night to Knee's Joint, though she hasn't figured out exactly how to go about that. She thought about it during her drive home, and she has a couple of ideas, but she hasn't put anything into motion yet. Since Kate won't be here tomorrow night, at least she won't have to fret over what to tell Kate when she leaves to go to the Meskwaki bar. Maybe it's a good thing that Kate won't be around tomorrow evening to ask questions. One less thing to worry about.

Despite this, Cheney remains concerned about Kate returning to DeKalb. "No," she answers Kate's question. "I'm not angry: Just concerned that's all."

"You don't believe me that I'm not going to see Nic do you?" Kate asks.

It's unlikely that Kate will see the jagoff, but still that possibility nags at Cheney. "I don't think you'll see him," she says. "Well, at least I hope you won't."

"I'm telling you, Cheney: I will never get back together again with that creep. Ever." Kate has stopped eating and is holding the phone in front of her and is texting quickly.

She sounds convincing, but then again, she's an actress. For all Cheney knows, Kate could be texting him right now. She hopes that is not the case. "I would hope you wouldn't, Kate, after what he's put you through. The guy is a raging asshole."

Kate nods. "I agree."

"Are you finished?" Cheney asks and Kate nods, absentmindedly, reading another incoming text.

"Honestly, Cheney, you don't have to wait on me."

Cheney ignores her and finishes clearing off the table and loading the dishwasher. Kate seems engrossed in her text message conversation. Her face is animated, her blue eyes are twinkling, and Cheney knows that look: it means she is full-fledged flirting.

As long as she isn't texting Nic Zafeiropoulos, Cheney doesn't really care with whom she is chatting, but she asks anyways, "Who are you texting?"

"Oh - it's this cute policeman I met the other night at the hospital. He's just checking to see how I am."

"You're flirting with the arresting officer?"

"No, no. Actually, he has nothing to do with my case."

"I would hope not! That would seem to certainly jeopardize the integrity of the prosecution if the responding officer was text messaging the victim."

Kate looks up from her text message conversation and smiles. "He was in the hospital trying to arrest a drunk driver that had been in a crash. The drunk guy was being treated for injuries in the area right next to me and so, the policeman had to stand outside in the hallway to keep guard over him. There was a point where the nurse had me sit outside on a chair in the hallway for like a half an hour waiting for some test results, and the officer and I started talking back and forth and he ended up asking if we could meet for a cup of coffee sometime, and so I gave him my number."

Cheney shakes her head. "You are the only woman I know who could be brought to a hospital *via* ambulance after being sliced in the head with a beer bottle and end up getting hit on by a cop. You are truly one of a kind."

Kate smiles. "Anyway, I think I might go meet him for coffee next week. I already have it planned how I'll wear my hair: I have this black velvet headband that I'm going to put over the patch where my hair was cut off and it will conceal everything perfectly."

"I just don't know if it's a good idea for you to go out so soon, Kate. You really need to rest."

"I'm not going to drink alcohol or anything. And besides, I can tell from talking to him that he's a compassionate man. My well-being will be his number one concern. You can see it in him. He has the most dreamy, lucid eyes. They just seized me from the get-go. The most vivid blue you've ever seen."

When Cheney asks the question, she knows what Kate's answer is going to be before Kate says it. "What's this police officer's name?"

"Brian. Brian Patterson. Why? Do you know him?"

# NAMES

*February 11*[th]

Although Cheney finds it hard to believe that Kate did not meet Brian Patterson at the house after the funeral, Kate insists that she doesn't remember ever seeing him before.

"I would remember seeing those blue eyes, believe me!" Kate says. "There were so many people here that day, we must never have been in the same room."

They have moved their conversation to the front parlor, and Kate is sitting on one of the green-velvet chairs and Cheney is curled up on the Victorian-era loveseat. Cheney had lit some wood in the fireplace, and the room is toasty, even though it is only five-degrees outside and the glass of the bay window is icy to the touch.

"Well, it's just odd that neither of you would have noticed each other, being that you're both single and so good-looking," Cheney observes.

Kate looks appalled. "It was Dan's funeral, Cheney. I had other things on my mind."

"Okay," Cheney says, though she smirks a bit, recalling Kate flitting about the post-funeral reception from officer to officer being her animated, flirtatious self. "Anyway, as I was saying before we came in here, he was the officer who was with Dan on the night he was murdered."

"Well, my last name is different than yours, so he probably just hasn't made the connection," Kate says.

"True," Cheney says. "Although most people say we look alike."

"Not enough that someone who doesn't know us would put it together that we are sisters," Kate says.

"I suppose," Cheney agrees.

"Do you think he won't want to go out with me when he finds out that you're my sister?"

"I don't see why that would pose a problem at all," Cheney says. "Although, the brass might have a problem with him going out with a Dom Batt victim in a case that is pending and where Loomisville is the arresting agency."

"Oh - you know I hate it when you refer to me as that," Kate says. "Can you please stop using that phrase?"

"I will. I will. Sorry," Cheney says. And, she is. The phrase 'Dom Batt Victim' had just slipped out. She'll try not to use it again around Kate.

"Anyway, he's not the arresting officer on the case against Nic," Kate explains. "He doesn't have anything to do with my case. I don't see why it would be a problem whatsoever."

"I don't know that it is," Cheney says, shrugging. "I'm just saying that, if anything would cause a problem, *that* would, more so than you being my sister. I mean, Dan's case is over. Derek Strozak killed Dan and Derek Strozak is dead. Case closed. There shouldn't be any issue at all with Patterson taking my sister out on a date."

"Well, I don't want to bring up a sore topic, but what about that Manuel guy? Do you think that case is closed too?"

"Yes," Cheney says. "I do. Manuel Rodriguez is dead. I don't think there's any more for the police to investigate concerning Manuel. They arrested the two people who were complicit in killing him in the Cook County Jail."

"Yes, but they asked all those questions about you. It seemed like maybe you were the one under investigation for something. At least, that's how it seemed to me when the Chicago Police questioned me."

Cheney bristles. "Well, I'm not. I'm not under investigation for anything." According to Patterson, the Chicago Police investigation into how Manuel Rodriguez ended up at her house was closed. Kate doesn't need to know that there was ever any investigation into the kidnapping of Manuel Rodriguez, and hopefully Patterson won't tell Kate anything about that situation, even if the two of them get close at some point.

"Okay, well, that's good to know," Kate says. "Now tell me, why do you have a copy of *Little House on the Prairie* sitting here with a bookmark in it?" Kate picks up the hardback book from the table between the two chairs, with a puzzled look on her face.

"It's not *Little House on the Prairie* - it's *The Long Winter*," Cheney corrects her.

"Okay, well why do you have a copy of a children's book here?"

"Because, I'm reading it."

Kate flips through the pages, delight in her eyes. "I can see that: hence, the bookmark at Chapter Eleven!" She smiles, clearly amused with herself. "Why is Cheney Manning, the literary snob, reading this?"

"I'm not a literary snob, and besides that, this is a wonderfully-crafted novel with its beautiful simplicity. It was one of my favorite books when I was child." She hesitates, apprehensive that this will just cause Kate to ask more questions, but then decides to add, "Actually, I'm reading it as part of a book club."

Oh, no. Here it goes. Kate looks amused. "A book club? When did you join a book club?"

"A couple of months ago," Cheney says and then asks, "Why do you find that so amusing?"

"Because a book club is such a chick thing," Kate says. "I can't see you being in a book club. A fantasy football league or a poker club, maybe - but a book club? Definitely not your thing. Besides, where is there to go to a book club around here? In the middle of the farm field? You're out in the middle of nowhere."

"It's a virtual book club. It's with Manuel's little sister, Carmen. She's nine. The two of us meet every Thursday night at nine for a half an hour virtually and discuss the book of the month. This month, we're reading *The Long Winter*."

"Wait a minute! Cheney Manning is in a book club with a nine-year-old? You must be kidding me! Is this the same Cheney Manning whom I know? The Cheney Manning who despises little kids and thinks they are annoying?! This head injury must be worse than I think. Maybe you should take me to the hospital."

"First of all, I don't hate kids. I just don't want any myself. I find them annoying as a general rule. But Carmen is different. She's a cool kid and she's fun to talk to. She's a real hoot actually."

"So, she is that Manuel guy's little sister?"

"Yes, she's 'that Manuel guy's' little sister.'"

It is evident that Kate wants to ask her questions about Manuel, and that she is dying to know whether there was anything romantic between Cheney and him, but she foregoes doing so. Instead, she just nods politely, and says, "Oh, well, that's nice. It's probably kind of fun going back and reading books that you read years ago."

"It is actually," Cheney says. "I'm enjoying it."

"Maybe you should write a children's book instead of a mystery novel."

"So, I can ditch my Hesperus Braun character?"

"Exactly!"

"Ha. Ha. It's not going to happen. I'm sticking with writing a mystery novel. Hesperus Braun's story is going to be written. You don't have to buy a copy if you don't want to."

"I'll be the first in line to read it. You know that," Kate says smiling. "Regardless of the ill-sounding first name of your heroine, I can't wait to read it when you're finished writing it. I'm sure it's going to be fantastic."

Between taking care of Kate and trying to assist Cassandra, it's been hard to find any time to work on the novel. At this pace, she'll be lucky if she gets the book finished by the end of the year. She is finally able to sneak some time in to write after Kate goes to sleep later in the afternoon, but even then, it's only for a couple of hours and her work is intermittent. She keeps thinking about how she is going to approach Dennis Rausch tomorrow night: what she's going to say, what she's going to wear. Despite that she is distracted, she does actually complete drafting the second chapter and she is already midway through writing the third one by the time Kate wakes up for dinner.

Cheney makes baked chicken, asparagus and mashed potatoes, and she is relieved to see that Kate's appetite is returning. Kate's energy, however, has not fully returned and she only watches television with Cheney for an hour after dinner before turning in for the night. Cheney ends up sitting in the parlor, stoking the fire on occasion, and thinking about her plan for tomorrow night.

She hasn't called Cassandra to fill her in on her conversation with Matthew Brockton, and she really doesn't want to talk to her yet until she can bring her some good news. There is still hope that she can convince Matthew to agree to DNA testing of the cigarettes. She just needs to come up with something that will persuade him that it is likely that this was a homicide and not a suicide. The only way she is going to be able to do that is by going directly to the source, just like Jack Stahl said. It would be too dangerous though to confront Dennis Rausch on her own. She needs to bring someone with her as back-up in case her plan fails. She originally thought maybe she would call Dan's brother, Dale, and see if he would help her out; but she really doesn't think he'll want to get involved with this, since he's a Chicago police officer, and he could get in trouble with his job. But it is obvious who is in the best position to help her and who would be the most willing to do so.

When she texts Solomon Wilson and asks him if he can talk on the phone, he calls her within seconds. He sounds genuinely ecstatic to talk to her. She congratulates him on the arrival of Alveda Isaiah, asks him how he is doing, and praises him on the pursuit of his studies. He talks about his baby with evident joy and enthusiasm, but he also talks about his classes as well, sounding excited and motivated. He tells Cheney about how he has a professor who is mentoring him, and who is encouraging him to pursue a career in the criminal justice field.

"Who knows?" Solomon says. "Maybe I'll end up being a lawyer one of these days: maybe even a public defender like you."

"That would be great, Solomon," she says, relieved that he is intent on setting and achieving educational goals. "But, in the interest of full disclosure, I should let you know that I'm no longer a public defender."

"What? I haven't heard that. Are you a private lawyer now? I can send some business your way. You're the best, Miss Manning. The absolute best."

"Well, I appreciate that, Solomon. Really, I do. But I'm not really practicing now. I'm taking a little break from the law: just doing some creative writing."

"You mean like books?"

"Yes. I'm working on a novel right now."

"Well, you should write a book about what happened to me and your husband and how Derek Strozak set me up and then tried to kill you when you found him out. That sounds like a good movie, actually."

"I'm writing a mystery novel, but it has nothing to do with what happened to Dan or to you. It is completely fictional: about a woman who is a Chicago police detective and she's trying to solve her sister's disappearance from two decades ago."

"What's your main character's name?"

"Hesperus Braun."

"Hesperus? I've never heard that name before: it's kind of funky sounding. I think you should change it to something else. I don't think anyone's gonna want to buy a book about someone named Hesperus Braun."

"Well, you're the second person to tell me that today."

"Oh yeah? Well, that might tell you somethin' then. I'm not a book publisher or anything like that, and don't be offended, but Hesperus? C'mon, what kind of name is that? Naw, naw: You got to ditch the name Hesperus and pick somethin' else that will sell books."

Cheney laughs. "Don't worry, Solomon. I'm not offended. I'll think about it; but for now, my heroine remains named Hesperus Braun."

Solomon chuckles and then says: "So, seriously, though: What's up, Miss Manning? Whatchya' reachin' out to me for? Just to say hello? I mean, it's nice hearin' from you and all, but you kind of seem like you have somethin' else you must be wanting to talk about. My cases are all done, so I know it can't be that. The only thing I got goin' on now is my civil suit against the police for arrestin' me for me somethin' I didn't do."

"Well, actually I called to ask for your help," she says.

"My help? You need my help on somethin'? Of course, of course, I'll help you out with whatever you need. You saved my life, just like I said in the email. Without you, I would still be sittin' in jail and probably end up being convicted and doin' life in the pen. I owe you my life, Miss Manning. I mean that."

"You can call me Cheney, Solomon. You're not my client anymore."

"Okay, Cheney, well what's up? What's it you need?"

"Do you have a car?"

"Yeah, yeah. I've got a car. I drive my mom's car."

"Okay. Well, would you be able drive it tomorrow night?"

"Yeah, yeah. No problem at all. But what's this all about, Cheney?"

"First, I need you to promise me that everything I tell you on this is confidential."

"Okay," he says. "No problem. I won't tell no one."

Cheney explains the circumstances to Solomon, including Cassandra's initial plea for legal assistance with the FOIA request, Cheney's review of the police reports, and Cheney's and Cassandra's joint belief that Dennis Rausch killed Jazzie Gonzalez. Cheney touches briefly on her meeting with Matthew Brockton and her subsequent conversation with Jack Stahl.

She emphasizes that she needs to go undercover at Knee's Joint to try to find out whether Dennis Rausch was a smoker thirty years ago.

"I need you to drive me there and then back to my house, and I need you to back me up in case something goes wrong," she says. "I don't know if this guy is going to be dangerous or anything; I doubt it, but I just have no idea how this whole thing is going to go."

When she is finished, Solomon does not hesitate to ask, and she can sense that he is eager to help. "What time should I pick you up?"

After the arrangements are made, and Cheney disconnects the call, she breathes in for a moment and holds her breath. She has no idea what she is embarking on, and what risks, if any, she faces. All she knows is that it can't possibly be as dangerous as when she lied her way into the Latin King safehouse three months ago. Or can it?

# HESPERUS

*February 12*<sup></sup>

*February 12*th

"Are you sure you want to go into this place alone?" Solomon asks her.

Not really: But she doesn't say it. Instead, she assures him. "Yeah, I'll be fine."

Knee's Joint is a shanty-like bar that looks like it would fall into the Fox River in a strong wind. It literally is a dive of a place, teetering only a few yards from the water, at the end of a dead-end road. It is the only commercial building on the street, which is dotted with mid-century once-upon-a-time summer cottages of rich Chicagoans, that have been converted in recent decades into year-round, over-crowded homes.

The bar's parking lot is really just a concrete slab of seven horizontal yellow-lined spaces in the front, though there is also parking available on the street in front of the residences, and four spaces on the side of the bar that are not visible from the front lot. Solomon had parked in one of the spaces along the side opposite from the entrance, to the rear of which is a clump of trees and a patch of dirt signaling the end of the raggedy lot. When they had pulled in, there had been only three other vehicles parked near the bar – though all those other vehicles were in the front of the lot, not on the side where Solomon ended up parking.

"I will text you if I run into any problems," Cheney says. "Thanks again for agreeing to do this for me. I really appreciate it, Solomon."

Right before she gets out of the car, her phone starts vibrating. It's Kate. She really doesn't want to pick it up, but there's no way she can ignore her sister's call under the circumstances. She needs to know that Kate is safe in the apartment; otherwise, she'll worry about her all night.

She says to Solomon, "I'm sorry. I've gotta take this," and when she hits the answer button, she asks, "Is everything okay?"

"Yes. I'm here safe and sound and I have Taleeka here with me," Kate says cheerfully.

"Hi, Cheney!" Taleeka calls out in the background, and it is clear that she's on speaker phone.

"Hi, Taleeka," Cheney says.

"I just wanted to let you know that Taleeka's here with me, and everything is fine, and I had a nice dinner with Dax and he's gone," Kate says.

"That's great," Cheney says. "I'm glad to hear you're doing okay. Give me a call in the morning after your appointment, okay?"

"Will do," Kate says. "I'll call you then. Love you!"

"I love you too," Cheney says and ends the call. She looks over at Solomon. "My little sister. She's down at NIU."

"Oh," he says, and then continues with their prior conversation, "Anyway, I'll just hang out here until you're finished. Take your time. No rush at all on my part. I set aside the whole night for you. My mom is watching Alveda for me while Renee is at work, so it's all good on my part."

Cheney nods, says "Thanks again," and heads into the bar. She's wearing a Chicago Cubs baseball cap with her auburn hair swept to one side, her black puffer coat, a plain gray zip-front hoodie, a pair of tight-fitting faded bootcut jeans, and short black leather booties.

There are only two men sitting at the bar, each on opposite ends, and she recognizes Dennis Rausch immediately at the far end. There was not a whole heck of a lot about him online, but she was able to find a picture of him from a newspaper archive when he caught a mammoth-sized Muskie in the Fox River four years ago. Even though he is in his mid-sixties, and wears the face of a decades' long drinker, he is still handsome in a rugged, Tommy Lee Jones meets Lee Majors kind of way. He has silver hair, dark, intimidating eyebrows, a pock-marked face, and eyes that look like hallways to an abandoned mansion. He is wearing a tan canvas long-sleeved button-down shirt over a black t-shirt, a pair of jeans, and suede construction worker style boots.

The bartender looks like he is in his eighties and he has a tracheotomy speaking valve, and he kind of nods at Cheney when she sits down on a stool only one down from Dennis Rausch. Without the bartender uttering a word, she orders a pilsner beer on tap that she hasn't had since she was in high school, before she realizes there aren't any taps. She then orders the same brand of beer, but in a bottle, and Dennis Rausch interposes, almost kind of testily, "They don't sell bottles here, lady. This is a can joint."

"Oh. I'll take a can then," she says and the bartender doesn't display any reaction other than pulling a beer out of the cooler under the bar, popping it open and sitting in front of her.

"Boy, I didn't know they still made this beer," she says to Rausch, before taking a gulp of it.

He looks at her like he wonders why she is talking to him, and he seems a bit annoyed. He doesn't even respond. Instead, he calls out to the old, fat guy sitting at the opposite end of the bar. "What time will Donley be here?"

"I don't know if he's coming at all," the man answers.

The bartender speaks, and when he does, it is evident it takes a great deal of effort to do so. "He said he'd be here after his office closes."

"Well, it's nearly six now," the rotund patron says. "He should've been here an hour ago."

"He must've got stuck with a client or something," the bartender says.

"He's gonna miss the beginning of the game," the patron comments.

Tadhg Donley is a well-known criminal defense attorney in Meskwaki. She's not sure that it is he to whom they are referring, but there's a good chance they are. Tadhg Donley is at least twenty-five years older than Cheney, and he practices mostly in Kent County, as opposed to Stickney County. She knows who he is, and it's unlikely he would know who she is, but still the possibility exists. After all, there was a picture of her near Dan's casket that had appeared in online newspapers and, brief video clips of her that had been shown on Chicago television networks when Dan was killed. Furthermore, since Derek Strozak and he worked for rival criminal defense firms, Donley probably had paid close attention to the news coverage when it had been revealed that Strozak had murdered Dan. Practically every attorney in the Fox River Valley had likely been riveted by the juicy details of a criminal defense attorney having killed a cop and having shot a public defender. It was possible that Tadhg Donley could recognize her as the public defender who had been married to the murdered Loomisville police officer; but then again, the risk remains that Dennis Rausch might recognize her from that same news coverage, regardless if Tadhg Donley shows up and blows her cover.

There is chit-chat – not much – between Dennis Rausch, the guy at the end of the bar, and the bartender, but all three of the men appear engrossed with the television screen that is angled at the top edge of the back of the bar. The two men occasionally order a drink for the other: Dennis Rausch is drinking whiskey and the other guy is drinking beer. She thinks about jumping into the rotation and buying a round for one or both of them, but she holds back for fear that such conduct will draw out more ire from Rausch and make him even more suspicious than he already seems. He already appears as though he may be trying to figure out why some good-looking woman in a Cubs hat is sitting in a dive bar on the Fox River during the work week in February.

The three men are watching a Bulls game, and they occasionally make a comment or emit a grunt or utter a curse about the game to each other. She is not a professional basketball fan, and could care less who wins. It's one of the few sports that she doesn't watch and she couldn't name a single player on the Bulls. She is afraid to say anything for fear of sounding stupid, so she stays silent, drinking her beer. She picks up her smartphone, which she has been keeping screen-down on the bar, and texts Solomon to let him know that she's still sitting at the bar, that it's going to be a while and that she's watching the Bulls game. Solomon responds with a thumbs-up emoji, but then sends a text asking: "Is he there?" She texts back with a thumbs-up emoji, and he asks, "How long will u b?" And she replies with a question mark.

A few minutes before half time, the old man at the end of the bar stands up abruptly, puts on his coat and hat, settles up with the bartender and says, "See you, Orv. See you, Denny. See you, whatshername." He heads out the door, calling out behind him, "It's starting to snow again. Better close early tonight, Orv. It's really coming down thick."

Since Denny Rausch has remained seated at the bar nearly the entire half, without making his way out to the parking lot for a single break, she is quite certain that he is not a smoker. What she really needs to know, though, is whether he was a smoker thirty years ago.

Even though her smartphone is on silent, Cheney notices an incoming text from Solomon that reads: "It's snowing really bad. How much longer?" She responds with another question mark.

Dennis Rausch orders another whiskey, but this time, he also says, "And one for whatshername," and does a quick nod over toward Cheney. Orv pops open another beer for her and plops it down in front of her on the bar. This is her fourth beer of the night, and even though it's a pretty low b.a.c., she's starting to feel it.

By the time the second half commences, Denny is actually talking to her, and she finds him both loquacious and flirtatious: surprisingly so, after an evening of being mostly ignored by him even though she's the only woman in the tavern, she's roughly half his age, and there's only one barstool between them. Now that the whiskey seems to have loosened his tongue, she sees why Jazzie Gonzalez found him so attractive three decades ago: there's an easygoing, smoldering way about him, a kind of mysterious half-agony in his eyes, a resolute confidence in his wide shoulders. When he smiles, there is such a slowness to it, that it's as if his hand is meandering along the small of her back.

He calls her "Cubs fan" or "whatshername" whenever he orders her a drink and he doesn't seem particularly interested in finding out what her actual name is, nor does he seem disposed to disclosing much details about himself either. He does inquire about her Cubs cap though,

216

and she takes it off and shows him the green underbelly of the bill where Harry Caray penned his name.

"It's my dad's cap actually, but he gifted it to me years ago," she says.

"Ah, that's pretty cool," he says, admiring the signature. "How'd you get him to sign it?"

"I was little, like five or six, and I really don't remember it much, except that I was with my parents at his restaurant after a game, and my dad was wearing this ball cap, and when we walked by Harry Caray's table my dad and mom said 'Hello' and my dad asked him if he would sign his cap, and he did. I'm a bigger Cubs fan than anyone else in my family, so my dad gave me the cap years later for a Christmas gift when I was in high school." She pauses. "Are you a baseball fan?"

"Nothing better than baseball," he says, taking a drink. "I played a little college ball for a couple of years up in Wisconsin, but I tore my rotator cuff. Had to have surgery. Ended up dropping out. Haven't played since."

"Were you a pitcher?"

"Yeah," he says. "How'd you know?"

"Rotator cuff," she says. "Just guessed."

He nods, but they don't talk about baseball after that, and he's kind of quiet for a while, seeming melancholy and brooding. It must be the mention of baseball, reminding him of the injury, and lost dreams. She won't bring up that topic again.

Not long into the second half, she has scooched over, at his beckoning, to the seat beside him; and there is a later point, about midway in the second half, where he puts his hand under her jaw and asks her if she knows that she is beautiful. When she says, "No," he says, "I find that hard to believe. Good-looking women usually know when they're good-looking and I suspect you're probably the same as the rest. So, tell me, what is a gorgeous gal like you doing in Knee's Joint?"

"I just came in for a few beers," Cheney says. "I needed to get out of the house for a few hours. My sister came to live with me recently, and I just kind of wanted to get away from her for a little while, and have some alone time."

Just then, Orv interrupts and says he's going to have to shut the bar down early for the night. "I'm sorry, Denny," Orv says, holding his cell phone away from his ear. "Pauly's on the line and he said that the roads are getting real bad. Wants me to come home. Says I should just leave my car here overnight. Says there no way that I can see in this. Says he'll come get me right now if I close down."

"Naw, naw, there's no need for Pauly to come out in this shit. I'll take you home, Orv."

"Are you sure, Denny?"

"Of course, I'm sure."

"Okay, I'm just gonna close both of you out," Orv says.

"Put 'em all on one. I've got whatshername's."

"Are you sure?" she asks. "You don't have to pick up my tab," she says to Denny and then she calls out to Orv, "You can do mine separate. I'll just pay my own."

Both men ignore her and Orv rings up the total, calls it out, and Denny slaps a couple of twenties on the counter. Denny says he's going out to the lot to warm up his truck and to scrape the windows.

When he returns a few minutes later, he asks her, "How'd you get here? I didn't see another vehicle parked out front. Did you walk?"

"Um – actually, I took a ride service. I'm gonna have to order one right now."

"How about you come home with me for a while and we'll watch the end of the game?" he asks, and then he adds, "Or not?"

It's clear what that 'Or not' means and his twentieth-century-throw-back forwardness is somewhat of a turn-on and a turn-off simultaneously. He is intriguing in an old-school kind of way. There is an alluring bravado about him, almost as if after hitting sixty he really doesn't give a damn if someone is offended by his masculinity. But somehow, she thinks he's probably always been this cocky, even before he was in his last quarter.

"You know, actually, I will take you up on that," she says, but then excuses herself to go to the bathroom. She's been in gas stations that had a cleaner, more spacious, bathroom than these crammed quarters. As soon as she closes the door, she texts Solomon and lets him know that she will be riding with Denny Rausch to his house. She knows his address from searching online yesterday, so she texts it to Solomon. She explains that she will need him to lay low until she is ready to leave Rausch's house and then she'll text him to come pick her up and that he needs to pretend he's with a ride service if Rausch comes outside to say 'Goodbye' to her.

Solomon's text back to her reads: "R U FKN CRAZY!!!!??"

She sees immediately that Solomon is calling her, but she's afraid to answer her phone, because the bathroom door is so flimsy, Orv has already turned the TV off, and she can hear Orv's and Denny's voices. Still, she hits answer, and whispers to Solomon, "I can't talk in here. I'm in the bathroom, but they're right outside."

"Listen, Cheney, I do not think this is a good idea for you to go to this dude's house. I mean, for all you know he could be a serial killer or somethin', and I mean, I didn't bring no gun or nothing like that with me. You know, I'm steering clear of all that shit. See, it's like this: I don't know how I can possibly back you up if you get in trouble in there, when I won't know what the fuck is going on."

She turns the water in the sink on to mask her voice and moves to the far wall by the toilet, crouching down on the floor, hoping her voice won't carry. "Listen, I can't talk right now. You said you were in. I need you."

He must sense how adamant she is, because he acquiesces, but only partly. "Well, I'm gonna follow you then when he pulls out. No way I'm lettin' you out of my sight."

"No," she says incisively. "I need you to back off. Just wait five minutes after we leave and then park a couple of blocks away from his house."

"Man, the snow is coming down like you wouldn't fucking believe. You want me to stay out there parked on a street with plows and shit coming by? I'm gonna be lucky if my mom's car don't get hit by some city plow." Solomon pauses. "Nothin' I say is gonna change your mind anyway, is it?"

She is quiet and then he asks, "How long you gonna be with this dude? How long I gotta wait?"

"You said you were in," Cheney reminds him. "You said you would help me out here. You said you had the whole night to help me." She almost says, "Remember, I saved you from doing life in prison," but she doesn't. She holds back.

It is evident he is agitated and wants to go home. "Yeah, that was before the blizzard came. This is nothin' like they said it was gonna be tonight. It's a lot of fucking snow out here. I can barely see out my windshield. I can't imagine trying to drive in this shit."

Again, she thinks about bringing up his email, his pledge to help her if she needs anything. Instead, she says just four words, still crouched down in the corner, hand over the right side of her mouth. "I need your help."

There is silence and then, he capitulates. "Okay. I'll help you. This whole thing sounds fuckin' crazy, but I'll help you. You saved my life. I guess this is the least I can do. I'll hold off, and I won't call you again. I'll wait for you to text me and then I'll come pick you up at his house. If anything happens though – if this dude tries to hurt you or somethin'- you'll text me, right?"

"I will," she says. "Thanks." She hits the red button on her cell-phone and then turns off the water.

The lights are down in the bar and Orv is waiting by the front door with it wide open, staring out at the snow tumbling down. Denny Rausch is standing next to the bar, his rangy six-foot-two frame, leaning against the bar top. He is wearing a camel-colored jacket with a cordu-roy collar and, now that he is standing, she notices for the first time how good he looks in a pair of jeans. He is staring at her - almost as if he knows she is up to something.

"Everything okay?" he asks her.

221

"Yeah. Why?"

"Just that you were in there a long time and it sounded like you were on the phone or something."

"Oh, I was just calling my sister to let her know I wouldn't be home until late."

He nods, but she can tell he doesn't believe her. She is nervous getting into his truck, but she slides into the back and then Orv sits in the front passenger seat. The two men make small talk, mostly about how unexpected this amount of snowfall is, and how slippery the roads are. The flakes are spiraling down hard, like angry ghosts falling from the sky, colliding with his windshield. It is a slow and tedious drive, and she can tell that Denny is struggling to keep the vehicle from fishtailing, so he moves at a cautious speed. When they pull into Orv's driveway, less than a mile from the bar, the old man's son, Pauly, comes out to the truck to thank Denny for driving him home and to assist his father on the snowy pavement in getting into the house without falling.

"Why don't you jump up here and join me?" Denny asks her, and she makes the switch from the backseat to the front seat.

His truck smells like the evergreen air-freshener that hangs from the rearview mirror. "Pickups are a bitch to drive in the snow," he says, eyes glued to the road.

"I know," she says. "I drive one."

"A girl who drives a pickup? I knew I liked you when you walked into the bar."

"Hey, you didn't even talk to me until the first half was over," she says.

"Yeah. I was playing hard to get," he half-grins, but he is still focused on the road.

It's only about a five-minute drive from Orv's and she has a tingling feeling of anticipation and nervousness when he pulls into the steep driveway. There is another sensation too: familiarity. She is not sure why. The house is only a block away from the Fox, and it is in a heavily-wooded subdivision of tired-looking homes that saw better times decades ago. His is an aluminum-sided chalky blue two-story home that looks like it was built sometime in the 1970s or 1980s. The house itself is set back at least a hundred yards or so from the roadway, and it is surrounded by mature pine and oak trees. It looks to be a sizeable lot, at least an acre, and the nearest house is visible, but still a fairly good distance away. There's a flagpole not far from the steps with a spotlight illuminating a thin blue line flag struggling against the blizzard winds.

It is nerve-racking when he hits the garage-door opener on his visor and the wide mouth of the two-stalls opens. It is even worse though when the doors close behind them and they are sitting in his garage in the dark. It feels like a tomb. She is sitting inches away from a man whom she thinks might have murdered a woman thirty years ago and no one knows she is here except her eighteen-year-old former client who is parked somewhere in a snowstorm. But somehow, for some strange reason, she kind of trusts Denny Rausch. It's probably attributable to alcohol and intuition, but, regardless of why, she is convinced that there is no way this man could be a killer. Is he a bit rough around the edges? Yes. But a murderer? No.

When they remove their seatbelts, he takes her right arm before she opens the passenger door and he pulls her over toward him. He removes her baseball cap, brushes her hair away from her face. When he kisses her, it is a forceful and well-practiced move. He has his right hand under her jaw, his fingers pressed gently into her cheekbone. She feels a shock go through her: a blend of passion, mystery and fear. She wonders where this night is going to take her.

When he leans back, he looks at her and grins. "Hey, what's your name, whatshername?"

She had a name picked out earlier in the evening, something kind of plain and innocuous, like Jenny or Linda, but for some reason, almost a half a six pack later, she abandons those, and says, "Hesperus Braun."

"Hesperus Braun," he rolls it around on his tongue as if getting a taste of it, and then smiles again. "I like the sound of that: a beautiful name for a beautiful lady. Let's go inside, Hesperus Braun, before we get snowed in here."

# NICOTINE

*February 12th*

Of course, he's got to be a big dog guy. He has the American-built truck. He has the house not far from the river; and, he's got two giant Labrador retrievers with square black heads and shiny eyes.

"Meet Bronco and Belle," he says, as she leans down to greet each of them.

The dogs ease away some of her anxiousness at being in this house with a strange man who might be a murderer. The Retrievers are disarming, all backside wiggles and smiles and licks. It's hard to imagine that a killer would volunteer to drive an old man home in a snowstorm, let alone own such lovable dogs.

"Are they siblings?" she asks.

He is removing his coat and hanging it up in a closet behind him. "Yes: same litter. I couldn't choose between them, so I took both of 'em."

He offers to take her coat and, at first, she thinks of saying "No," but instead she agrees. She stands up, unzips it and hands it to him, along with her baseball cap and gloves.

Immediately she crouches back down to play with the dogs. "Oh, they are beautiful," she says, letting Belle lick her face. "How old are they?"

"Four," he says. "Let's go let 'em out." He starts walking toward the back of the house, the two dogs charging happily ahead of him. There is an open staircase at the entry way that leads up to what looks like an exposed loft with a wooden railing. The front space on the lower level is a sunken living room with camel-colored leather furniture, well-worn tawny carpet and a large stone fireplace. She follows him along a linoleum walkway along the edge of the living room, which leads to an open dining room. Along the wall, there is an open door which appears to lead to the main bedroom. He leads her to a kitchen in the back of the house, and he lets both dogs out in the backyard. He asks her if she wants a beer.

She says "Yes," looking for a place to sit. The kitchen is small, outdated, and somewhat of a mess. It is obviously a bachelor's dining area. There is a pizza box on the counter, and a bunch of plates stacked haphazardly in the sink. There are dog bowls on the floor near a small round table with two chairs, and scattered remnants of Belle's and Bronco's vigorous mastication dot the linoleum. There's only one chair at the table, and it looks like one that was a garage-sale find.

He hands her a can of beer, and she smiles. "This is a can joint too, huh?"

"Yes," he says, grinning. "No bottles. Just cans."

"Do you want anything else?" he asks. "Potato chips? Nachos? Pizza?"

"Oh, no, thank you though," she says. Outside of the same tiling from the front of the house, which appears relatively modern, the kitchen looks like it needs some serious remodeling.

He lets the dogs in the house and then walks away toward the living room. She notices for the first time that there is another door next to the opening to what she assumes is the bedroom, and she guesses that is the first-floor bathroom. The dining room area is actually quite beautiful compared to the kitchen, with what looks like fresh-painted dark beige walls, and a barnwood dining room table, not unlike the one in her own house. There's also a matching hutch and buffet, along with a collection of waterfowl replicas.

Though the rust-colored carpeting in the living room appears dated, the furniture looks to be in good shape, and the layout of the room gives the feeling of being in a much larger house with its open floor plan and the magnificent stone fireplace. There is what looks like a fairly modern sound system along the back wall of the living room. He puts on a classic rock station and asks her if that's okay.

"Yeah," she says. "I like rock. I like just about everything."

"Just about everything, huh?" he asks; and, he is so close she can feel his breath against her face. "That's promising."

His confidence makes her shiver, but in a good way. And he tells her he's "going to put the dogs upstairs" and he'll "be down in a minute." He disappears with the Retrievers and she sits down on the sofa in the living room. Her heart moves a bit with either anticipation or anxiety, for she wonders whether, if, when he returns, he all of a sudden is going to put the moves on her as soon as he sits down on the couch. He does.

His kisses are direct and convey a meaning of which is purely sexual. She really only wants to find out whether or not he smoked thirty years ago, but his hand is already underneath her hoodie and t-shirt, almost professionally so, and he has already unclasped her bra, so that the underwire chafes uncomfortably and awkwardly against her breasts. It is all feeling really good, and she is melting beneath his kisses and his touches. But there's that telltale bullet scar that mars her right shoulder, which he'll probably see as soon as he unzips her hoodie and eases off her t-shirt. She suddenly recoils, sending a silent signal that he's being too forward, too fast. She takes a gulp of her beer, and asks him if he has a light.

She had brought with her a pack of cigarettes in her hoodie pocket that were left over from the packs she had bought for Manuel back in November. Her plan all along, had been to ask Dennis Rausch whether he had a light. But there really had not been an opportune time to do so. Until now.

"No, I don't," he says, rubbing his hand through his hair, looking a bit confused by the abruptness of her change of direction. He drinks some beer. "I don't smoke."

"Oh, I thought maybe you might have a lighter or some matches around here somewhere."

"Nope," he says, and then, after thinking for a few seconds, he suggests: "Well, actually, I have fireplace matches, if you want to use one of those." He stands up, but she tells him, "No, no. That's okay. I just thought if you had a lighter or a regular match, I would smoke, but don't go to any bother. I'm not itching for one or anything right now. It's better if I don't smoke one anyway, because once I start, I'll want to smoke another one right away."

He sits back down, and drinks some more beer. "Actually, I gotta say I'm kind of surprised that you smoke," he says. "You don't seem like a smoker. In fact, I haven't seen you smoke all night."

Suspicion seems to perhaps, be impelling his directness. Is he figuring out that she's here for some other purpose? "I'm trying to quit," she says, attempting to sound nonchalant. "I can usually go a half a day or sometimes more without smoking, but then I will binge and smoke like two or three in a row. You probably know how that is, though, if you ever used to smoke."

"Actually, I hate those things – cancer sticks," he says, his jaw flinching a bit with what appears like contempt. "My grandfather and one of my sisters – Pat - both smokers- both died of lung cancer."

"Oh, I'm sorry. Was that a long time ago?"

"Yeah, yeah it was. Actually, my grandpa died when I was just a kid, and Pat died when I was twenty. She was seventeen years older than me.

"So, you never smoked then?" It's a leading question and as soon as she asks it, she wishes she could take it back, and ask an open-ended one in its stead. It's too late.

"I tried 'em when I was a kid, but it's not really my thing," he says.

Now, she's got to seek more clarification and this may be tricky. She drinks more beer, smiles. She can't ask, "What do you mean by that?" or "When was the last time you smoked a cigarette?" because both questions sound overly-probing and he'll probably shut down, so she kind of tosses her hair and asks: "So, after you tried smoking when you were a kid, did you ever smoke again as an adult or was it one of those things where you never smoked again?"

"I've probably had a couple since then, when I was shooting the shit with friends at a bar or something, but I've never been a smoker or anything like that. As I said, it's just not my thing."

She has to ask it, so she does. "So, you were never a regular smoker though, where you would like smoke a few in a row or keep a pack of cigarettes around or anything like that?"

He eyes her and she can now definitely tell that he is suspicious of her. "Man, what's with all the smoking questions? You sound like a cop."

When she answers, she can sense the nervousness in her own voice, but she tries to remain steady. "I'm just curious, because I'm trying to break the habit myself, and I'm always wondering how other people could possibly have smoked, but not gotten hooked on nicotine, like I did. Maybe I think that will somehow help me break my addiction. I don't know. Sorry, if I offended you by asking questions."

"No. It's alright," he says, though he seems a bit agitated. He adds, "Like I said, I never was a smoker. I've tried a couple here or there over the years, and I never got hooked. I don't think I've ever bought a pack of cigarettes in my life. It's just a habit I've never picked up. I've got enough bad habits as it is."

A part of her wants to find out what exactly those bad habits are, a part of her wants him to kiss her again, a part of her wants to go too far, but she suppresses all of these desires. Instead, she asks him where the bathroom is and he points her to the door which she had assumed was the place. She tells him she'll be right back and when she gets there she takes off her sweatshirt, and then readjusts and reclasps her bra, which had been digging into the skin beneath her breasts. She then texts Solomon to come pick her up in ten minutes, and she turns on her cellphone's ringer. As soon as she gets a 'K' text from Solomon in return, she fluffs up her hair with her hands, studies her face in the mirror for a few seconds, goes to the bathroom, washes her hands and heads back out to the living room.

For some reason, she is mesmerized a bit by this sixty-something retired cop, and the attraction she has toward him surprises her. She is still grieving the loss of her husband, and she is not ready to get into a sexual relationship with anyone right now. But there is a mysterious ruggedness about him. A part of her feels like she is missing out on something when she tells him that she is going to have to head home and that she has already ordered a ride service to pick her up and that it will be here in about ten minutes.

He is standing near the fireplace, stoking the wood, and the flames are just starting to dance. He doesn't particularly look disappointed, just possibly mildly surprised, which is one of the things that she already likes about him. It is also a trait which mitigates against the chance that he is a murderer. He is not a man who appears to be easily rattled or upset. He almost seems as if he has another gorgeous young woman waiting in the wings on standby, so that Cheney's departure is Cheney's loss, not his. He gives off an air as if he would have made love to Cheney if she was willing, but now that she's made her choice to leave, he's indifferent. He doesn't try to persuade her to stay and he doesn't seem like he really cares if she goes.

He simply shrugs, dangling the fire poker in his right hand like a golf club, and says, "Okay. Do you want another beer while you wait for your ride?"

She says, "No. Thank you, though."

When she sits back down on the sofa, he doesn't sit next to her this time. Instead, he reclines in one of the leather armchairs, observing her, almost as if he is studying her. She can't help but think he must know this whole thing has been a bit odd, and he's trying to figure her out.

Along those lines, he starts to probe a bit, for the first time. "You said your ride's comin' in ten minutes?"

"Yes."

"That's pretty quick for a ride service in a blizzard, isn't it?"

"Oh, I suppose so, but he must've been in the neighborhood. That's how those ride services work. You never really know if a driver will be able to pick you up right away or whether it will take a half an hour or so."

He nods, and then says, "So, you never did tell me what you do for a living."

"You never told me what you do either," she says. "You go first."

"I'm retired."

"From?"

"Law enforcement."

"Oh," she says. "Where?"

"Here. Meskwaki. I was on the job for thirty-four years. Retired when I was fifty-seven."

"Do you work now or are you fully retired?"

"Just part-time at a friend of mine's shop." He pats the large wooden coffee table in front of him and then nods up toward the dining room. "We make furniture out of reclaimed wood, mostly from old buildings."

"This is your work?"

"Yes," he says. "Well, mine and Bob's."

"Amazing," she says. "I love this piece, and I noticed that dining room set when we walked by it. It's beautiful. I can't even imagine the craftsmanship that goes into making something like this." She glides her hand along the top of the table, studying it. "The patience, the attention to detail...I just want to take this table home with me. It would look great in my living room."

He laughs. "You can have it."

"Can I take the hutch too?" she asks jokingly. "I need one of those, too."

He laughs again. "Sure. Why not? But you have to tell me what you do first."

"I'm a writer," she says.

He looks mildly surprised. "Oh yeah, what do you write?"

"I write poetry, short stories, plays, things like that."

"Well, maybe I could read something you wrote sometime."

"I'd like that," she says.

"Where'd you say you live again?"

"I didn't," she says. No reason to lie about this part, so she tells the truth: "You never asked. I live out on a farm about fifteen minutes southwest of Hanley."

"You live out on a farm all by yourself?"

233

"Yes," she says. "Well, kind of. I have a dog. But like I said earlier, I also have a sister who's been staying with me. But, that's a temporary thing."

"The dog or the sister?"

"The sister."

"Oh," he says and she can tell he is reading her, trying to figure her out.

"What kind of dog?"

"A Rottweiler. Patton."

"Patton? After General Patton?"

"Yep. You got it."

"One of my favorite movies of all time: George C. Scott as Patton."

She knew she liked this guy. There's no way he's a murderer. "It's one of my favorites too."

"Well, we'll have to watch it sometime together," he says. "I've got it on DVD upstairs."

Her phone pings and it's Solomon. She jumps up, probably too eagerly so, and rushes over to the closet to grab her jacket and cap. She puts her boots on, balancing herself by placing one of her hands on the stair-railing post. When she finishes, he takes her by the hand, looks her in the eye, and she thinks he's going to call bullshit on her. Instead, he kisses her and she enjoys it. Again.

234

When he lets go of her hand, he puts his boots back on as if he is going to head outside with her and, he talks to her, looking down, as he's doing so, "What are you doing Thursday night?" he asks.

"Thursday? You mean, Valentine's Day?"

"I guess that's what they call it." He looks up at her, and he is so direct, she feels her heart teeter a little bit.

Thursday evenings are, of course, reserved for the Spinach Omelet Book Nerds, but she can text Carmen tomorrow and tell her that they'll have to postpone the meeting until the following week. She hates doing that, because she knows the child will be disappointed, but she hasn't even had a chance to finish reading her assigned chapters of *The Long Winter* anyway, and it's unlikely she'll finish before Thursday evening. She's got too much on her mind, between the situation with Kate and this investigation into Jazzie Gonzalez's death. It's doubtful that she'll do any reading tomorrow or Thursday.

So, she answers him. "Nothing. At least nothing that I know of at this point."

His boots are on and he looks at her as if he is sizing up how to fix a problem on a ranch, or on the streets, or at a construction site. "I'd like to take you to a nice steak dinner. There's a good place on the river: The Branded Blue."

He goes into the closet and takes a cellphone out of his coat pocket and asks, "What's your number?"

She had prepared for the possibility that he might ask for her number, by driving into Hanley and buying a burner phone earlier in the day. She gives him the number to that phone, instead of her permanent one, and she watches him enter the number into his contacts. He then calls her number, but disconnects it immediately, and says, "Now you have mine too."

He steps away, opening the door for her. "Your ride's out there," he says, eyeing the car. "I can walk out there with you. I need to shovel tonight anyway. It looks like it's stopped snowing – at least for now."

"No, no, - you don't have to walk me out. I'm fine."

"Well, be careful on that sidewalk," he says. "Text me when you get home, so I know you made it there okay."

She nods and is halfway out the door when he tells her to also text him her address and he'll pick her up at five-thirty on Thursday.

She turns around and says, "No, that's okay. I'll just meet you here."

"You're not going to take a ride service again, are you?"

"I don't know yet. I might," she says.

"Do you have a driver's license?"

"Oh, of course," she says. "I just don't do a lot of night driving. Poor eyesight."

"Oh," he says, but he looks dubious. "Well, since you live way out in the country, that's one helluva expensive ride. Why don't I just pick you up?"

"No. No. It's fine. I don't mind at all. Besides, I may drive myself - I don't know yet. See you Thursday!"

"Okay, I'll make reservations for six then," he says.

She turns her back and starts walking. He says something else, but she can't hear exactly what it is, because she moves pretty quickly over the snow toward the car.

She gets into the back-passenger seat as if she is taking a ride service. Solomon turns around and looks at her, "You okay?"

"Yes," she says. "Let's go."

In truth, she's not sure that she's okay. Her heart is racing and her mind is kind of jumbled. It's a little bit of fear and anxiousness, but mostly, a lot of thrill. She is relieved to be back in the safety of the vehicle with Solomon and away from the risk of harm. She is trembling, but it is not from the cold, nor the fear. It is from coming so close to letting Dennis Rausch's kisses knock down her walls.

# GUT

*February 12*th

"So, did he do it?"

She does not process Solomon's question at first. Instead, she is thinking of how long of a drive it will be to her house, and how dangerous it will be for Solomon to have to drive all the way back from her house to his grandma's house in Washburne by himself in a compact car. It's not even ten yet, but, still, if he has to drive her all the way home, he won't be back to Washburne until past midnight with the condition of these roads. If Patton wasn't waiting to be let out at home, she would just ask Solomon if she could stay overnight at his grandmother's, but instead she offers to let him stay at her house, rather than drive home.

"Naw, naw; that's okay, Cheney. I'm fine to drive. I want to get home to see my baby. Besides, after we talked earlier, I figured I might be in for a long night. I couldn't figure out what you were doin', but I thought you might even stay over at the dude's house. I wasn't sure what was goin' on. I'm still not sure. So, what's the deal: Did he kill her or not?"

"I don't think so," Cheney says.

"You're not sure, though?"

239

"I'm not sure," she confirms. And she's not. She hopes he didn't though. Maybe her physical attraction to him is clouding her judgment.

"Did he smoke back then?" Solomon asks.

"It doesn't sound like it," Cheney says.

"What does that mean?"

"It means, he smoked once in a while, but not much. He's not really a smoker and never was. That's the best I could glean from him. Obviously, I couldn't ask him if he was smoking on his back porch when Jazzie Gonzalez took a bullet to the chest."

"I see," he says. "And that's why you think it wasn't him?"

"Well - that, and my gut. He doesn't seem like a murderer."

"What do you mean by that?"

How does she explain this? Is it because he's a big dog guy with two happy-faced Labrador Retrievers? Is it because he drove an old tavern-keeper home in a snowstorm? Is it because of the absence of malice in his eyes, in his kiss, in his scent? It's probably a combination of all of these things, none of which she cares to disclose to Solomon, so she says, "I don't know. I'm not sure how to explain it really."

"Well, did *I*?" Solomon asks.

She looks at him puzzled, and he clarifies without turning his head, focused on the roadway. "Did I seem like a murderer?"

"No," she says.

"That's how you knew that I didn't kill your husband, right?" he asks. "That's why you believed me and went out to go get the King to help you find the killer. It was your gut, right?"

"Yeah," she says. "Mostly, it was my gut."

"Then, you're probably right," he says. "I mean, you were right about me, so you're probably right about him. He's probably not the killer. So, she killed herself then? Is that what your gut tells you?"

"No," she says, staring out the side window, into the darkness. "I still think she was murdered: just not by him."

"So, who was it then? You said when he got to the house, she was supposedly dead on the back porch, right?"

"Yes."

"So, do you think it was some, like, random shit? Some dude that just broke into the house and shot her for the hell of it?"

"No," she says. "I think it was someone she knew."

"Who?"

"I don't know that. That's what I have to figure out."

"So, whatchya gonna do next then?"

"I'm meeting him for dinner Thursday night."

"What!? You gotta be kiddin' me. You're going on a date with this dude?"

"I guess you could call it that, but I prefer to refer to it as going undercover."

"On Valentine's Day? Are you fucking kidding me!? You're going to go out with this dude on the same night he shot and killed his girlfriend?"

"I told you, I don't think he killed her."

"Well, you did a few hours ago when you had me pick you up and drive you out here. C'mon, Miss Manning, you can't be serious? You're really going to go on a Valentine's Day date with this dude knowing that he might have killed a woman on Valentine's Day?"

"Yes."

"What if this dude is like a serial killer or somethin' and he gets off on killing women on Valentine's Day?"

"He's not a serial killer, Solomon," she insists.

Solomon just shakes his head. It's quiet in the car for a minute, before he speaks. "Miss Manning, are you feelin' okay? I mean you've got a lot of shit that you been through lately and I'm just wonderin' if maybe you aren't thinkin' straight. I know you probably don't want to talk about it, but there's talk that you busted into the Latin King house in Humboldt Park and threatened to shoot the whole place up and that's how you got Manuel Rodriguez to cooperate with you: and then that the two of you started gettin' it on together, you know what I'm sayin'?

"Now, I hope you're not pissed off at me or anythin' for tellin' you this, but this is what I've heard. And, I'm not sayin' that any of it's true: it's just what I've heard, that's all. And don't think I'm not grateful or anything, because I am. I really don't care how you ended up findin' out that it was Strozak who killed your husband and not me. I don't care if what they're sayin' is true or not, but I'm just sayin' that maybe you need to take a break from all of this private investigator shit, or whatever it is you're doin' for a while - take a break or somethin', maybe go on a cruise."

She soaks this all in, thinks about it for a while, and sighs. It's clear that Solomon is genuinely concerned about her, but his revelation about what people are saying concerning the situation with Manuel and her is disturbing. But it is not the rumors about how she coerced Manuel into cooperating with her investigation into Dan's murder that troubles her, particularly since it is rooted in truth; rather, it's the gossip about their relationship that she finds perturbing. The characterization of the two of them 'getting it on together' disturbs her. It's as if the phrase itself diminishes the depth of their relationship, which was, in truth, primarily emotional - and only minimally physical - in nature. She wants to defend herself, and defend Manuel, but instead, she remains silent.

After a few minutes or so, she says: "You're the second person who's tried to convince me recently that I should go on a vacation. My friend Lauren's on one right now and she tried to get me to go with her. Maybe I should have."

"Yes. Yes, that's what I'm sayin'. Maybe you should take a vacation or somethin' and get away from all of this murder and shit. Besides, who wants to be up here in Illinois this time of year anyway? Get away, go down to Miami or somethin'. Get some sun. You look like you could use some sun." He pauses, and she can tell he cares and is trying to help. "Anyway, Miss Manning, I just hope you're okay, that's all."

"I am, Solomon. Really, I am. And remember, you can call me Cheney. I'm not your lawyer anymore."

"Anyway, Cheney, it just seems like a good time for you to get away from all of this. I mean, didn't you tell me on the way out here tonight that you didn't even really like this Cassandra chick?"

"That's right: I said I used to not like her, but I also said she's kind of growing on me now."

"Well, it just doesn't make any sense to me," Solomon says, shaking his head, but still staring at the road. "I mean, I understand why you helped me out and all. You and I went way back to when I was just a kid and you were my lawyer all those years so we had a bond - I guess you could call it. And then, also, you had an interest in my situation, because it involved your husband. I mean, don't get me wrong: I'm not tryin' to say that you only stuck your neck out for me because you wanted to find out who killed him, but I'm just sayin' that it had somethin' to do with why you helped me. It had to of. But this situation: I just don't get it. I'm sorry. I don't. I just can't understand why you would be going around stirring up shit about some old case just to help out some lady you don't even like."

"It just feels like the right thing to do," she says softly. "Sometimes, you just got to do things that you might not really understand why you feel compelled to do them. That's how I feel about this, I guess. I told you on the drive out here that I used to not like Cassandra and that she treated me like shit in the past, and all of that is true. But it's also the past. Now, she seems changed, for the better. She seems like a different person now. She seems a lot nicer than she was.

"But maybe it's me. Maybe it's me who's changed. I don't know. Maybe the little things that used to irk me in the past, really don't matter anymore. Dan's death put a lot of things in perspective for me.

For whatever reason, Cassandra Cantoni just doesn't seem that bad anymore. Now she just seems like a person who needs help and I guess I feel like I'm the one who can help her."

"I still don't think it's a good idea for you to go meet this dude for dinner," Solomon says adamantly. "You don't know that he didn't kill that girl. Maybe he did. Maybe he'll think you're askin' too many questions and he'll do to you what he did to her."

"I'm going to be fine, Solomon. I'm not scared of him. I trust him."

"You don't even know this dude. How can you possibly trust him?"

Of course, Solomon is right. She really doesn't know Denny Rausch and there's no way she can really trust him at this point. There is an undercurrent within him, a cowboy-like reticence, that she can't quite pinpoint: it could be dangerousness, or it could be mysteriousness, or it could even be shyness. She's not really sure how to characterize his demeanor, or the reason for her reaction to it, but regardless, she finds it desirable – and distracting. His kisses and his touch are still on her mind, regardless of her ability to field the barrage of questions from Solomon during the ride. It will be nice to get home and to be alone to deconstruct these feelings about Denny Rausch that she finds exciting, but, nonetheless, confusing.

"How about I drive you again? I don't have plans on Thursday night anyway. Renee has to work and my mom can watch the baby. I'll come pick you up and take you again."

"No, no. It's okay, Solomon. I do appreciate it, though. I'm telling you, I'm not afraid of him. I'm going to be just fine."

"Well, I don't really get why you have to go out with him again. What's he gonna tell you that you couldn't have already asked him?"

"I don't know that I'll find anything more out, but I've got to try. I've got to find out who could've been in the house with Jazzie Gonzalez that night. If it wasn't him: who killed her?"

"Well, you don't really know for sure that it wasn't him. Like I said, this dude could be the one who killed her. It's also possible that the cops got it right all those years ago, and she shot herself. I mean, from what you've told me it sounds like the cops got it wrong or that maybe they were even covering it up for one of their own, but, maybe it went down just like they said it did. Maybe she did kill herself."

"Perhaps," she says.

"And don't you think if she didn't kill herself and he knew who killed her that he would've told the police back then?"

"Probably so," she says. "But maybe not."

"You mean maybe he's covering for someone else?"

"Possibly," she says. "Or maybe he doesn't know someone killed her, and he really believes it was a suicide."

"Maybe it was one of her ex-boyfriends or somethin'," Solomon says. "Or maybe it was Rausch's ex-wife. You said he was divorced, right?"

"Yes," Cheney says.

"Yeah; maybe she was jealous that he was dating some hot young babe and she came into the house and killed her on Valentine's Day. She might've even had a key to that house. Did Rausch live there before he was divorced?"

"I don't know that, but it wouldn't surprise me if he did," Cheney says.

"Did the police ever interview the ex-wife?"

"I don't think so," Cheney says. She likes where Solomon is going with this, as his brainstorming is helping her formulate the possibilities. When she gets home, she'll jot down some of his ideas.

"What about kids?" Solomon asks. "You said no one else lived in the house with him and Jazzie, but did Rausch have any kids?"

"He did actually," she says contemplatively. "The reports didn't have much in them about his kids. Their names were redacted because they were juveniles at the time. The reports indicated he had a daughter, but she was really young at the time, like ten or eleven and she lived with his ex-wife. And then, he also had a son who was in high school – I think he was like seventeen."

"And the son didn't live with them?"

"No. He lived with his mother too."

"In Meskwaki?"

"Yes," Cheney says.

"Maybe the son killed her because he was jealous of the attention that his father was giving to her. I could see that happening. Divorce can really fuck up kids. Maybe the son was like possessive of his dad or somethin' and blamed Jazzie for the divorce."

Interesting theory, yet unlikely to be correct. Cheney discounts it. She explains, "Rausch had been divorced from his ex-wife for a couple of years before he even met Jazzie. That's clear in the reports. So, there wouldn't be any reason for his son to bear a grudge against her, since Rausch didn't even know her when he was married."

"Don't matter," Solomon says. "What goes on in kids' brains is completely different sometimes than the truth. The son might have subconsciously blamed Jazzie for breaking up his family, even though it wasn't true. Or maybe he was just pissed that his dad moved on so quickly and felt that his dad abandoned him. Maybe he was angry at the dad for replacing his mom so fast. I'm guessin' your parents aren't divorced, or otherwise you would know some of this. You see, it's like this: Divorce fucks with kids' brains. I should know. I've been one of those kids who's had it happen to them. Unless your parents are divorced, you don't know what it does to you."

Solomon's right, of course. Her own parents have been married for thirty-five years, so she wouldn't know what it's like to be a child of divorce. Solomon gives her a perspective that is insightful, truthful, and raw. His words make her mind formulate, contemplate, analyze.

It's entirely possible that Dennis Rausch's ex-wife had a key to the house and shot Jazzie Gonzalez. Jealousy or revenge makes people do unimaginable things. And, as horrific as it is speculative, it's just as likely that it was his son, or even his daughter, who pulled the trigger that killed nineteen-year-old Jazzie Gonzalez.

# VALENTINE'S DAY

*February 14*[th]

The outfit she picks out for Valentine's Day dinner is one that Dan bought last spring for her at her favorite boutique in a small town in the western part of the state, not far from Iowa. They had gone out for a weekend trip to stay in the Desoto House Hotel in downtown Galena. The mid-nineteenth century hotel has a historical, and spectral, aura about it, being that it had served as Ulysses S. Grant's campaign headquarters.

It is rumored to be haunted, and during that particular trip, Cheney had an unusual experience herself, though she couldn't aver it was paranormal in nature. She had been sitting on a loveseat on the second-floor landing at the top of the magnificent winding staircase, writing poems past one in the morning, when the crystal chandelier began shuddering violently. The experience had caused Cheney to take her journal and head back to the hotel room, where Dan had been curled up snoring.

She had wanted to wake him up, but had resisted doing so, and in the morning, when they ate breakfast together in the indoor courtyard, she shared with him the strange occurrence with the chandelier. He had admitted that it was odd, but Dan had not been one who believed in the paranormal, so he had simply shrugged and said that it must have been from foot traffic upstairs or perhaps reverberations from the elevator. When Cheney had pointed out that it was so late, and that it was unlikely that anyone would have been riding the elevator at that hour, Dan had appeared skeptical and had asked: "So, you think it was a ghost, right?"

She had replied that she wasn't sure, but maybe it was. He had smiled and said, "C'mon, Cheney. You know there's no such things as ghosts."

Sometimes, she isn't so sure of that, particularly these days. Ever since Dan's death, she has become convinced that the individuals of the spirit world tend to interact with the living. There have been dozens of times when she has rolled over in the morning sensing Dan was there, or has gone to sleep physically feeling his arms around her. There have been times when she has caught a whiff of his aftershave or the scent of his sweat, and still other occasions, when she has walked into an unlit room, anticipating he will appear to her.

And one time, she had been asleep in bed, taking a nap, a few days before Christmas, when she had heard the unmistakable sound of his voice say her name. It woke her up from a sound sleep, and she had no doubt that she had heard him. Perhaps these were simply psychological effects of being traumatized by his death. Yet, it certainly seemed at times as if his spirit still lingered in the old farmhouse.

Because the outfit she decides to wear for her dinner with Dennis Rausch is one that Dan had bought her the preceding year, she hesitates at first in wearing it. It just kind of feels strange to do so, almost as if she is betraying Dan by wearing it on a date. But then again, this is not really a date: it's an undercover assignment. She's trying to solve a murder, not looking for romance. Still, though, she is attracted to Dennis Rausch, and this feeling of desire bothers her. Dan's death is too fresh, only three months' past, and it's too soon for her to get emotionally or physically involved with another man. She had been growing too close to Manuel in the weeks after Dan's murder, and she had tried to shut down that emotional attachment back then. Yet, there is still some residual guilt over her feelings toward Manuel that lingers. Instead of being intrigued by Dennis Rausch, what she really needs is time to mourn, a mental space to process Dan's death. But her life continues moving at such a hectic pace, and there never seems to be any sign of it slowing down.

"Oh, you look so beautiful," Kate gushes when she comes down the stairs into the kitchen. Kate is looking up from her laptop computer which she had retrieved from her apartment in DeKalb. "But pink? You never wear pink. It looks great on you."

The outfit is a blush-pink pantsuit, with a jacket and high-waisted skinny flares, paired with an oatmeal-colored slightly-cropped cashmere mock turtleneck, and a pair of beige suede booties. She accessorized with a rose-gold heart bracelet that Dan had bought for her as an anniversary gift and a matching triple-strand necklace. Kate is right. Pink is not her usual color, but she had wanted this outfit the moment she had seen it in the display window in downtown Galena. At the time, she had thought she would wear it on their next Valentine's Day together, not knowing then, that she would not have that opportunity.

Cheney thanks her and grabs a bottle of water for the road. Before she leaves, she studies her sister for a moment. Kate had her stitches removed in the morning before she drove back from DeKalb, and she is no long wearing any bandages. The harsh kitchen light exposes the jagged, healing wound at the top of the left side of her forehead, as well as the bald patch and raised red scab along the section of scalp from the most grievous wound. Still, Cheney is relieved that Kate's injuries were not more severe. The shorn hair will grow back, concealing the deepest damage, and any scar along her top forehead can be covered by the side swept bangs of the gloriously thick red locks. Yes, it could have been much worse: He could have killed her. Cheney shudders.

"Are you sure you're going to be okay without me tonight?" Cheney asks her sister.

"Yes. Yes. I'm fine. Go. Have fun. Enjoy yourself. You deserve it," Kate says cheerfully.

Still, something tells her she shouldn't go. Maybe she should text Dennis Rausch and let him know she has to cancel. She can reschedule for another night. But she is being silly to be so worried about Kate. Even though the house is secluded, there are multiple firearms in the house and Dan had given Kate shooting lessons years ago. Kate is actually a better shot than she is. Besides, Patton is here and someone would have to be insane to break into the house with the giant Rottweiler roaming around. But then again, this Nic guy seems like he is crazy: crazy and an asshole – not a good combination.

Ultimately, even though she has a sense that maybe she shouldn't, she leaves for the night. The drive is unremarkable as she heads toward Meskwaki. It hasn't snowed since Tuesday and there is only the slightest of winds, so the roads are clear. She worries about Kate being alone in the house, but she also is filled with a nervous energy with the thought of seeing Dennis Rausch again. There is a thrill to it all, pretending to be someone she isn't – the mysterious Hesperus Braun – and with the idea that no one knows she is going to meet with him other than Solomon.

She had been evasive when she had told Kate earlier in the day that she was going on a dinner date that night. When Kate had inquired, she had simply told her that her date was with an older man who was a retired police officer. She had also given Kate the name of the restaurant at which she was meeting him in Meskwaki. She thought she should provide Kate with just enough details so that, in case she didn't make it home safely, Kate would be able to give the police some information by which to find out what happened to her. Thankfully, Kate had seemed more surprised, as well as happy, that Cheney was actually going out for the night, as opposed to being curious for more information.

The only time Kate had pried a bit for details concerning her date, was on the topic of his age. "He's retired? How old is this guy?"

When Cheney had told her that he was in his mid-sixties, Kate had looked floored. "Far be it from me to judge anyone's dating selections, but I think that sounds kind of old for you, Cheney. Good heavens, you're only thirty-one! He's more than twice your age. I mean, he's older than Dad!"

"I know," Cheney had said. "You went out with that hockey player when you were only eighteen that was nearly twice your age."

"First of all – he wasn't just a hockey player. He was a Chicago Blackhawk," Kate had said. "But moreover, he was only in his thirties - not his sixties! Big difference! Unless this old cop looks like a movie star, I can't imagine dating anyone that old."

"Actually, he does kind of have a Lee Majors' way about him," Cheney had said wryly. "I've always had a thing for Lee Majors."

"Who's Lee Majors?"

"The Bionic Man," Cheney had said.

Kate had looked at her blankly.

"Heath from *The Big Valley*," Cheney had added.

Kate still had a look of cluelessness, and had started scanning her smartphone for images of Lee Majors.

"He was married to Farrah Fawcett," Cheney had said. When her sister had continued scanning her phone as though she had no idea about whom she was talking, Cheney had ended the conversation, "Just forget about it. Take my word for it: Lee Majors was a really good-looking man and he still is. Age doesn't mean a thing."

Besides her sister, she had also mentioned to Carmen the previous day that she was going out to dinner with a friend for Valentine's Day and so she would not be able to attend this week's Spinach Omelet Book Nerds' meeting. She had also confessed that she had not had time to read the assigned eight chapters anyway. Carmen had seemed disappointed, but had said she understood and Cheney promised that she would complete the reading assignment before the next meeting.

As for the person who would have the greatest interest in knowing she was going to dinner with Dennis Rausch – Cassandra Cantoni - Cheney had not revealed to her that she was doing so. When she had talked to Cassandra mid-week she had simply told her that she had met with the State's Attorney on Monday and that he would not agree to DNA testing of the cigarette butts without more evidence to support such a request. Cheney had not told Cassandra about her meeting with Jack Stahl, nor had she revealed to her that she had gone under-cover to Knee's Joint to meet Dennis Rausch. She hadn't wanted to get Cassandra's hopes up, when it seemed so unlikely that she would be able to find out anything to persuade Matthew Stockton to agree to DNA testing of the evidence. She thought it would be better for Casssandra to be surprised with positive information, if she were to uncover anything helpful, as opposed to having her hopes dashed.

Cheney has conflicting emotions about this meeting with Dennis Rausch. While the attempt to find information that would support DNA testing is her overarching goal, it really seems kind of pretextual at this point. The nervous energy she feels is not only borne of the covert nature of her mission, but also her excitement to be with Dennis Rausch again. He got to her in some way the other night: his dark eyes, his craggy features, the lean-aged body that looks great in a pair of jeans. She has thought about him a lot over the past couple of days, and the overriding feeling she has is one of desire. This feeling troubles her though: not only because, she had initially suspected he had murdered Jazzie Gonzalez, but also because it feels wrong to be attracted to a man so soon after Dan's death.

When she gets to his house, he greets her by coming out onto the stoop. He kisses her, intimately so, when she walks up the steps, almost as if this isn't a first date. He then says, "Happy Valentine's Day, Hesperus Braun. I thought you might be a no-show."

It is uncharacteristic of her to be late, but she had procrastinated before she had left, by talking to Kate. In truth, she had actually thought of canceling up until the moment she had pulled out of her driveway, particularly when Kate had mentioned the owls.

"I forgot to mention," Kate had said nonchalantly, "there were two owls hooting to each other that woke me up in the middle of the night: like two or three in the morning. I could hear them out there calling to each other. It was cool, but kind of eerie."

Those damn owls were back. The harbingers of death. The owls that Dan and she used to hear before he was murdered; the owls that Manuel had heard the night before he was killed. But Cheney had not mentioned any of this to Kate. Instead, she had just said, "Yeah, Dan and I used to hear them too."

Still, the thought of the owls returning had bothered her to a point of where she had lingered, afraid to leave her sister alone in the house and concerned about meeting with Dennis Rausch by herself. When she had finally left the house, she carried with her a nagging feeling of foreboding.

When Denny greets her at his door, she doesn't apologize for her tardiness, nor does she offer an explanation. She just says, "I was running a few minutes late and I don't text and drive."

He nods in acknowledgment and says, "I've got the truck warming up already. So, let's get going. They're booked tonight and I don't want them to give away our reservation."

When he holds the door for her and she gets into the front passenger seat of the trunk, she is greeted by the evergreen scent of the air freshener and the sound of classic rock. He looks over at her, kind of half smiles, and says, "By the way, you look beautiful. I should've told you that the moment I saw you standing on my porch."

"Thank you," she says. She thinks he might kiss her again, but instead he backs up, and heads toward the restaurant.

It's only about a five-minute drive to the Branded Blue Steakhouse, and he asks her if she's ever been there before.

"Yes, actually, I've been there before, but not in a while." She does not elaborate, but she and Dan had been to the restaurant together a handful of times, although it has probably been two or three years since they had last been there. "It's known as being one of the best steakhouses in the area," she adds.

"Yes, actually, I was friends with the old owner," he says. "He just moved down to Florida and it's under new ownership as of just last week. I'm hoping it's as good as it always was. Should be the same chef, from what I understand. I don't think the new owner brought in anyone new."

"Oh, I hadn't heard that the Branded was sold," she says. "I've been going there for years. My parents used to take my sister and I there when we were little kids."

"Yeah: some guy from Loomisville bought it. He owns some place in Loomisville that's supposed to be pretty good and another restaurant in Chicago."

Loomisville. Chicago. Is it possible that her favorite steakhouse has been purchased by that asshole who scarred her sister? She pauses before asking, "Have you met the new owner?"

"No, no. Not yet. This will be my first time going there since it switched hands."

"Do you know the name of the guy who bought it?"

"Yeah; it's Nic something: a Greek last name. Begins with a Z. I can't pronounce it, let alone remember it."

Unfuckingbelievable. What are the odds of this happening? She's never met Nic Zafeiropoulos, but, still, he may recognize her. The thought of this – combined with her utter contempt for him - makes her heart rate go up and her mind race, though she tries to calm her nerves. She and Kate certainly look a lot alike, but there are enough differences that he may not recognize her as Kate's sister. It's possible though, that he may have seen pictures of her on Kate's phone, or on Kate's social media pages. After all, even though Cheney only saw him from a distance in the driveway, she knows what he looks like, because Kate has shown her photos of him on her phone and from the Internet. It's entirely possible he saw photos of Cheney at some point. Still, even if he sees her and recognizes her, it is unlikely that he would approach her and engage her in conversation. After all, what would he say to her, "Are you the sister of the woman whose head I just sliced open with a beer bottle?"

She's so quiet, and staring out the window, such that Dennis Rausch must suspect something is wrong, because he asks her: "Why? Do you know him or somethin'?"

"No," she says truthfully. "I don't know him. I just heard of him, that's all."

"Oh?"

"Yeah," she adds, surprised that she is letting anger seep into her own voice. She doesn't know how she'll react if she sees this jagoff after what he's done to Kate. "He dated a friend of mine not that long ago. I heard he's a real asshole." As soon as she says it, she's concerned that she's revealed too much.

He doesn't show much of a reaction but he must sense the degree of anger in her voice, for he asks her if she wants to go somewhere else. He says that most places are going to be booked, but he has a friend who owns a fantastic steak restaurant in Hanley at which they could get a table. She knows the restaurant of which he is referring, and it is much more likely that she would run into someone she knows there than the Branded Blue Steakhouse, since the other restaurant is in Stickney County, and most of her friends and former colleagues live in that area.

"It's kind of a drive, but, if you don't mind waiting to eat, all it will take is a call," he offers.

"No, that's okay," she says. "Thank you, but I'd like to stick with where we're going."

And she does. She's apprehensive, but at the same time a part of her really wants to see this little weasel that wounded Kate. It would be satisfying to stare him in the eye and to unsettle him with her knowledge that she knows he is a piece of shit. It would be well worth it: even if it might mean blowing her cover.

# MOONLIGHT

*February 14*[th]

She never sees anyone who looks remotely like Nic Zafeiropoulos while they're at the Branded Blue SteakHouse, and, after a couple of beers, her edginess wears off such that she stops panning the restaurant trying to find him. Instead, she relaxes and settles in for dinner, enjoying the conversation with Dennis Rausch, while at the same time, waiting for an opportunity to ask questions about his past.

The segue comes naturally from his questioning of her. They are eating her favorite appetizer, Oysters Rockefeller, and they are sitting near a window overlooking the ice-covered Fox River. When he looks at her, she is uneasy at times, from either guilt, fear or passion, or perhaps all of these things. She's not sure exactly. There is a directness about him that she appreciates, but at the same time, she worries he may be able to see through her charade.

He tells her: "I'm surprised a gorgeous girl like you was available on Valentine's Day. I figured you must have a boyfriend or a husband. I was sure you were going to text me and say you had plans tonight and had to cancel or that you would just ghost me altogether."

She smiles, coyly so. "No."

"So, what's your story, Hesperus Braun?"

"What do you mean?" she asks.

"Well, it sounds like you're single. Are you divorced? Any kids?"

This is easy. "Yes, I'm obviously single or I wouldn't be here tonight. No - I'm not divorced. And – No - I don't have any kids. How about you?"

"I'm divorced. Two kids: both grown."

"Oh," she says, feigning ignorance. "How long have you been divorced?"

"Oh, God, what's it been? Thirty-four years? Something like that. I've probably been divorced longer than you've been alive."

"Yep," she says. "I'm thirty-one."

"I figured you were somewhere around there, late twenties, early thirties."

"I take it that your kids are older than me?"

"Oh, hell, yeah. They're older than you, by a lot. My son is – what is he now? – he would be, uh, forty-seven; yeah, forty-seven. It's hard to believe. My son is almost fifty. And then my daughter, Lilly, she just turned forty a few months ago. She's an insurance adjuster downtown. Lives in Lincoln Park. She's like you: not married, no kids. Calls herself a career woman."

"So, your son, what does he do?"

"Not much, that one, unfortunately," he says. "He's kind of job hopped a bunch over the years."

"You, said your daughter lives in Lincoln Park, but you didn't mention where your son lives. Does he live in Chicago too?"

"No. The last I heard he was living in McNamee. I don't talk to him much, you see." He pauses and his jaw flinches a bit. "You don't have kids, so I don't know if you'll understand this: but you don't ever want your child to feel like you're disappointed in him. You try never to communicate that to a child. It's kind of part of being a good parent. But, my son, you see, I've tried over the years to get through to him, and he's kind of gone down a different path: one I don't much agree with. I saw it coming when he was a kid, but by the time I tried to change it, it was probably too late. He didn't want to hear any advice from me. He's pretty hard-headed: maybe too much like his old man, who knows? Anyway, we haven't talked to each other in years."

"I'm sorry," she says.

"Hey, nothin' to be sorry for. It's just the way it is."

"Do you have any grandchildren?" she asks.

"No. Well, at least none that I know of. It's possible that Jason's had a child and I wouldn't even know. As I said, we haven't talked in years."

"Were you ever close?" she pries.

He looks like he may be putting some walls up; she sees his jaw clench, but then relax a bit when he takes a drink. He puts his glass down and says, "Yes. When he was a kid, we were. We both loved base-ball. I was his coach when he was growing up. Jason was a great fielder, and a pretty good pitcher. He was an over-the-fence hitter: the kind of batter who either hits a homer or strikes out. But then, when he hit high school, he quit all sports. Well, actually, I think he played his freshman year, but after that, he quit. Started smoking dope and drinking beer. Didn't do much of anything but that for four years, except play video games and listen to music. Spent more time in the detention hall than he did in his classes. His mother couldn't handle him and he came and lived with me for a while, but Jason never cared for my rules much, so he moved back home."

"When was that?"

A strange look flashes in his eyes when she asks the question, and she can't tell if it's suspicion, annoyance, or a struggle to recall, but, none-theless, he answers. "Part of his junior year, I think. Could've been his sophomore year, but I'm pretty sure it was when he was a junior. Why do you ask?"

"Just curious, that's all," she says. "I find human relationships, par-ticularly between parents and children, to be interesting. I'm a writer, so I tend to ask a lot of questions of people that maybe other people wouldn't ask. I'm sorry if I went too far."

"No worries," he says, and takes a drink.

It is evident, though, that even if he loosens up from a couple glasses of whiskey, that he's got too much cop in him for her to ask questions about whether Jason smoked cigarettes without him shut-ting down altogether. Besides, she was able to get enough information tonight which will be helpful: his son's name, by which she'll be able to track him down. Also, the disclosure that Jason was troubled in high school and that he smoked marijuana are factors which would suggest that he likely was a cigarette smoker too, though not necessarily.

After dinner, they take a walk along the concrete path that parallels the river. It comes naturally when he takes her by the hand. It just feels right, and this surprises her and excites her in a way, almost as if she is back in junior high when a boy first held her hand. It's the first relatively warm night in weeks, as it is in the low forties and there is only the slightest of winds. The moon is spectacular over the river, suspended in the dark blue suburban skyline like a child's finger-painting of a winter nighttime scene.

The path is not long, for it butts up against private property, and there is a cul-de-sac pavement area for cyclists to make U-turns. The moon is so remarkable in the clearing, and they stand for a minute silently looking out over the silvery ice-bound river. He takes his smartphone out of his jacket, scans it for a moment, as if searching for something.

Once he finds what he is looking for, he looks around the circle and says, "No ice patches. This is the perfect spot for a Valentine's evening dance."

"Oh, I'm not much of a dancer," she says, and she isn't.

But he faces her anyways, and looks her deeply in the eyes, and says, "Don't worry. I'll do the leading."

"That's my problem," she says. "I always want to lead."

"Well, we'll change that," he says. "I won't let you."

He starts playing *Moondance* by Van Morrison, and he puts his smartphone back into his pocket, taking both of her hands. He leads her

265

through a makeshift hybrid waltz kind-of fox trot, and she can tell he is an excellent dancer, for he even makes her feel like she is not awful at it. More than once though, he kind of jingles her wrist a bit, reminding her gently not to fight him and to let him lead. Not only can the man dance, but he can sing too, and he serenades her to the Irish rock balladeer's song as he twirls and guides her along.

When he finishes, he kisses her briefly on the lips and then says, "Not bad for a girl who can't dance."

"I tried to lead the entire time," she admits.

"I know, but I wouldn't let you," he says. "You were doing better toward the end."

They linger in the area, holding hands, and she comments about how clear one can see the man on the moon.

"Man? How do you know it's a man and not a woman?" he jokes.

"I guess I don't," she says.

"You're one of these twenty-first century types. I would've thought you would have referred to it as the gender-neutral 'person on the moon', and not used a sexist phrase like an old outdated grouchy guy like me would use."

"Oh, I don't think you're old, and you're certainly not grouchy," she says.

"Sometimes I think I've lived way beyond my expiration date," he says gloomily. "I'm pretty out of sync with what's going on in society right now. Time is just kind of passing me by at a rapid pace: leaving me behind, I suppose."

"Oh, I wouldn't say you're past your expiration date," she says. "You can still dance well, you can still sing well, and I'm guessing you can probably still do some other things pretty well, too."

"Like what, Hesperus Braun?" he asks.

But she blushes, and turns away. She's not really one for engaging in coy sexual banter, so she really isn't sure how to move past her last comment. It is so unlike her to make that type of remark, so she is uncomfortable, wanting to change the topic.

Thankfully, he doesn't continue along the opening she gave him, and when she doesn't respond to his teasing question, he returns to the topic of age. "It's just that – when you get to this age, it doesn't feel like there's a lot of time left. My parents are gone. My brothers are both gone. All my first cousins, gone. I've got a lot of friends who are gone too. Some by cancer, others by gunshot. I know a lot of coppers who've killed themselves after they retired: good friends of mine. It kind of pisses me off really. I'm angry at them. I wish they were still here."

She wonders if he'll open up about Jazzie Gonzalez, but she doesn't have to speculate for long, because he starts talking about her. "I had a girlfriend once: a beautiful girl like you – she shot herself."

"Oh," Cheney says. "I'm sorry." And she is. But not only does she feel empathetic, a part of her feels guilty for having deceived him: not guilty enough to tell him the truth though. Instead, she just listens, soaking it all in, storing it away.

"Yeah, she shot herself with one of my guns. Shot herself in the heart. Today's the thirtieth anniversary."

"Oh my God," Cheney says, feigning shock. "I'm so sorry. She killed herself on Valentine's Day?"

"Yes," he says. "I was coming home from work. We were supposed to go out to dinner that night: actually, to this same restaurant. It was her favorite place. I found her on the back deck off the second story. Bullet wound to the chest. She was dead when I found her. It had been snowing, and it was clinging to her face and her hair. She had black hair, real long like, the most beautiful hair. It was like a pretty pony's tail. That's what I used to call her, 'mi poni bonita.'

"When I found her laying there, she was on her back, dressed to go out. Her eyes: they were wide open. She had these brown eyes that just grabbed you, ya' know? And they were just staring up at me: like she was waiting for me to close them for her, to let her sleep, to let her go." He chokes a bit, and it seems as though he is about to start crying, but he doesn't. He seems to catch himself and he just says, "But you don't want to hear about all this. That's not what you came here for: This is your night. I shouldn't be talkin' about the past."

"It's okay," Cheney says, touching his arm. "It's part of you, part of who you are. I'm glad you told me. What was her name?"

"Jasmine Gonzalez. But we all called her Jazzie. Jazzie Gonzalez." He pauses. "Do you believe in love at first sight?"

"Yes," Cheney says.

"Well, that's how I felt about Jazzie. The first time I laid eyes on her, I fell in love with her and that's what she used to tell me too. That she fell in love with me as soon as she saw me. She was one helluva girl, one helluva girl."

"Do you know why she killed herself?" Cheney asks.

And when he looks out over the sleeping river, he seems mesmerized and he is silent for a moment. When he speaks, his voice, though a whisper, is filled with anger.

He does not seem to be addressing Cheney, but rather, a ghost: "Jazzie Gonzalez. Jazzie Goddamn Gonzalez. I wish I knew. I have no fucking clue why you did what you did. No fucking clue at all."

# DISTRUST

*February 14th*

When they reach his driveway, she already has made up her mind that she is going to go into his house if he invites her inside. When he pulls up in his truck, she notices a car parked about fifteen yards down the street, on the opposite side of the road. It's a black Grand Am with tinted windows: just like the one that Solomon Wilson drives.

Is it possible that Solomon has followed her here tonight? No. It is so unlikely. He wouldn't have done that. It's Valentine's Day night and Solomon has more important things to do than conduct surveillance of her date with Dennis Rausch. But then again, it's strange that a car that looks like Solomon's is parked so close to Rausch's house. But with the tint on the windows, she can't even tell if anyone is in the car, let alone identify anyone, and she doesn't want to stare, because to do so might cause Dennis Rausch to get suspicious.

Instead of the living room couch, this time they end up in his bedroom, with the door shut to keep the dogs out. Between his kisses and his guiding, she finds herself lying on his waterbed with amplified seventies and eighties rock in the background. He turns the overhead lights off, but leaves on a floor lamp near his closet that casts a partial glow over the room. She has never been on a waterbed before, and she makes a joke about it when its squishy insides give way to her weight.

"You really do like the 1970s," she teases.

271

"What?"

"This waterbed. I've never been on one of these before. I didn't even know they made these things anymore."

"Yeah, they don't make a lot things that they should anymore," he says, and then kisses her. "But they still make waterbeds. Not many. But they do."

Outside of having removed her pink suit jacket when she first came into the house, she is fully clothed; she intends on staying that way, so it was probably a bad idea to join him in his bed. His touches move her to a point of near-ecstasy, despite that her clothes are a barrier to his roaming hands. His kisses are steady, assuring, passionate, and they compel her to reciprocate in stroking him too. He moves quickly, this time starting with her pants, instead of her bra, but when he goes to unzip her pants along the side, she gently stops him with her hand. This touch- and-go continues to amp up, and she is getting lost in the feel of it all, until he loops around and tries again with the zipper. This time, she stops kissing him, takes his hand, and says, "I'm sorry. I'm just not ready for this yet."

He doesn't say much, just that he understands, and he brushes her hair away from her eyes, strokes her face, looks at her lovingly, and kisses her again on the lips. She is falling for this man, and it confuses her, and excites her, and frustrates her, all at the same time. She wants to tell him – well, she wants to tell him a lot of things, but she doesn't. She kisses him for a while, lets him hold her; and ultimately, they both fall asleep, fully clothed, in each other's arms.

When she wakes up, she sees on his digital clock that it's almost eleven-thirty. She needs to get going. Kate is probably going to be worried about her, as she had told Kate before she had left that she thought she'd be home by ten or ten-thirty at the latest. She tries to rise out of the bed without waking him, but with the movement and the sloshing, he rouses too and gets up with her. She tells him that she's sorry, but she has to get back home.

He follows her into the living room and she scoops up her blush-pink jacket from the back of one of the leather chairs, and then heads toward the front closet. When she gets there, she sits down on the steps, pulls her boots on, and starts opening up a little bit, offering some truth: "I don't know if you remember me telling you, but my sister is staying with me for a while."

"Yeah, I do," he says, leaning up against the wall next to the front door, arms crossed, watching her. It is evident he really doesn't want her to leave.

"Anyway, I've got to get home to make sure she's okay," she explains. "I don't like leaving her alone for too long. I hadn't told you this part, but, you see, she was in a situation last weekend where someone struck her with a beer bottle in the head."

He looks concerned, shifts his weight in his feet, keeps his arms crossed. He brushes his hand through his dark, silvery hair. "Your sister was in a bar fight?"

"No," she says. "Unlike me, my sister tends to avoid bars. It was a domestic."

"Oh," he says. "Her husband?"

"Boyfriend," she says.

"Is she okay?"

"As okay as she can be. She had a concussion, but she's doing okay now. She's got two pretty nasty cuts: one on her scalp and the other on her forehead. They're healing okay and she got the stitches out yesterday. She's gonna have scars, but it could've been much worse. She should be able to cover up the scars with her hair. At least that's what we hope.

"She's an actress," she continues. "A stage actress: you know, just college stuff for now. She's majoring in theater at NIU. And, she's done some modeling: not like a runway or magazine model, but she's into all of that social media influencer stuff. She's got like some ungodly amount of followers on her social media pages. And right now, she's just going through a lot, trying to heal really. Just keeping private, hanging out at my house. It's all been real rough on her."

"Is the s.o.b. in jail?"

"No," she says. "He bonded out almost right away."

"You said you live out in the country, right?"

"Yes."

"Are you going to be okay out there: just the two of you – if he shows up?"

"Yes," she says definitively. "I've got guns. I've got Patton. We'll be just fine."

"Well, if you ever need me to come stay out there with you and keep an eye on you, as long as you don't mind two big dogs coming with me, you just let me know."

"I appreciate that, really," she says. There's some irony in her drawing comfort in an offer of protection from a guy whom she only a few days ago thought might be a murderer. She kind of smiles at that thought, and he picks up on it and asks her, "What?"

"Oh, nothing," she says.

When he keeps watching her, waiting for her to explain, she stands up, takes her coat and hat out of the closet and says, "It's just nice that you are willing to do that, when we've only known each other for a couple of days."

He steps forward and buttons her coat for her, and then puts his hand under her chin, looking her in the eyes. "It feels like I've known you a lot longer than that."

"Me too," she says. And it's true. It does feel like she's known him for years.

He kisses her again, and then insists that she give him the keys and that she wait inside while he goes outside to scrape her windows and warm up her truck. He jogs upstairs, lets the big dogs out, and the Retrievers come barreling downstairs, gathering joyously around Cheney. She leans down to pet and hug them, while he quickly throws on his jacket and boots. When the dogs and he leave to go out front, she hesitates for a few seconds before she decides to walk upstairs. If he comes back inside before she comes down, she'll just explain that she was looking for a bathroom, that she guessed that there may be one at the head of the stairs on the second floor, and that she thought it might be quicker to just go up there than to go to the first-floor bathroom.

When she gets upstairs, she scans the open loft area above the dining room with built in bookcases against the righthand wall and a couple of cozy cloth-covered chairs. To the left is a doorway, and she flicks on the light and sees a small bedroom and a second door that is ajar within it; and which she assumes leads to a bathroom. She doesn't go inside though. She turns the switch off and heads to the far wall above the kitchen and opens the sliding-glass door. She doesn't turn the light on for the deck, and instead walks out onto the suspended platform in the dark, though the moonlight partially illuminates its expanse. It is strange, but she feels compelled to do this, to visit the site where Jazzie Gonzalez either shot herself or was shot by someone else thirty years ago. Maybe while standing here in this place where the violence occurred, Jazzie's spirit will send to her a sign of some sort. Perhaps it will arrive as an image, or a sound, or an intuition, that will lead her to the truth about what happened here.

When she moves across the wooden deck and stands in the area where Jazzie's body was found, she closes her eyes, and tries to imagine what happened that night. She wills herself to see, compels herself to feel, what fury, what hostile hand took the young dispatcher's life. She feels anxious, and she can hear her own breath, but she neither sees, nor senses, anything beyond her own heartbeat.

She jumps when she hears the sound of the giant canines bounding out onto the porch, and she opens her eyes. He is walking out behind his dogs, and he looks pissed off.

"What are you doing out here?" he asks and there's an edge to his voice that she hasn't heard before. It is evident that he is suspicious, as well as a bit angry, and he has reason to be both. She is standing out on the spot where he found the bloodied body of his girlfriend thirty years ago, and this is likely to evoke some negative reaction. For the first time around him, she is fearful. What if she is wrong about him and he did kill Jazzie Gonzalez? What if he suspects she is probing into the old case and decides he is going to stop her from doing so? What if that old Meskwaki gossip about his violent temper is true?

"I just---I just—". She can't use the bathroom excuse. She has to make up a reason why she went outside. "I just came to get some fresh air. I came up here to use the bathroom, and then, for some reason, I felt dizzy and real hot all of a sudden: almost like I was going to pass out. Maybe I'm coming down with a flu bug or something."

"I thought maybe you came out here to smoke or somethin'," he says and he holds her eyes, studying her.

"Oh, no," she says. "I was just getting some fresh air. That's all."

"For someone who's just quit smoking, you sure don't seem to get that itch very much. You haven't mentioned wanting to smoke all night."

She smiles and takes out a pack of cigarettes from one of her pockets, holds them up weakly. "Will of steel. But I've got 'em right in here if I fold. Just like a pacifier."

It is evident he is on to her, but yet his stream changes course, and his eyes gentle a bit. "Do you think you're going be okay to drive?"

"Yeah. Yeah, I'll be fine," she says.

"Are you sure you don't want to go lay back down for a bit?" he asks.

"No. No. I really need to get home to check on my sister," she insists.

"Well, let me at least get you a bottle of water," he says.

"No, no, that's okay. I feel fine now. Really, I do."

They walk together back into the house, the two dogs bounding in front of them, and he shuts the sliding glass door, resolutely. He looks over at her and she can tell he is gauging whether to buy into the story that she just told him. He probably wants to believe her, but he seems to be struggling to do so.

"Why'd you come up here?" he asks. "Why didn't you just use the bathroom on the first floor?"

"I just figured there was a bathroom on the second floor, and that it'd be quicker to just come up here, since I was at the stairs anyway."

He just nods, says nothing, and they head down the stairs. He doesn't believe her: it's clear from his eyes. Regardless though, he doesn't ask her any more questions and, when she leaves the house, he follows her to the truck to make sure she gets inside okay. She notices the black car still parked on the other side of the road, but she tries not to stare at it, because she doesn't want to draw his attention to it. He kisses her one more time before she gets into her vehicle; and when she pulls away, he is standing outside under the garage door lights, his arms crossed, with his two dogs alongside him.

There is a pang, a guilty longing that she feels, almost as if she may never see him after she pulls out of his driveway. But then again, she probably won't. After all, there's no reason to arrange another meeting with him at this point. She has all the information she needs from him. Maybe it's the kisses, maybe it's the riverside dance, maybe it's the way he looks in a pair of jeans. Whatever it is, chalk it up to instinct, but she's convinced that he's not the killer. It's time to move on to her next suspect: Jason Rausch.

# COINCIDENCE

*February 15*[th]

She's two stop signs away from Denny Rausch's house, when she pulls over into a poorly-lit parking lot by the river. The black Grand Am pulls in behind her, but she's not afraid, because she's certain that it's Solomon following her. She's right.

He walks up to her passenger side door and she hits the unlock button. "C'mon, Solomon, I told you that you didn't have to worry about me."

"Don't matter, Miss Manning," he says, rubbing his gloveless hands together. "I was going to worry about you anyway. No way I was going to let you go to some killer's house without me watching your back."

"Were you at the restaurant, too?" she asks.

"No," he says. "Just the house. I waited for you there. I drove by there a little after seven and saw your truck parked there, and I figured you must have left it there and went with him to dinner, and that you would have to come back to get your truck."

"Well, you were right," she says. "But I can't believe you sat out there for hours waiting for me. You should have been taking Renee out for Valentine's Day."

"Like I said, she had to work anyway," he says. "So, it was no problem – no problem at all. I had my laptop with me and I had a bunch of reading to do for class. I got a lot done while you were in there. But I tell you this: I wasn't gonna wait much longer though. I was about to go knock on his door right when you came out. You were in there so long, I thought he might've pulled a Jazzie Gonzalez on you."

He's clearly trying to help, but still the comment about Denny killing Jazzie Gonzalez gets to her. "I told you he didn't kill Jazzie Gonzalez," she insists.

"You told me you thought he didn't, but you weren't sure," he reminds her.

"I'm sure now," she says definitively.

"So, who killed her then?"

"Well, you got me thinking about his son," she says. "I found out more about him tonight, and I think your instincts may have been right."

"Really?" he says, looking pleased.

"Yes," she says.

"Whatdya' find out?"

"Well, that he lived with his dad for a bit when he was in high school, but it doesn't sound like it was during the time frame that Jazzie lived there: it sounds like he lived there a year or so before she was killed. And he smoked a lot of dope, which means that he probably was a cigarette smoker."

"You didn't find out if he smoked cigarettes?"

"No," she says. "And I couldn't ask because I think he would've found it too odd if out of the blue I asked him if his son used to smoke cigarettes thirty years ago."

"Yeah, yeah. I get that," he says. "But just because he smoked dope, don't mean that he smoked cigarettes."

"True," she says, "but a person who smokes pot probably smokes cigarettes too."

"Not necessarily," he says. "I know a lot of people who smoke dope, but who don't smoke cigarettes."

"Okay, well, I'm still thinking there is a possibility that he is the person who was on the back porch with Jazzie."

"What else makes you think that?"

"Well, you got me thinking when you talked about children of divorce. I think you might be on to something. There are some indicators from what his father says that his son was troubled in high school; and, if I have the time-frame right, it sounds like his troubles started right around after his parents got divorced."

He doesn't look impressed with her detective work. "Anything else?"

"I've got nothin'," she says. "Oh, except my gut."

"We're back to the gut, then?" he jokes.

"Yes," she says.

"Well, that may be all you got," he says smiling, "because this really doesn't sound like much to go on, Cheney."

"It's not," she says. "But I know his name now, so I can do some digging."

"What's his name?"

"Jason. Jason Rausch."

As soon as she says it, Solomon starts searching on his smartphone. Seconds later, he finds a picture on a social media account and shows it to her. "This is a Jason Rausch in McNamee. That him?"

"It's gotta be," she says, studying the image. His face is fleshy; he's got a scruffy goatee and mustache, a load of tattoos on his arms and one on his neck, and the look of a guy who has spent most of his adulthood in taverns. There are some slight physical similarities between the unattractive chubby son and his handsome father. Something about the eyes. Same color, same shape, same thick eyebrows.

"He's a lot heavier than his dad, but I can see the resemblance," she says. "And he's about the right age: late forties."

"Yeah, he looks like a doper," Solomon says, still scanning, studying his phone. "And he's a dumbass too, because he's got his social media all public – no privacy controls on - so I can see everything about him."

Cheney has her own smartphone out too, and she is scanning as well. There are lots of pictures of Jason Rausch on his social media pages drinking beer and smoking cigarettes. She holds one up to Solomon.

"Bingo," she says.

"Don't mean he smoked thirty years ago," he says dismissively.

"True," she replies. "But again, it's just one more indicator that it was more likely him on that back porch than his dad."

"He works at Foxy's Tail," Solomon says, staring at his phone. "Claims he's the bar manager: At least, if this is current." He tilts his phone toward Cheney and she can see Jason Rausch's profile on his phone.

"That's just bizarre," Cheney says.

"Why's that?"

"Because that's the same bar that Jazzie Gonzalez worked at before she quit and became a dispatcher. Different name now, but same bar. It used to be called Hijinks back then. Just a strange coincidence." She is scanning her phone and she says, "He *does* still work there. He's working there tonight."

She holds up one of Jason Rausch's social media pages and plays a fifteen-second video of him doing shots with a couple of overtly-intoxicated patrons. "This was just posted an hour ago," she says.

"So, what do we do next?" he asks.

"I've got to call home and check on my sister," she says. "But if you have time to swing by McNamee with me, let's go see if we can go get us some DNA evidence."

"How are we going to do that?" he asks.

"I know that bar. I haven't been there in a few years, but a lot of the Loomisville cops used to hang out there. Once in a while they would have a party there. Even though neither Dan nor I were smokers, some of his co-workers were. I remember how they used to hang out on the side of the building smoking with the servers. Sometimes we'd stand out there too with them."

"Don't you think it's kind of late to be doin' that? It's past midnight."

"No," she says. "This is the best time to go. They'll be winding down for the night, closing soon." She can see he is weighing whether to go to the bar or to head home and she asks, "Are you in?"

"Yeah," he says. "I'm in."

They drive separately to Foxy's Tail, and she calls Kate on the way.

"I hope I didn't wake you up," she says.

"You didn't at all," Kate replies sleepily. "I was just watching TV downstairs."

"Is everything going okay?" Cheney asks. "I'm probably not going to be home for the next couple of hours."

"Everything's fine," Kate says. "I take it your date is going well then?"

"Yes," Cheney says. "Actually, it's going great."

"Well, I've got to hear more about this guy when you get home."

"Oh, don't wait up for me. Like I said, it may be past two until I get there."

"I may anyway," Kate says. She is probably scared to fall asleep in the creaky old farmhouse without anyone with her, and Cheney feels guilty about that. At least she has Patton with her.

"Well, I'll be home as soon as I can," Cheney says.

"Don't rush, Cheney," Kate insists. "Enjoy your time with him."

Cheney pulls in alongside Solomon in the lot and ends her call with Kate. They have each parked advantageously with a view of the side of the building, and Cheney leaves her truck and gets into the passenger seat of Solomon's car.

"What do we do now?" he asks.

"We wait," she says.

And they don't end up having to do so for very long, before it's less than fifteen minutes later, when Jason Rausch appears on the side of the bar and lights up a cigarette near the commercial garbage can. It's unmistakably him: goatee, pudgy face, round body, neck tattoo. He's taller though than he looks in the photos: maybe six-feet or six-one even. He's with two other people – a young woman and a man – both of whom look like they're probably employees. All three are smoking: at times looking like they are arguing, and at other times, laughing. The woman, in particular, is animated, flailing her arms on occasion as if angrily describing some incident.

"How are we gonna know which cigarette butt to pick up?" he asks. "All three are smoking."

"I see that," she says. "We just gotta watch closely and see where he puts his down."

All three of them finish smoking around the same time. The woman cuts over to a cigarette dispensary stand near the building, rubs her cigarette down into the sand, and disposes of it; the man follows her and does the same. Jason Rausch on the other hand, simply flicks his butt carelessly down on the cement, and then stomps on it with his right foot.

"Now what?" Solomon asks.

"Do you have any napkins?"

"There should be some in the console," he answers.

There are: when she lifts up the console, she takes out a napkin, and folds it neatly in her pocket.

"We're going to go up there and just smoke ourselves," she explains. "I'll just flick mine down on the ground near his when I'm through smoking, and then I'll pick his up and put it in this napkin."

"Isn't your DNA gonna be on it?"

"Maybe," she says. "But they can always exclude my profile if they have to eliminate it."

"Won't mine be on there from those napkins in my car, along with the fast-food worker's DNA who gave them to me?"

"Again, maybe - but then again, maybe not," she says. "It depends. But the bottom line is that Jason Rausch's DNA will likely be on there, because he was actually putting the cigarette into his mouth. They should be able to get a DNA sample of his from the cigarette to compare up against the DNA on the butts from thirty years ago."

"How we gonna pretend we're smoking when we don't have any cigarettes?" he asks.

She takes the pack out of her pocket and he looks surprised. "I didn't know you smoked," he says.

"I don't," she says. "I brought this pack along as part of my cover."

"Got it," he says. "Well, let's go. I don't have all night. Renee's probably home already from work, wonderin' where the hell I'm at. She texted me about a half an hour ago, and I just told her that I had somethin' to do for the next couple of hours. She didn't text me back after that, which means she's pissed."

Cheney doesn't remind him that he showed up tonight without invitation and that she had encouraged him to stay home in the first place. After all, she's relieved he's here. It's much safer having someone do this alongside her, and, besides, she enjoys the camaraderie between her and her former client. It is refreshing to be around him when he's not behind bars, and when his young life seems on such a positive and inspirational path. It is nice to see him so interested in criminal justice and enthusiastic about his educational studies. Perhaps Solomon's involvement with the investigation into the thirty-year old case could be viewed as a kind of mentoring program. Hopefully, though, she is not doing any damage to his trek toward obtaining a career in the field, since this informal, and dangerous investigation is unorthodox and certainly not one that would be endorsed by his community college professors.

The entire operation only takes about five minutes and they are back in their respective vehicles. Cheney places the napkin with the cigarette butt gingerly down on her passenger-side seat and then texts Solomon, "Thx."

He writes back to her: "What now?"

She texts: "We need to come back tmrw. I need to talk to Jason and try to get info. from him before I go to the SA."

Solomon's reply text reads: "Can't you just take the cig in to SA and get him to test it?"

"No," Cheney writes back. "We still don't have enough. We need more. He'll never agree to DNA testing without more."

Solomon's reply is: "More what????????"

"Not sure yet," she writes, "but we need more of *it* whatever *it* is." She tops off her text with a smiley-face emoji.

"What time tmrw?" he texts.

"Late."

"How late?"

"Does midnight work?" she texts.

His reply text is a thumbs-up emoji.

She texts: "C you then."

When she goes to back the truck out of the parking lot she turns on the radio, and is surprised what song is playing: Van Morrison's *Moondance*. She smiles at the coincidence of it all, the thought of Dennis Rausch gliding across the bike trail's cul-de-sac under a wintertime moon. She hadn't heard this song in years until Dennis Rausch sang it to her, and now it just happens to be playing on her radio. This has got to be an omen of some sort. She just hopes that it's a good one.

# ROSES

*February 15*[th]

She passes an ambulance with its lights and sirens on when she approaches the hill on the road less than a quarter of a mile from her property, and immediately she has a sinking feeling of doom. As she reaches an unobstructed view of her driveway, a sheriff's squad car pulls out without its emergency lights oscillating, and heads east in the same direction as the ambulance. This cannot be good. It could be Kate in that ambulance. Her sister could be injured or dead. But even though her heart is pounding, she is strangely calm, almost like she was when the police came to her house in the middle of the night to tell her that Dan had been killed.

There is still another squad parked in her driveway, up toward the house, and she recognizes John Hardy's truck parked behind it, but there is no one outside. It is almost like she is moving in slow motion, but she knows she isn't. She parks her truck, and jogs in her suede boots toward the house, unconcerned about slipping on the slick driveway. It is as if she is trapped in a dream, one in which everyone around her that she loves dies.

But when she enters the house, Kate jumps up from the loveseat and hugs her. She is dressed in sweats and slippers, and her long hair is pulled back in a pony-tail, with her wounds exposed. Cheney puts both of her hands on the side of her face, and looks her in the eyes, "You're okay?"

291

"Yes. Yes -I'm fine," Kate assures her.

John Hardy is standing there too, with his warm and sympathetic eyes, looking concerned, and a bit awkward, as if he's trying to figure out whether he should leave the two of them alone to talk privately.

Now that she's done an assessment of Kate, her next thought is of her dog. "Where's Patton?"

"Oh, he's fine," Kate says. "He's in the first-floor bedroom with the door closed. I put him there before the deputies came so that he wouldn't scare them."

"What happened? Where are the deputies?"

"They're in the kitchen interviewing Dax," Kate says. "They've already interviewed us," she says, gesturing to John Hardy, "and now they're just finishing up with him."

"What happened, Kate? Who's in that ambulance?"

"It's Nic," Kate says. "He showed up pounding on the door, screaming at the top of his lungs, threatening me that I needed to open it. And I knew that the sheriff wouldn't be able to get here in time before he broke it down or shattered a window, so I called Dax and he and his dad came here right away. He pulled a gun on them, Cheney. He shot at them."

"What? Is Dax okay?" she asks John.

"Yes," John says calmly. "He's fine, but my truck isn't. I've got a windshield that looks like it took a piece of concrete. But I'd much rather it be my truck than my boy."

"He shot at you when you guys were in the truck?" Cheney asks, astonished at what she is hearing.

"No, actually, we were already out of the truck and heading toward the house, trying to talk to him and he just pulled the gun out and shot. I think he panicked really. I don't know that he was trying to shoot us; but, if he was, he's got to be about the worst shot I've ever seen. Thank God for that. Dax just lunged for him and tackled him like he was out on the football field. Between the two of us, we had him down on the ground and tied up with hay bale twine before he could fire off another round."

"Well, thank you. Thank you for helping my sister. It means a lot to me." Uncharacteristically, she starts to cry. It is just such a relief that Kate is safe and that Nic is locked up, and the release comes in the form of tears.

Kate hugs her. "It's okay, Cheney," Kate says. "I'm fine. Really."

"It's just that – I don't think I could handle anything happening to you," Cheney says, stepping back and heading toward the hallway bathroom for a tissue. "I'm just so glad that you're okay." When she returns, after wiping her tears away, she says to John Hardy, "And Dax, too - and you, of course - you too, John. I'm just glad everyone's okay." She pauses, composes herself and asks, "Not that I care what happens to him, but how did Nic Zafeiropoulos end up in an ambulance?"

John explains: "After we had him tied up pretty good, he first started swearing at us -calling us every name in the book - and he seemed fine. But then when the sheriff's police showed up to untie him and take him into custody, he all of a sudden started complaining about chest pains, moaning that he was having a heart attack. So, the sheriff called the ambulance and we all had to wait awhile for the ambulance to arrive and then they drove off and took him to the hospital."

"The hospital won't release him from there, Cheney, will they?" Kate asks nervously.

"No," Cheney says. "They'll have deputies at the hospital to take him into custody as soon as he is discharged from the hospital."

"That's what the deputies told me," Kate says, "but I wanted to make sure."

The deputies' and Dax's voices and footsteps can be heard walking down the hall, and when Dax comes into the parlor he walks over to his dad, but the deputies stand in the hallway, outside of the parlor, evidently taking in that a newcomer has arrived to the house. The deputies both look relatively young, in their early twenties: a man and a woman.

"This is my sister, Cheney Manning," Kate says to the deputies.

"I'm the home owner," she says.

"Oh, ma'am, we just have a couple questions for you. Could you please come with us back to your kitchen so we may talk to you?" the female deputy asks.

Cheney follows them down the hallway to the kitchen, and they ask her some perfunctory questions, aimed at confirming that Cheney was not home when the incident happened, and that she has never given Nic Zafeiropoulos permission to be on her property. They ask her when was the last time her sister spoke to Nic, and she says she can't say for certain, but that she believes Kate has not talked to him since the night he was arrested last Friday.

It is impossible not to notice that there are two dozen long-stemmed roses in separate vases displayed on the kitchen table. These roses were not at the house when Cheney left.

"Do you know who sent your sister these roses?" the male deputy asks.

"No," she says. "These weren't here when I left for the evening."

"What time was that?"

"Oh, it had to have been around 5:15," she says.

"You have no idea who would've sent her these?" the female deputy asks.

"Well, that's a different question than whether I have actual knowledge who sent them to her," Cheney says defensively. "I don't know who sent them to her. If you're asking me to speculate, I could probably come up with a long list. My sister has a lot of admirers." She pauses. "Honestly, I'm not sure how this is relevant to your investigation, but, if you are curious as to who sent her the roses, just ask Kate. I'm sure she'll tell you."

The two deputies look at each other, ostensibly silently communicating with each other, and then the female deputy says: "We did. She told us a dozen were sent to her by Dax Hardy and the other were sent to her by someone else, but she wouldn't tell us who sent them."

"She wouldn't tell you?" she asks in disbelief.

The deputies don't say anything, and she takes their joint silence to mean, "Yes."

"May I ask what is the relevance to your investigation?" Cheney asks.

Her burner phone starts vibrating and she looks down and sees that it's Denny calling, probably wondering if she arrived home safely. She had promised him before she had left that she would text him when she was home, and he is probably worried about her, since she hasn't done so.

"I've got to take this for a second," she says. "I'm sorry." She answers the call and before he can say 'Hello' she says: "I'm home okay, but I actually have two deputies in my kitchen right now, so I'm going to have to call you back."

"Is everything okay?"

"Yes."

"Your sister? Is she alright?"

"Yes. She's fine. I'll explain tomorrow when I talk to you," she says.

"Well, if you need anything, please let me know," he says. "I could drive out there right now."

"No," she says hastily. The thought of Dennis Rausch showing up at her house and all the explaining she would have to do is not what she needs right now. Her voice is edgy and she raises it a bit when she says adamantly, "No, that's not necessary, but thank you. I appreciate it."

She ends the conversation with another assurance that she'll call him in the morning, and then she disconnects the call, sets her phone on the countertop and leans back against it, folding her arms.

"Going back to what I was asking: how are those roses relevant to your investigation?"

"Your sister says that both of these were sent to her," the male deputy explains. "Dax Hardy confirms that he ordered a dozen roses online for your sister and your sister was able to show us a message card from Dax that came with the roses, along with a delivery slip confirming that those roses were delivered *via* currier this evening. But as for the other dozen roses, she can't produce a delivery slip or a message card."

"You're thinking that Nic Zafeiropoulos brought them to her?" Cheney asks them directly. "You're concerned that she let him into the house and then all of a sudden changed her mind and wanted him to leave? You think maybe that he didn't try to break into the house at all?"

Again, her questioning is answered with silence. The two deputies just look at her, and Cheney says, "I'm going to talk to Kate right now. I'll get her to clear this up. If you want to know who gave her those flowers, you're going to know before you leave." She starts to head out back toward the parlor, but before she does, she asks, "Can I tell John and Dax Hardy that it's okay to leave or do they need to stay?"

"Oh, they can go," the female deputy says.

"Thank you," Cheney says and heads down the hallway, ready to give Kate an earful. She cannot believe that her sister would be concealing the truth to the deputies and she is ready to get to the bottom of it. She wants to get this finished, send the deputies on their way, and maybe even get a little sleep.

When she gets to the parlor, she tells both of the men "Thank you, again," and she says that "she owes them dinner" and that, "after all of this settles down," they "will invite them over for a ham or a pot roast."

297

John Hardy says: "That sounds good, but you don't have to go to any trouble," and Dax is gazing at Kate like he wants to hold her or kiss her or keep her nearby. But, despite this, it only takes a few seconds to usher the men out the door. After all, it's two-thirty in the morning, and it's clear that John Hardy has had enough of the drama for the evening and is ready to head home, even if his son has a crush on Kate.

"Are the deputies still here?" Kate asks after John and Dax leave.

"Of course, they're still here. You didn't see them walk by, did you?"

"Well, I didn't know if they went out the back or something. Why are they still here?"

"Kate, I need you to tell me the truth. No lies. Okay?"

"Cheney, you're scaring me. What did I do?"

"Kate, I need to hear this from you. Agree that when I ask you this, you are going to answer me with the truth."

"Okay," Kate says, and she is clearly worried.

"There are two sets of a dozen roses on the kitchen table that weren't there when I left. Where did each dozen come from?"

"One dozen were delivered after you left and they're from Dax."

"Okay – and the other dozen?"

Kate sighs and it is evident that she is conflicted. "You won't tell the deputies this, if I tell you who gave them to me, will you?"

"Yes, I'm going to tell them," Cheney says. "That's exactly what I'm going to do. Listen, Kate, I'm not bullshitting you here. You have to tell the deputies the truth about this. You need to tell me who sent those roses to you. I can't see why you wouldn't tell the deputies the truth about this."

"I just can't," she says.

"This doesn't make any sense, Kate. Listen, this is a serious case. Two of my neighbors got shot at because of your choice to date a jagoff. And now this asshole is facing the possibility of attempt-murder charges. This is not some rinky-dink disorderly conduct case. You need to come clean with the police, Kate. Did you let Nic Zafeiropoulos into my house? Is he the one who brought you the roses?"

"No," she says, recoiling a bit with visible indignation. "How could you possibly think that after what he did to me?"

"Then what is it you're hiding, Kate? Why won't you just tell the police who sent you the roses?"

"Because I'll get him in trouble if I do," Kate says softly, and a bit defensively.

"What - Is the guy married or something?"

"No," Kate says firmly. "You're the one who said he could get in trouble for dating me."

"Oh, my God," Cheney says. "Brian Patterson."

Kate nods guiltily.

"Patterson had the roses delivered to you?"

Kate shakes her head.

"He was here? In the house?"

"Yes," Kate says, and then quickly adds, "I didn't want to tell you, because I thought you might get mad, because you said he might get in trouble with his job for dating a Dom Batt victim or whatever it is you keep calling me. Anyway, he came over tonight and I made him dinner after you left, and then he had to leave for work at ten for the midnight shift." She pauses, and then charmingly quips, "By the way, there's left-over chicken alfredo in the refrigerator if you want any."

"Oh, Sweet Jesus, Kate" Cheney says. "C'mon with me to the kitchen."

"Cheney, you cannot make me tell them."

"Kate, listen to me: you cannot lie to the police. It's called obstruction of justice."

"I didn't lie to them. I just refused to tell them who sent me the roses."

"Kate, they think you are lying to them and that Nic Zafeiropoulos gave you the roses and that he was in the house with you. It affects your credibility. Your failure to tell the deputies the truth may impact the prosecution. Do you want Nic to walk because you won't tell the deputies the truth about Brian Patterson giving you those roses?"

Kate doesn't answer the question; she just says, "I really like him, Cheney. I really don't want to get him in trouble with his job."

"I get it," Cheney says. "But now is not the time to worry about Brian Patterson. Brian Patterson is a big boy. He'll be just fine. I doubt he's going to have any repercussions at his job anyways, since he's had no involvement in your dom batt case whatsoever. But listen to me, regardless of what may or may not happen with Brian's job, I need you to be concerned about yourself for a minute here. I need you to think about what might happen if the deputies don't believe you about what you told them tonight. The truth always has a way of coming out eventually, Kate. You know that. It's best to be the one who brings it out."

Kate sighs. "Okay fine. I'll go with you. I'll tell them it was Brian and that he was here. Can I call him first though to let him know what happened and that I'll be telling the deputies that he was here earlier in the night?"

"You haven't talked to him yet then, I take it?"

"No," she says.

"You didn't call him or text him to let him know that Nic was trying to break in the house?"

"No," she says. "I knew he was working tonight and I didn't want to bother him and I knew he was too far away to help me anyway. That's why I texted Dax. I knew he could get here within minutes, and he did." Kate pauses and asks again: "So, is it alright if I call Brian to let him know what's going on in case the deputies contact him and ask him questions?"

"Go ahead," Cheney says resignedly. "But make it quick. The deputies are waiting for us."

Kate goes into the library and shuts the pocket doors to the room for privacy, even though Cheney can overhear most of the conversation. Kate does keep the call brief, and after a few minutes, she pulls back the doors and says: "He's worried about me, of course, which I didn't want him to be while he's at work; but I told him I'm fine and that you're here now, too. He said if we need anything, that either one of us could call him."

Cheney nods and then heads down the hallway with her sister. Hopefully, once Kate's disclosure is made, the deputies will leave, and she'll be able to finally go to bed. But she knows that it's unlikely she'll fall asleep, since there is so much adrenaline fueling her. There is just way too much to unpack, to iron out, to unfold. With her luck lately, she probably won't be able to doze off until the sun is coming up.

# AUTOGRAPH

*February 15ᵗʰ*

She would be lying if she said it wasn't strange to see Brian Patterson and Kate together. The two of them are sitting next to each other on the loveseat in the parlor, just like Dan and she used to do. It is evident from the way Patterson looks at Kate that he is absolutely taken with her. Even though he is nice enough, Cheney has always thought of him as a bit robotic, gloomy and standoffish. But now, in the presence of Kate Costello, he is expressive, animated and doting. He actually smiles and laughs frequently. Cheney hasn't seen this side of him before, as he has always seemed so doleful and serious.

Though they seem as if they would be mismatched, it's nice that Kate and Patterson have evidently connected with each other, because Kate could do much worse: like reuniting with Nic. At least with Patterson, his gentleness is apparent, and it appears that he would never raise a hand to Kate. Besides, he's somewhat multifaceted in that he's not only a police officer, but a poet, which is a unique combination. With Kate's theater background, and his creative mind, they should, at least, have the arts in common. Sitting on one of the wing-backed green velvet chairs trying to converse with the two of them, is kind of like watching two teenagers who are flirting with each other in a study hall: It's all a bit nauseating.

Cheney's about to leave anyway, and it's a relief that Patterson will be here with Kate while she's gone. Nic was only charged at this point with Reckless Discharge of a Firearm and Violation of an Order of Protection. While the prosecutor had called Kate earlier in the day and had told her that it was possible that the charges may be upgraded to attempt murder, that decision had not been made yet. Thankfully, the prosecution had filed a motion to revoke his bond on the aggravated domestic battery case, and so Nic was still confined, pending a hearing on that motion.

Despite that Nic is locked up, Cheney still doesn't like the thought of leaving Kate alone again after what happened last night. It is good that Patterson will be here with Kate, particularly since Cheney doesn't know how long she'll be gone. Patterson has the night off and is planning on staying over in the guest bedroom on the first floor. Cheney is purposely vague with both of them, telling them that she is going to McNamee to meet friends and that she doesn't anticipate that she'll be home until well past midnight and that she might even stay overnight.

Kate point blank asks her: "Are you going to meet the retired cop that you went out with last night?"

"No," Cheney says truthfully. At the same time, she looks down at Patton who is sitting next to her on the floor, and she pets the top of his mammoth head.

"Retired cop?" Patterson asks. "Who is it? Maybe I know him?"

"You wouldn't know him," Cheney says, focusing on petting Patton, feigning disinterest in the topic of her Valentine's dinner date. "He's been retired for a long time."

"From where?" Patterson asks.

"Meskwaki."

304

"Well, what's his name?" Patterson presses. "I know some retired guys from there."

Cheney stands up, stretches, and Patton stands up too. "Well, it's time for me to head out. You guys have a good night and please try not to have lights and sirens here when I get home. I barely had any sleep night last night as it is. I can't take another night like that."

"Wow," Kate says laughingly. "Miss Mysterious. You're not going to tell us this guy's name?"

"Nope," Cheney says and heads toward the door, patting Patton on the head and telling him 'Goodbye.' Then to Kate and Patterson she quips: "You guys have a good night," and she walks out the front door.

The night is fairly warm for the middle of February, in the low forties, and she ditched her puffer coat for her three-quarter length black leather jacket. She's wearing a black beanie, a black cashmere turtle-neck, a pair of faded bootcut jeans, and black leather booties. She's normally a fan of rap or country when she drives, but tonight, she turns on a classic rock station.

The first song that's playing is good driving music: Stone Fury's fast-paced angst-filled *Break Down the Wall*. She plays it loud, gets lost in the drumming, and the beat fuels her with the courage needed for tonight. She's going it alone. Solomon had texted her earlier in the day and said that Alveda Isaiah was sick and that he was unable to make it tonight. He apologized and had asked her if they could move this to another night, but she had just texted back with: "No worries." When he had pressed her to make sure she wasn't going to "do anything stupid" and "go without him", she had just sent a smiley-face emoji back. There was no sense in lying to him, but she had her mind made up already. She was going tonight, with or without him.

It's only seven, and she is planning on meeting Cassandra at her house before she goes over to the bar in McNamee. She doesn't want to get to the bar too early, but she doesn't want to raise her sister's suspicion by leaving at eleven o'clock at night. She had texted Cassandra in the morning and had asked her if it would be okay to stop by the house later in the evening and give her an update on the status of discussions with the State's Attorney concerning DNA testing. She had been purposely vague though and had not actually come out and disclosed that she had met with Matthew Brockton nearly a week ago. She had avoided Cassandra's calls for the past several days, and had not returned any of her voice mails or texts until today.

Cassandra had responded immediately to her text, letting her know that tonight would be perfect, that Jeff would be at work, and that her daughter was going to stay at her aunt's house. Cheney suggested stopping by around seven-thirty or eight, and Cassandra had sent back a thumbs-up emoji with a "Perfect!"

Cheney isn't sure how this meeting is going to go, though she is concerned that Cassandra might get upset that she can't share a lot of details with her. She wants to let Cassandra know that she is positive that Dennis Rausch is not the killer, but she doesn't want to go in to why. She also wants to tell Cassandra that she has a suspect in mind, but she is not prepared to say who that person is until she is sure.

Unfortunately, the meeting goes about as well as Cheney had suspected. Cassandra is immediately agitated that Cheney won't tell her why it is that she has ruled out Dennis Rausch and whom she suspects killed her mother.

"I don't understand why you can't tell me, Cheney," Cassandra says, her dark eyes flashing.

"You've just got to trust me, Cassandra, when I say this, but I am quite convinced that Dennis Rausch is not the killer."

"But you still think my mom was murdered, right?"

"I do," she says.

"But by someone else?"

"Correct."

"And you can't tell me who?"

"That's right."

"Why exactly is that?" Cassandra demands.

"Because I'm not going to tell you who I suspect it is until I have some corroborative information. If it were to leak out, it could jeopardize our chance of solving the case. Moreover, quite frankly, it's defamatory if not true."

"Well, it's not like I'm going to tell anybody," Cassandra says flippantly.

"C'mon, Cassandra. Like you're not going to want to share the information with your grandparents and uncles right away? With how quick a disclosure is commuted into a mass media posting nowadays, I just can't take a chance on the name being publicized. I'm sorry, but I just can't tell you yet, until I'm sure."

"So, does the State's Attorney know who you think it is?" Cassandra asks, clearly miffed.

"No."

"Have you even met with Matthew Brockton yet?"

"Actually, yes, I met with him on Monday."

It is evident that Cassandra's irritation is heightened upon hearing that Cheney has been holding back information. "I tried to call and text you a bunch of times and you never responded until today," Cassandra says testily.

"I've been a little busy," Cheney replies. "My sister's having some issues with an ex-boyfriend and she's living with me now."

"Oh," Cassandra says, the anger in her eyes softening a bit. "Jeff mentioned something about your sister to me. I'm sorry about that."

"Oh yeah? What did Jeff tell you?"

"Just that, your sister was beaten by the guy who owns our favorite restaurant in Loomisville and now we're not going to eat there any-more." Cassandra clearly wants to hear about Cheney's meeting with the State's Attorney, as opposed to talking about Cheney's sister, so she returns to the topic she wants to address. "So, what happened with this meeting? Will Brockton agree to DNA testing?"

"No," Cheney says. "Not without more."

"You told him, though, that you believe my mother was mur-dered, right? You told him that, based on your experience, in looking at the reports and everything, it looks like a homicide, not a suicide, right?"

"Yes," Cheney says. "But my opinion is just that: an opinion. It's not evidence. He wants evidence in order to justify reopening the investigation by agreeing to DNA testing of thirty-year-old cigarettes."

Cassandra looks defeated and exasperated for a moment, almost as if she is shrinking in her chair. "How are we going to do that? After all these years, how could we come up with more evidence?"

"I don't know," Cheney says. "But I don't want you to give up hope, Cassandra."

"What does that mean, Cheney? My family has been hoping for thirty years that the truth would come out about my mother. How much longer do we have to keep holding on to hope?"

"A while longer," Cheney says and she stands up from the couch to leave.

"What are you doing, Cheney?" Cassandra asks, standing up from her chair and following Cheney to the front door. "You're doing something on this case that you're not telling me about, aren't you? Like some kind of undercover private investigative work like you did when Dan was killed, aren't you?"

"If I was, I couldn't tell you," Cheney says, her hand on the door knob.

Cassandra abandons her accusatory tone and her voice mellows. "Well, if you are doing something like that, Cheney, thank you. And if you aren't, well, I want you to know, that I do appreciate everything else you've done for me and my family. I know I sound frustrated, and I am, but I'm not mad at you or anything. I am grateful – my whole family is grateful – really."

When Cheney opens the door, Cassandra touches her shoulder and says: "One other thing, Cheney. Whatever you're doing, be careful."

When Cheney gets to the parking lot of Foxy's Tail, it is pretty crowded, but she's able to find a spot to park. She sits in her truck, and she waits. She doesn't want to go into the bar until an hour or so before closing time. She had picked up a cheeseburger, some fries, and a diet cola, on her way here, so she eats that in her truck. Then she spends a couple of hours surfing the Internet and her social media accounts on her smartphone. The lot gradually thins to a point where it's only her truck and a handful of other cars.

She had texted Denny earlier in the day to briefly explain to him, vaguely, about the incident with Kate's ex-boyfriend having shown up at her house last night, and she had also told Denny that she was going to stay home with her sister tonight since Kate was pretty shaken up. When Denny had responded with a text asking whether she would have time to talk to him, she had responded that she would give him a call on Sunday. That's how the text conversation had concluded, so she is surprised when her phone starts buzzing and it's Denny.

"Hello," she says.

"Hey," he says. "I kind of wanted to hear your voice. Make sure I wasn't dreaming."

"Dreaming?"

"That there's some beautiful writer named Hesperus Braun who was in my arms last night."

"You weren't dreaming. I was there." And because she can't help being kind of a smartass, she adds, "On the waterbed. With a can of beer. With a classic rock station blasting."

"So, when am I going to see you again?" he asks.

"I don't know," she says. "There's a lot going on with my little sister right now, and I kind of want that to settle down a bit before I leave her alone at night."

"So, this asshole showed up at your house last night, huh?"

"Yes."

"Did he get into the house?"

"No. But it sounds like he was trying. My sister texted my neighbors and they showed up and they were able to tackle him and get him tied up until the sheriff's deputies came. But he pulled a gun on my neighbors first and actually took a shot at them."

"You got to be kidding me."

"No. Shattered my neighbor's truck's windshield."

"All this happened last night while you were gone?"

"Yeah."

"How's your sister doing?"

"She's okay. Just a bit shaken up."

"Is the guy still locked up?"

"As far as I know, yes. There's a hearing on the State's motion to revoke bond on a different case on Monday."

"Well, you lead kind of an exciting life for a country girl, Hesperus Braun. You could write a book about your escapades."

She almost says, "If you only knew the half of it," but instead she kind of snorts and says, "Yeah, I probably could. I don't know if anybody would read it though."

"I would," he says. "As long as you promised to give me an autographed copy."

She laughs. "You would definitely get a signed copy."

They talk for a few moments more, and she says she'll call him tomorrow. He doesn't seem like the kind of guy that likes to talk on the phone much, so he sounds content with keeping the conversation brief. Not long after she disconnects, she sees his son come out from the side of the bar along with a woman co-worker and she watches them smoke cigarettes on the cement slab. It's a couple of minutes until midnight. Now is a good time for her to inconspicuously go into the bar and get an advantageous spot: one where she can flirt with Jason Rausch.

# JAZZIE

*February 16*[th]

She's literally on the bar stool for less than sixty seconds when Jason Rausch and the woman bartender come back inside. The woman heads off to assist a group of raucous men at the opposite end of the bar and Jason Rausch approaches Cheney with a, "What can I get for ya'?"

She orders a pilsner and he opens the bottle for her, plops it down and says, "Three dollars." She hands him a ten and he plops a five and two singles on the bar. Other than the bartender, Cheney is the only woman in the bar. It's not going to be tough to get Jason Rausch's attention, and she can sense his interest immediately.

He starts chatting her up, making a comment about women who show up alone at bars right before closing time. As if in an onstage routine, he brings over the bartender, whom he calls "Joy-dee", and tries to involve her in banter with Cheney too; at times, Joy-Dee -if that's her real name - appears receptive, but more often she seems to find him annoying, and just walks away when he tries to get her to join in on a conversation with Cheney. It is hard to believe that Dennis Rausch produced this as his child: The cool bravado that Denny exudes - the rough, silent ranger mystique - is definitely lacking in his offspring. Jason Rausch is obese, sweaty, loquacious and unkempt.

There is little to find appealing about him, though he seems popular with what appear to be the regulars in the bar: paunchy middle-aged

313

men with a variety of Chicago sports team shirts, who converse with him about games and gambling. Like a chubby comic, he seems to have a routine of oscillating jokes: three parts sexist and one part self-deprecating. The regulars laugh at his routine and buy more drinks. She may have to come back a different night, because it doesn't seem like she'll be able to segue into any type of conversation that will lead to information about Jazzie Gonzalez: at least, not while the audience is still here.

She's on her second beer when she notices the photograph behind the bar. It's not framed or anything, and it's just a small picture wedged into a corner of the bottom frame of the bar mirror about the size of a senior class photo. It's a young Latina woman with long dark hair, bangs, luminous brown eyes, and a beautiful smile. She recognizes her immediately: It's Jazzie Gonzalez.

When he comes over to chat with her again, she asks, "Who is that girl in the photo?"

He looks at her strangely, and then turns to where she is pointing, but he doesn't actually look at the photo. "Oh, her. That's a girl who used to work here."

"What's her name? She looks familiar to me."

"You wouldn't know her," he says, bristling a bit. "She's been dead for thirty years, probably before you were born.

"She's beautiful," Cheney says.

"Yeah. She was beautiful," he says, sounding irritated.

"You knew her, then?"

"Yeah. I knew her."

"She looks so young. How did she die?"

He looks at her and says, "You want to know how she died, huh?" It almost sounds like a threat.

"Yeah," she says, not liking the look in his eyes.

"Stick around after close and I'll tell you." Then he winks, turns and starts attending to the rest of his customers.

Her instincts are telling her to get the hell out of here, but still, she stays. Cradling her beer. Drinking slowly, wanting to remain extraordinarily alert. After she finishes her first beer, the final stragglers start leaving and fifteen minutes past last call, she's the sole customer remaining in the bar.

"You wanna another one?" he asks her and she says, "Sure." He opens another bottle, sets it front of her. "This one's on the house."

He and Joy-Dee go through a routine of closing for the night. They clean off the bar, wash glasses, shut down the lights in the back room, wipe down the tables, put chairs up on the tables, sweep the floor. It's the first time he's actually jokeless and quiet, seemingly focusing on shutting everything down and getting out of there. Watching them close down, is kind of like observing a dance of sorts: the two of them gliding along, knowing without talking, all the things they need to do to tuck the bar in for the night.

While Joy-Dee is cleaning out the bathrooms, he asks Cheney if she wants to step out back for a smoke, and she says, "Yeah."

The two of them stand out on the cement slab, the same area from which she and Solomon had retrieved the cigarette, and there is an adrenaline rush to all of this, as Jason Rausch makes small talk with her. It is possible that she is close to finding out if he shot Jazzie Gonzalez, but she isn't quite sure how to segue from first-phase flirting into probing a homicide suspect. He told her he would tell her how Jazzie died, but it doesn't seem like it would be a good idea to push it at this juncture. Instead, she'll just have to wait until later to see if he opens up.

"So, what's your name?" he asks her.

"Hesperus Braun," she says.

He doesn't say anything. His eyes just grow wide and she can tell he wants to make some kind of sarcastic remark about her name, but he doesn't. After a few seconds of silence he says, "Hesperus. Never heard that one before."

"And you're Jason," she says, "I picked that up from hearing the guys in the bar."

"Yep."

"I'm actually trying to quit these," she says, holding out the cigarette. "It's a tough habit to break. I've been smoking since I was a freshman in high school."

"Same here," he says. "I started when I was fourteen and I haven't been able to put 'em down since."

Bingo. Jason Rausch was the smoker on the back porch. But she goes a bit further, just to confirm. "Did you ever try to quit?"

316

"Nope," he says. "Don't see no reason why I should."

After they go back inside, she continues drinking her beer at the bar, while he finishes the last of his closing duties. She's almost halfway finished with her beer when Joy-Dee puts on her coat and says she is going out to the lot to start her car and that she's gonna let it run for a few minutes before she heads out. Cheney catches Joy-Dee glance at her when she walks by and Cheney knows that look: it's the secret intuit of a woman warning her that she's leaving and that maybe she should go too. But even after Joy-Dee comes back in and then leaves altogether for the night, Cheney stays.

He turns off the lights in the place except for the ambient lighting directly behind the bar, which casts an eerie glow over the assemblage of green and gold liquor bottles. He pours himself a glass of whiskey and then he asks her if she wants to smoke. She thinks he means cigarettes and she says, "Sure," thinking they're going to step outside again and chat on the side cement slab, but instead, he takes out a bowl from behind the bar and lights it up.

She hates the smell of marijuana and she doesn't want to be around it. It would probably be an opportune time to just abandon this investigation and leave. She's not really sure how to segue into asking him questions about his past without raising his suspicions anyway. She hadn't quite figured that out before she came here tonight. If she leaves now, after gaining some familiarity with him, she can regroup, reassess, and plan on how she can best approach him about his whereabouts on Valentine's Day thirty years ago. Now does not seem like a good time to bring the topic up, for he appears sullen and withdrawn all of a sudden, and his face has a pallid and strange glow to it, cast by the eerie reflection of the soft light hitting the liquor bottles.

Now, with the absence of the audience of men and Joy-Dee, he is not chatty at all, but, instead, seems brooding and quiet. The switch in his mood alarms her somewhat, and she feels the hairs on the back of her forearms raise, her heart-rate amp up, and beads of sweat start forming on her forehead. It's time to get out of here. He tries to hand her the bowl to take a hit, and she says, "No, I thought you meant cigarettes. I don't smoke weed."

He nods. "Just take a little. It will mellow you out a bit."

"Do I seem nervous?"

He nods, inhaling some again. When he finishes, he says, "Uptight. This will help."

He tries to hand it to her again, but she holds up her right hand and she says, "No. No, really. Weed's not my thing."

"Oh, yeah," he says. He comes around the bar and she shuffles a turn in her bar stool, and faces him. "Yeah, what is your thing?" he breathes into her, only inches away from her face.

And it is then that she notices that he has exposed himself, and it is sticking out with his jeans unzipped.

"Um, not that," she says bluntly.

"Yeah, well, we can change that," he says and he takes her by the face and kisses her forcefully, with lots of thick froggy tongue and gross saliva. She goes from being in control - to not - in a heartbeat. The fear has arrived full force: no one knows she's at this place, it's dark, and it's at the end of a dead-end road alongside the river.

She doesn't like where this is heading, and she's got to break this up somehow. She sits back for a minute, attempts to suppress any outward manifestation of her nervousness and repulsion, and says, "Hey, you prom-ised you'd tell me about the girl in the mirror."

"Uh huh," he says, "I did". He puts her hand forcibly on his penis. When she takes her hand away, he starts stroking himself.

She's lost control of this situation and she has to get out of here, but there's no way she can brush by him without him grabbing her. He weighs a good two-hundred-and-seventy- plus pounds and he looks like he could snap her in half.

"So, what's the story?" she asks, calming her voice, trying to sup-press her fear.

"You want to know the story, huh?"

"Yes," she says.

He stops stroking himself, and zips up his pants, and he goes behind the bar. It might be a good chance to bolt for the door, but she is afraid he will catch her and hurt her if she tries to do that. It is better to remain calm and to try to cajole him into letting her leave. Besides, he hasn't actually forced her to stay in the bar; maybe he won't do anything at all if she simply just starts nonchalantly walking toward the door.

He picks up the bowl and smokes more, eyeing her. He pours two shots of whiskey and slides one toward her.

"Drink up," he tells her.

"I don't drink whiskey," she says.

"You do now," he says, grinning. "You know what you came here for. You know what you want. You're gonna get it. Drink up."

This does not sound promising. Her heart feels like it has dropped into her stomach and it is being strangled by her intestines. She can barely breathe. He pours her the cheap stuff in a shot glass and, as much as she despises whiskey, she drinks it.

The alcohol is an immediate rush and it gives her a bit of cowboy courage. "So, let's get back to the beautiful girl in the photo. You said you would tell me about her."

"Whatd'ya want to know?"

"Who she was: How she died."

"Her name was Jazzie," he says, taking another hit. When he's finished, "Jazzie Goddamn Gonzalez. Finest piece of ass in the county."

"Was she your girlfriend?"

He laughs. Pours two more shots of whiskey. Demands that she drink up.

She drinks the shot and feels it sear through her esophagus into her belly. She hates whiskey. It does, however, put her a little more at ease, though that may not be a good thing.

"Yeah, I guess you could say she was my girlfriend. At least, that's what I thought she was – *my* girlfriend. But she wasn't. She was just a little whore, really. She fucked me over and she fucked my dad over. My dad, you see, he really was duped by her. So was I, though. So was I."

"How did she dupe you?" Cheney asks.

"My dad, my dad, yeah, he really was pussy-whipped by her," he says. "Said he loved her. But, shit - my dad was way too old for her. He was like in his thirties and she was like two years older than me. She would never have been happy with my dad. She would've kicked him to the curb after a couple of years. I'm sure of it."

"Yeah, but you said she duped *you*. How did she dupe you? I don't understand," Cheney says.

It is evident he is getting agitated. "Oh, she was like all you fucking women are, ya' know? Leading guys on, making them fall in love with you," he says, slurring his speech. "Giving 'em hard-ons and shit and then just walking away."

"I don't understand: were you and your dad both dating her?"

"Like I said, my old man was fucking her, but she wanted me. I know she did. She told me she was gonna leave him. Told me "just to be patient", "just wait a while". That's what she kept saying. She told me that we would be together. But then when I went there that night, she was supposed to have already told him she was leavin' that day, but she had lied to me, ya' see? She was stayin' with him: all dressed up and ready for him to come home and take her out. It was all lies. All fucking lies. She wasn't ever gonna leave him like she told me she was."

"But how did she die?"

"How did she die?" he asks, sneering a bit. He takes another hit of marijuana. "You want to know how she fucking died?"

Cheney doesn't say anything, fearful of the rage in his eyes. He walks around the bar and stands in front of her again, inches away, towering above her. "I'll tell you how Jazzie Gonzalez died. I fucking shot that bitch in the heart. That's how she died. Is there anything else you want to fucking know?"

There is, actually. But she is frozen with terror and she is silent. She senses he is going to rape her or kill her or both.

# LOSS

*February 16*[th]

"Did your dad know?" When she is finally able to breathe after a few seconds, this is the question she poses.

"My dad? Naw. He had no fucking clue that I shot her. He thinks she killed herself. Lived his whole life wallowing in guilt that he could've done something to save her. He's a sap, my dad – a fucking pussy-whipped pussy. That's what my dad is."

She is no longer frozen, and her reaction is swift. She rises up from the stool and knees him hard in his crotch and she runs toward the front door. She makes it outside, but only a few paces before he grabs her by the jacket, whips her around, slaps her with an open palm across her face. "Where do you think you're going, you fucking whore?" he yells. He rips her coat and pulls her back into the bar by the left side of her body. She hits him in the back and shoulders with her free hand, but it's like striking the side of a whale. He literally drags her, and she wriggles with her weight, trying to resist with the heels of her boots scouring the cement walkway. But, she has no chance with the disparity in size and strength. He throws her down on the floor of the bar, then slams the door shut. Her first thought is that this is how she is going to die.

The notion is short-lived for there is immediate pounding at the door. It has to be the police or maybe a passerby who saw him assault her.

323

"Did you fucking call the cops?" he asks her.

She shakes her head, still cowering on the ground, holding her face where he struck her.

The pounding continues and then there is a familiar voice commanding: "Open the fucking door, Jason. Now! Open it or I'll fucking bust it down. You know I will."

Jason capitulates and goes to the door, opening it and, as soon as he does so, Dennis Rausch barrels in and punches him so solidly with a left jab and a right hook combination that it knocks his son down to the ground.

Denny doesn't waste any time in coming over to Cheney, helping her stand up, brushing the hair out of her eyes, asking her if she's okay.

"I'm okay," she says, but she is eyeing Jason cautiously, who is standing up woozily. Jason has his fingers pressed against his jaw and is moving it back and forth. He lunges toward his father, who has his side to him.

"Watch out, Denny!" she cries out.

The two men exchange punches, though Denny is clearly getting the better of his overweight son. She is about to call 9-1-1 when she hears sirens and sees oscillating emergency lights. By the time the police officers enter the bar, the men have stopped swinging and have stepped back from each other. Both are breathing heavily. Jason seems far worse off than Denny, and Denny is kind of leaning over like a baseball player, with his hands on his knees.

"Who called 9-1-1?" one of the officers asks, and Denny kind of half raises his right hand and looks up at them, still leaning over. "Right here," he says and then adds, "He attacked her."

"Are you okay, ma'am?" one of the officers asks her and she nods. "Do you need an ambulance?"

"No, no," she says.

"What's your name, ma'am?"

"Cheney Manning," she says, and when she looks over at Denny he meets her eyes, but he does not seem surprised.

Two more police officers arrive, and they escort Cheney to the back room past the hallway bathrooms to interview her, while the other two officers remain in the main part of the bar to speak with the two men. It wraps up fairly quickly, in less than a half an hour's time, with Cheney signing a complaint for battery, and Jason being taken away in handcuffs. The rest of the story though is too complex to be resolved by midnight-shift patrol officers in McNamee who are responding to a bar fight; instead, Cheney is instructed to contact the Meskwaki Police Department later in the day to discuss Jason's confession to her concerning the thirty-year-old death investigation of Jazzie Gonzalez.

She is hoping that Denny will invite her to stay the night at his house, and she is relieved when he does. Between the whiskey and the excitement, she has no intention of driving a vehicle, and if he hadn't asked her to stay with him, she would have had to of called Kate to ask her and Patterson to drive all the way to McNamee to pick her up.

In his truck, on the way to his house in Meskwaki, she asks him, "Did you know my name was Cheney Manning before tonight?"

"Yes," he says.

"How did you know that?"

"Your face was plastered all over TV and the Internet when your husband was killed and then again when that whole thing went down about that lawyer from Loomisville being involved."

Her phone buzzes, and she sees that it's Kate wondering if she's coming home or staying over, and she texts back: "Staying here. See you in the morning." She adds a purple- heart emoji, and Kate sends a single letter - "K" - back.

She returns to her conversation with Denny and asks, "You mean, you knew it was me when I walked into the bar?"

"No," he says. "I knew I recognized you when you walked in, but I didn't know from where. Then, when you gave me that fake name – Hesperus Braun – I knew right away that you were bullshitting me. So, I started digging a bit on the Internet and eventually I remembered where I had seen you before; and, I was right."

"You did this last night?"

"No," he says.

"When, then?"

"The first night, after you left my house."

"You mean: you already knew who I was when you took me to dinner on Valentine's Day?"

"Yeah," he says.

"How did you know I was at the bar tonight?"

"Because you were there last night," he says.

"You followed me?"

"Yeah," he says.

"Why?"

"Trying to see what you were up to," he says.

"What was I up to?"

"You think my son killed Jazzie Gonzalez," he says.

"How do you know that?"

"I saw you and the kid watching him," he says. "I saw you collect Jason's cigarette last night."

"But how did you know that it had anything to do with Jazzie Gonzalez?" she asks.

"My gut," he says," and all the probing you were doing about whether I smoked and how I found you standing out on the porch right near where I found her. You had no reason to be up there, other than

327

that you were snooping around. I just knew. But then again, maybe deep down I always suspected Jason killed her. There was no reason for Jazzie to shoot herself: no reason at all. And Jason was always hanging around her, his tongue practically hanging out, like a puppy dog. I could tell he was infatuated with her."

"Jason did kill her, Denny," she says softly.

"What makes you think that?" he asks, sounding agitated.

"Because that's why I ran out of the bar: He told me that he killed her."

He's quiet then and it is evident that all of this is overwhelming for him. When they get to the house, he seems different, reflective, maybe shocked or angry. He doesn't ask her to sleep with him on his waterbed, and instead sets her up in the bedroom upstairs, and tells her if she needs anything to let him know. He doesn't kiss her or hold her, and she understands why. It is clear he feels betrayed by her deception, and that his heartbreak over the loss of Jazzie Gonzalez is refreshed and exacerbated by the events of tonight.

In the morning, he drives her back to the parking lot to get her truck, and they don't say anything about the previous night, except that she tells him she is sorry for having lied to him. When she says that, he does not acknowledge, nor accept, her apology. Instead, he says simply, "I'm sorry about your husband. I knew a few coppers who knew him. They all said he was a good guy."

She nods, and says, "He was," and then adds, "Thank you for that. I appreciate it."

He doesn't say anything in response, just nods.

Before she gets out, she asks him, "Will I see you again?"

He looks at her, but just glancingly so, and then looks straight ahead out the windshield and answers, "I'm not sure."

"I get it," she says, and she does. He looks over at her, and she continues, "For what it's worth," she says, "I'm sorry. I'm sorry for any pain I caused you. It's a terrible situation and I'm sure I've made it worse for you, dredging all of this up."

When she finishes speaking, he turns his head back toward the windshield again, studying the distance. His silence is confirmation, and she says "Thank you for the ride." As soon as she exits his truck, he takes off, and doesn't wait to see if her truck starts okay, even though the temperature had dipped below zero over the course of the night.

She won't hear from him again. She's certain of it. She starts her truck and scrapes the ice off from the windows, while the vehicle is warming up. She has never felt so lonely in her life: even in the weeks following Dan's murder, or the moments in the hospital bed after having been informed that Manuel had been stabbed to death. She had felt lonely then, too, but not nearly as overwhelmingly so as now. It's as if all that trauma - a series of misery and loss - has been kept in a storm-cloud, bottled up, suppressed, and it charges into her heart now like a blizzard of pain, tapping its icy knuckles against her arterial walls, and then squeezing tight.

She can't go home right now. She needs a relief. She needs to dip herself into some happiness, even though it may be temporary. It will do her some good to bring some positive news to someone. She gets into her truck and heads toward Cassandra Cantoni's house. Certainly, it will lift her spirits to share with Cassandra that she knows definitively that Jazzie Gonzalez did not commit suicide and that she is certain of the identity of the shooter. The closure that this will bring to Cassandra and her family will be uplifting, and hopefully, it may also be kind of an elixir to her own misgivings about lying to Denny. It will make what she has done worth it somehow.

She texts Cassandra from the driveway of Cassandra's house, letting her know that she has information she'll want to hear about Jazzie and asking her if she has time to meet.

Seconds later, Cassandra texts her back: "Yes! When?" and Cheney texts back, "How about now? I'm in your driveway."

The text she gets back from Cassandra reads, "Jeff is here," followed by a frown-face emoji. Cheney can see Cassandra appear in the bay window, looking out at Cheney's truck.

"That's okay," Cheney texts back. "Maybe it's time to let him into the loop. He'll want to hear this too."

"U R right," Cassandra's text reads. "C'mon in. Miranda's here too, but she's still sleeping."

Cheney does not stay long. She sits at the dining room table, opposite Cassandra and Jeff. Cassandra had insisted that Cheney have a cup of coffee and a donut.

When Cheney starts by telling Cassandra that she went undercover last night and that Jason Rausch -Dennis Rausch's son – confessed to murdering her mother, Cassandra becomes overwhelmed and bursts into tears.

Jeff looks dumbfounded and asks, "What is this about Cassie?"

Cassandra addresses him quickly in Spanish between her tears. Cheney only understands bits and pieces of what Cassandra says, but she picks up "my mom" "thirty years ago", "murder" and "I went to Cheney for help."

When Cassandra is finished talking, Jeff still looks stunned and a bit irritated, and Cassandra tells Cheney it's okay to move on. Cheney delves into an abbreviated and sanitized version of the backstory. She doesn't say much about Denny, other than that she had met him at a bar, and that she had learned that he had never been a cigarette smoker from their conversations. She skips over details like going to his house, kissing him, and dancing next to the river in his arms.

As Cheney continues talking, Jeff's face gets redder and redder and he looks like he is going to explode. He starts interposing Cheney's narrative with questions and snide comments such as: "Why the hell would you think this was a good idea?" When she gets to the part about Jason Rausch attacking her, he says sarcastically: "This is exactly why you should leave police work to the police. You're lucky this guy didn't fucking kill you."

Finally, Cassandra raises her hand to him, and says, "Jeff, can you please just let Cheney finish?"

But when he persists in interrupting Cheney and questioning her actions, Cassandra says, "Please, Jeff. Just shut up."

He says nothing after that. He takes his coffee cup, puts it in the sink, and leaves down the hallway.

"I'm sorry, Cheney," Cassandra says. "I'm sorry you had to see that. You know how he gets."

"I do," Cheney says, recalling how angry Jeff Cantoni was when she had started questioning his investigation into Dan's murder.

"Well, I just want you to know that I am truly appreciative of everything you have done for me," she says. "This is going to mean so much to my grandparents and my uncles. You just don't know." She starts crying again, but she is smiling too through her tears. "We all knew that my mother would not kill herself, but none of us could prove it. You brought us the truth and for that, I will always be grateful."

Cheney winds down with a closing summary of the events of last night, answers a few questions for Cassandra, and then tells her that she really needs to get home and get some sleep.

"But you said you are going to contact the Meskwaki detectives today, right?" Cassandra inquires.

"Yes," Cheney says. "I've got to do that sometime this morning. And, like I said, since it's a homicide, my guess is that they'll want to talk to me today."

"Well, do you really want to drive all the way out to the country and then have to turn around and come right back to this area again? Why don't you just stay and sleep here in our guest room for a couple of hours and then call the police?"

"No," Cheney says. "I really just want to get home."

"But why, Cheney? Who's there to go home to?" And as soon as Cassandra asks it, she looks like she realizes, too late, the unintentional hurt that is carried with that question.

No one. No one is really there to go home to. Her husband is gone. It's been almost four months, and it seems like only a day has gone by since she had last seen him.

But she has Kate. And she has Patton. And so, she says so. "My sister. My dog. My own bed. That's who's waiting for me at home."

When she heads out to her truck, she feels a bit more alighted than when she first had pulled into Cassandra's driveway. Still, though, there is an emptiness, a sadness that clings to her and she thinks about how much she misses Dan the entire ride home.

# WISCONSIN

*February 27*[th]

She is not much of a skier, but she had left it up to Solomon and Carmen as to where they had wanted to spend the day: And, the two of them had, following deliberations, jointly decided that this is what they wanted to do. The decision was an official one - adopted by resolution of the Chair and Member of the Spinach Omelet Book Nerds - at its most recent meeting. Solomon had appeared as a guest at the meeting remotely *via* computer from his grandmother's home in Washburne.

The problem would be transportation, particularly since Carmen lived in Humboldt Park in Chicago and Solomon lived in Stickney County. Cheney had no qualms about driving to the Rodriguez house to pick Carmen up. It was clear that the Latin Kings no longer posed a risk of harm to Cheney. Dale had called Cheney the prior week and had let her know that any chatter concerning her had ceased, and that it appeared that the Kings who had wanted vengeance for Manuel's death were no longer focused on Cheney and had moved on to other activities. Even though Dale hadn't specified, she was pretty certain that it had been Manuel's brothers who likely had run interference for her with the rest of the Kings, and they must have worked to convince the gang to just leave her alone.

Solomon, however, was an entirely different story altogether. He was a former Gangster Disciple, and it was possible he would be recognized and targeted if he were to venture on the streets of Humboldt Park.

It would be best to try to come up with another way to all meet to go to Wisconsin and back in a day's time.

Ultimately, one of Carmen's uncles agreed to bring her out to Cheney's farm early in the morning and another one of her uncles agreed to pick her up later in the evening. Cheney arranged with Solomon to have him drive to her house to be there before Carmen arrived. Solomon, Kate, Patterson, Cheney and Patton awaited the child's arrival in the parlor, and, while they were sitting there, Cheney's phone started vibrating.

When she had observed it was Matthew Brockton's number, she had walked back to the kitchen to take his call. She was filled with a flood of various emotions when Brockton told her that the lab was able to recover DNA from one of the cigarettes found near Jazzie Gonzalez's body. The DNA profile matched that of Jason Rausch. He told her that the arrest warrant for the first-degree murder of Jazzie Gonzalez had already been served and that he would be presenting the case to the Grand Jury later in the week.

By the time that Carmen showed up at the house, Cheney was already filled with a fantastic energy from the news delivered over the phone by Brockton. She had already felt that the day was going to be a special one, a day of celebration and remembrance, and the good news about the Jason Rausch prosecution had only added to her exuberance. When Carmen had first entered the house, Solomon had greeted her in the parlor and had told her that he wanted to thank her in person for Manuel having saved his life.

"I've already thanked Cheney here for helping me out - but your brother, Manuel, he's not here for me to thank him - so I just wanted to tell you that I appreciate everything he did to help me out and that without him I would've died in a prison cell." Solomon had started to get choked up, but he continued: "He stuck his neck out for me – someone he didn't even know - a rival gang member - and it cost him – it cost him everything. And I feel really bad about that. I do. I feel bad that I'm here and that he's not. So, I just want you to know that I appreciate it. I appreciate it and my family appreciates everything he did for me. I wanted to meet you and tell you in person, so thank you for coming all the way out here."

"You're welcome," the child had said, her eyes tearing up at the mention of her brother, and seemingly humbled by Solomon's gratitude.

"Well, I wish I got to meet your brother," Solomon had said.

"I wish my brother was still here," Carmen had replied. "But I know where he is and I know that I'll get to see him again someday. And I know he would say to you to not feel bad about anything, because he wouldn't have helped out if he didn't think it was the right thing to do. That's how my brother was. A lot of people thought he was a bad person. But he wasn't bad. He wasn't bad at all. Right, Cheney?"

Cheney had nodded, holding back tears herself. "That's right, Carmen. He was one of the good ones."

Before they had left the house, Solomon had handed Carmen a card with a note in it from his mother, along with a cloth purse with a horse handstitched on it, made by his grandmother. He also had given the child a book - a hardbound copy of *The Secret Garden* by Frances Hodgson Burnett.

"Cheney told me that this was the next book on your reading list, and that you picked it," he had said.

"I did! Thank you! I can't wait to read it!" Carmen had exclaimed and her face had lit up with joy.

They had packed into Patterson's SUV and he had driven the entire group, *sans* Patton, to the ski resort. Cheney had been quiet during most of the ride up to Wisconsin, preoccupied with thoughts about Dan. The only times she had skied in her life had been with Dan. He had been a capable skier, and had tried to teach her to have confidence going down the slopes. They had come to this same ski resort several times before they were married, and Dan had patiently tried to teach her to ski. Despite her affinity for most sports, she had awkwardly moved about in the skis, feeling stiff and robotic, as if she were going to snap an ankle or knee joint at any moment. She had struggled to control her speed and movement down the slopes, and even had difficulty dismounting from the ski lift, tumbling down more than once. She was really not looking forward to a day of skiing, particularly with her shoulder injury still causing her occasional pain.

Once they arrived at the ski lodge, Patterson and Kate parted ways with the three of them. Patterson and Kate were experienced skiers, so they hit the big hill. Occasionally, Cheney caught a glimpse of their sparkling smiles shining from atop the lift, or their graceful bodies zigzagging down the slopes, or the two of them kissing and holding hands on level ground. Contrastingly, Cheney, Solomon and Carmen spent most of the day either struggling down the bunny hill or sitting in the dining area of the lodge drinking soft drinks and eating giant soft pretzels.

Toward the end of the day, when the sun is riding low on the horizon, she is alone with Solomon in the lodge, sitting around a small round café table, drinking hot chocolate. Carmen is in the middle of a half-hour beginner's lesson with an instructor for which Cheney had paid, and Cheney is keeping an eye on the little girl out of the expansive windows that border the cafe to make sure the child is safe.

"That still bothering you?" Solomon asks, nodding toward Cheney's right shoulder.

"Is it that obvious?" she asks.

"Well, you spent the whole time with us on the bunny hill," he says.

"I'm not much of a skier, Solomon," she says. "Like I said on the way up here, I've only skied a few times before, and it's a sport that I'm not very good at. But to answer your question – yes - it does still bother me a bit. I try to keep pressure off of it as much as I can."

"Aww…man, I should've thought of that before we picked skiing. We could've just gone to dinner or a movie or somethin'."

"No, no. It's fine, really. It's just kind of a nagging pain. Nothing bad really. Shoveling the driveway makes it feel much worse than this. But I'm just going to take it easy today. Otherwise, I'll be paying for it tomorrow."

"Yeah, well, I should've thought of that before and suggested we do somethin' else besides skiing."

"No, no, really - this has been a fun a day. I'm glad we came here. I haven't been here in years. Besides – it's been good for you, good for Carmen. She's really enjoying herself."

"She's a good kid," he says. He pauses, and moves on to a different topic. "What do you think you're going to do now that you're not a public defender and now that you figured out who killed Jazzie Gonzalez?"

"*We* figured that out, Solomon. Not *me*. *W*e. I couldn't have done it without you. You're the one who came up with the idea that it might have been Denny Rausch's son. It turned out that you were right."

Solomon nods. "I can't disagree with you on that. I just kind of guessed that it might be the son, and it turned out it was." He pauses.

339

"So, going back to my original question: Do you think you'll go back to practicing law or are you going to stick to writing that book you told me about?"

"I'm going to stick to writing the book," she says. "I actually wrote a few chapters last week. I'm about a quarter of the way finished now."

"Are you still staying with that terrible name, though, Hespala or Hesperene or whatever?"

"Hesperus. Hesperus Braun. And yes; I'm sticking with that name."

"Where'd'ya come up with that name anyway?"

"It just came to me, I guess," she says, and she's not really sure. Maybe she dreamt it. It just sounded right: Hesperus Braun.

"What does it mean: Hesperus?" he asks.

"I don't know that it means anything," she says.

Solomon takes out his smartphone and starts typing and searching. "Everything means something," he says absentmindedly, scanning. After a few seconds, he says, "Here it goes: Hesperus, comes from Greek mythology, son of Eos, goddess of the dawn. So, it's a dude's name. It means 'Venus at Night'."

"Ahhh…" she says dreamily, "the Evening Star. That makes sense."

"You mean you really didn't know that's what it meant when you came up with the name?" he asks, seemingly perplexed.

"No," she says. "I really had no idea what it meant. But now that I know what it means, I feel vindicated. Venus, the Evening Star – Hesperus - what perfect imagery for a beautiful, strong, fearless heroine."

He snorts. "I still don't know about that. I don't know how many books you'll sell with a character named Hesperus."

She laughs with him and says, "I don't know either, but I'm sure enjoying it nonetheless. It sure beats the practice of law."

Still smiling, but a bit more serious now, he says, "Miss Manning, I've got to ask you somethin', and I hope you don't take offense at it."

"Okay," Cheney says. "It must be serious, since you're back to 'Miss Manning,' and not 'Cheney'."

He laughs. "Okay, okay, 'Cheney' then, let me ask you: What ever happened between you and that old guy?"

"You mean Dennis Rausch?"

He nods. "Yeah. You were kind of digging him, right?"

"You could tell that?"

"Could I tell that?" he laughs. "You've got to ask me 'Could I tell that'?" He laughs louder, holding his stomach, rollicking.

"It was that obvious?" she asks.

He just smiles, shaking his head.

"So, what's goin' on between you two? Are you gonna see him again, or what?"

"I don't think so," Cheney says.

"You're still missing your husband, aren't you?" Solomon asks.

"I am," she says, "I miss him a lot."

"Well, you can't be alone forever," he says.

"It's only been four months, Solomon," she reminds him. "I haven't had time to even really mourn Dan's loss with everything that's gone on since he was killed."

"I get it," he says. "Really. I do. But four months can turn into four years and four years can turn into forty years in the blink of an eye before you know it. What I'm sayin' is, it's like this, Cheney: You've got to live your life. You can't be stuck in the sadness of the past. Time marches on, and all that shit. You're a smart lady; you know that. You got to keep moving forward, or else you'll get run over by time. It'll just pass you by, ya' know what I'm sayin'? See, it's like this: if your husband loved you, then he would want you to be happy. And you can't be happy being by yourself out in the farm fields writing some books about some lady detective that no one's ever going to read unless you change her name to something better than Hesperus."

He's bringing up valid points, but she deflects from the seriousness of the conversation, and half-jokingly asks, "So you're recommending that I go out with Denny Rausch?"

"Hell, no!" Solomon says, recoiling a bit, and chuckling at the same time. "That's not what I'm sayin' at all. That dude's way too old for you.

You need a guy like your own age, or maybe a couple of years older, but not some guy who could be heading to the nursing home anytime soon."

"You're probably right," Cheney says, smiling, and he is. Denny is more than twice her age and has his own demons with which he is wrestling - with which he will always be wrestling. Any relationship with him would likely be doomed from its inception. Still, she can't help but thinking about him. In fact, she thinks about him often, his 80s rock, his squishy waterbed, his whiskey kisses. Solomon is staring at her, almost as if he knows she is thinking about Denny, so she adds, "But it's not like I have a choice in the matter anyway, Solomon. He's not talking to me right now."

Solomon looks stunned. "*He*'s not talkin' to *you*? I find that hard to believe. I mean, you're *you*- the whole package - and he's just some old retired cop. Man, that's his loss, not yours."

"He's upset, you know, and he should be: I lied to him. I pretended to be someone that I'm not."

"You really like the old dude, huh?"

"I do," Cheney says. "I really like the old dude."

"I can tell," he says. "Now, listen: You didn't pretend to be anyone that you're not. The only thing you gave him was a fake name. That's all. No one gives a fuck about a name anyway. It's just a name and a bad one at that. Cheney Manning sounds a lot better than Hesperus Braun. You didn't fake anything with him. You're the real deal. He knows who you are. Don't matter if you go by Hesperus Braun or Cheney Manning, it's all the same; it's all you."

"Again, you're probably right, Solomon," she says. "But I still don't think I'll ever hear from him again."

343

"Well, you can change that. Some public defender once told me, when I was locked up in a jail cell, that I always had the power to choose my path in life. And you know what? She was right. So, why wait for this dude to call you? I mean, what are you waiting for? Why don't you just call him? What would Hesperus Braun do? Just sit around waiting for the old man to call her?"

"Well, I don't…" she's about to say 'know', when she stops. There is background music playing in the lodge and she wasn't really paying attention to it before. But she is now. It's Van Morrison's *Moondance*.

It's the end of February, the briefest month, the coldest month. And though so much has happened over the past twenty-some-plus days, it seems like it has all gone by in a millisecond. She is dancing with Dennis Rausch alongside the Fox River with the papier-mache moon chaperoning them. He is holding her steadily, but not overpowering her, and he is moving her body along, convincing her to trust him, and to let him lead.

She smiles, stands up and starts heading for the door, taking her smartphone out of her ski jacket.

"Wait - are you going back out on the hill?" Solomon calls out to her.

"No," she says, turning around slightly, phone in hand. "You can stay in here. I'll be back in a few minutes. There's a call I have to make."

She steps into the chill, into the retirement of the day, and she is grateful that the gray month of brevity is almost over.

# ABOUT THE AUTHOR

Donna Kathryn Kelly is a former prosecutor, who practiced law in the Illinois criminal justice system for many years. Kelly began her legal career as an assistant public defender handling felony and juvenile cases in Kane County, Illinois, and subsequently worked as an assistant appellate defender for seven years for the Office of the State Appellate Defender, Third Judicial District, Ottawa, Illinois. Kelly has successfully argued cases before the Appellate Court of Illinois and the Supreme Court of Illinois.

After devoting the first decade of her legal career to criminal defense, Kelly subsequently worked as a prosecutor at the McHenry County State's Attorney's Office in northern Illinois, where she tried numerous felony cases to jury verdict. In 2007, she was honored by the Alliance Against Intoxicated Motorists with the Outstanding Assistant State's Attorney (Illinois) of the Year Award for her commitment and dedication to seeking justice for victims of impaired drivers. Later in her career, Kelly served in executive-level managerial positions as Chief of the Civil Division and subsequently, First Assistant State's Attorney.

Kelly's poetry has appeared in various literary journals such as *Heart of Flesh*, *Snapdragon*, and *Oakwood*. Her poem, *Assumpsit*, was selected as the First Place Entry in the South Dakota State Poetry Society's 2018 Annual Poetry Contest (Portrait Category).

IN HEELS, SHE GOES, is the sequel to Kelly's crime novel, COP EYES, featuring an Illinois public defender turned amateur sleuth, Cheney Manning.

Made in the USA
Monee, IL
06 September 2022